Dear Reader,

Thanks so much for ch[...]
This delightful collecti[...]
to warm the corners of your heart and bring you
endless seasonal joy.

We're proud to present you with *New York Times*
bestselling author Linda Howard's classic romance,
"Bluebird Winter." This story of a blizzard, a baby
and an unexpected love is one to cherish. Bestselling
author Joan Hohl delivers a brand-new story with
"The Gift of Joy," about a burned-out lawman and a
feisty city gal who experience some memorable
holiday moments. And "A Christmas to Treasure,"
by award-winning author Sandra Steffen, will deliver
its share of special smiles as two determined children
set about finding themselves a daddy for Christmas.

Please accept our warmest wishes for a happy holiday
season for you and yours!

The editors at Silhouette Books

ABOUT THE AUTHORS

Linda Howard

New York Times bestselling author Linda Howard says that books have long played a profound role in her life. She cut her teeth on Margaret Mitchell, and from then on continued to read widely and eagerly. In recent years her interest has settled on romance fiction, because she's "easily bored by murder, mayhem and politics." After twenty-one years of penning stories for her own enjoyment, Ms. Howard finally worked up the courage to submit a novel for publication—and met with success! Happily the Alabama author has been steadily publishing ever since.

Joan Hohl

lives in southwestern Pennsylvania, where she was born and raised. A bestselling author of over forty novels, including twenty-five for Silhouette Books, Joan has won numerous awards, including the Romance Writers of America Golden Medallion Award and two *Romantic Times Magazine* Reviewer's Choice Awards. One of the industry's most popular authors, Joan writes both historical and contemporary romances.

Sandra Steffen

has been called a rising star in the romance writing industry. Her first Silhouette Romance® novel won the prestigious 1994 Reader's Choice Award. Eighteen of her heartwarming stories have followed, charming and delighting her fans. Several of those titles have appeared on national bestseller lists. Married to her high school sweetheart, this proud mother of four sons makes her home in Michigan.

LINDA HOWARD
JOAN HOHL
SANDRA STEFFEN

Delivered by Christmas

Published by Silhouette Books
America's Publisher of Contemporary Romance

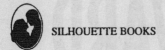

SILHOUETTE BOOKS

DELIVERED BY CHRISTMAS

Copyright © 1999 by Harlequin Books S.A.

ISBN 0-373-48387-2

The publisher acknowledges the copyright holders
of the individual works as follows:

BLUEBIRD WINTER
Copyright © 1987 by Linda Howington

THE GIFT OF JOY
Copyright © 1999 by Joan Hohl

A CHRISTMAS TO TREASURE
Copyright © 1999 by Sandra E. Steffen

Visit us at www.romance.net

Printed in U.S.A.

CONTENTS

BLUEBIRD WINTER

Linda Howard

Chapter 1

It wasn't supposed to happen like this.

Kathleen Fields pressed her hand to her swollen abdomen, her face drawn and anxious as she looked out the window again at the swirling, wind-blown snow. Visibility was so limited that she couldn't even see the uneven pasture fence no more than fifty yards away. The temperature had plummeted into the teens, and according to the weather report on the radio, this freak Christmas Day blizzard was likely to last the rest of the day and most of the night.

She couldn't wait that long. She was in labor now, almost a month early. Her baby would need medical attention.

Bitterness welled in her as she dropped the curtain and turned back to the small, dim living room, lit only by the fire in the fireplace. The electricity and telephone service had gone out five hours ago. Two hours after that, the dull ache in her back, which had been so constant for weeks that she no longer noticed it, had begun strengthening into something more, then laced around to her distended belly. Only mildly concerned, she had ignored it as false labor; after all, she was still three weeks and five days from her due date. Then, half an hour ago, her water had broken, and there was no longer any doubt: she was in labor.

She was also alone, and stranded. This Christmas snow, so coveted by millions of children, could mean the death of her own child.

Tears burned her eyes. She had stolidly endured a bad marriage and the end of her illusions, faced the reality of being broke, alone and pregnant, of working long hours as a waitress in an effort to keep herself fed and provide a home for this baby, even though she had fiercely resented its existence at the beginning. But then it had begun moving inside her, gentle little flutters at first, then actual kicks and pokes, and it had become reality, a person, a companion. It was *her* baby. She wanted it, wanted to hold it and love it and croon lullabies to it. It was the only person she had left in the world, but now she might lose it, perhaps in punishment for that early resentment. How ironic to carry it all this time, only to lose it on Christmas Day! It was supposed to be a day of hope, faith and promise, but she didn't have any hope left, or much faith in people, and the future promised nothing but an endless procession of bleak days. All she had was herself, and the tiny life inside her that was now in jeopardy.

She could deliver the baby here, without help. It was warm and somehow she would manage to keep the fire going. She would survive, but would the baby? It was premature. It might not be able to breathe properly on its own. Something might be wrong with it.

Or she could try to get to the clinic, fifteen miles distant. It was an easy drive in good weather...but the weather wasn't good, and the howling wind had been getting louder. The roads were treacherous and visibility limited. She might not make it, and the effort would cost her her own life, as well as that of her child.

So what? The words echoed in her mind. What did her life matter, if the baby died? Would she be able to live with herself if she opted to protect herself at the risk of the baby's life? Everything might be all right, but she couldn't take that chance. For the baby's sake, she had to try.

Moving clumsily, she dressed as warmly as she could, layering her clothing until she moved like a waddling pumpkin. She gathered water and blankets, an extra nightgown for herself and clothes for the baby, then, as a last thought, checked the telephone one more time on the off-chance that service might have been restored. Only silence met her ear, and, regretfully, she dropped the receiver.

Taking a deep breath to brace herself, Kathleen

opened the back door and was immediately lashed
by the icy wind and stinging snow. She ducked her
head and struggled against the wind, cautiously
making her way down the two ice-coated steps. Her
balance wasn't that good anyway, and the wind was
beating at her, making her stagger. Halfway across
the yard she slipped and fell, but scrambled up so
quickly that she barely felt the impact. "I'm sorry,
I'm sorry," she breathed to the baby, patting her
stomach. The baby had settled low in her belly and
wasn't kicking now, but the pressure was increasing.
It was hard to walk. Just as she reached the old
pickup truck a contraction hit her and she stumbled,
falling again. This contraction was stronger than the
others, and all she could do was lie helplessly in the
snow until it eased, biting her lip to keep from
moaning aloud.

Snow was matting her eyelashes when she finally
struggled to her feet again and gathered up the articles she had dropped. She was panting. God, please
let it be a long labor! she prayed. Please give me
time to get to the clinic. She could bear the pain, if
the baby would just stay snug and safe inside her
until she could get help for it.

A dry sobbing sound reached her ears as she
wrenched the truck door open, pitting her strength
against that of the wind as it tried to slam the door
shut. Clumsily she climbed into the truck, barely
fitting her swollen stomach behind the wheel. The
wind slammed the door shut without her aid, and for
a moment she just sat there, entombed in an icy,

white world, because snow covered all the windows. The sobbing sound continued, and finally she realized she was making the noise.

Instantly Kathleen drew herself up. There was nothing to gain by letting herself panic. She had to clear her mind and concentrate on nothing but driving, because her baby's life depended on it. The baby was all she had left. Everything else was gone: her parents; her marriage; her self-confidence; her faith and trust in people. Only the baby was left, and herself. She still had herself. The two of them had each other, and they didn't need anyone else. She would do anything to protect her baby.

Breathing deeply, she forced herself to be calm. With deliberate movements, she inserted the key in the ignition and turned it. The starter turned slowly, and a new fear intruded. Was the battery too cold to generate enough power to start the old motor? But then the motor roared into life, and the truck vibrated beneath her. She sighed in relief and turned on the wipers to clear the snow from the windshield. They beat back and forth, laboring under the icy weight of the packed snow.

It was so cold! Her breath fogged the air, and she was shivering despite the layers of clothing she wore. Her face felt numb. She reached up to touch it and found that she was still covered with snow. Slowly she wiped her face and dusted the flakes from her hair.

The increasing pressure in her lower body made it difficult for her to hold in the clutch, but she wres-

tled the stubborn gearshift into the proper position
and ground her teeth against the pressure as she let
out the clutch. The truck moved forward.

Visibility was even worse than she had expected.
She could barely make out the fence that ran alongside the road. How easy it would be to run off the
road, or to become completely lost in the white
nightmare! Creeping along at a snail's pace, Kathleen concentrated on the fence line and tried not to
think about the things that could happen.

She was barely a quarter of a mile down the road
when another contraction laced her stomach in iron
bands. She gasped, jerking in spite of herself, and
the sudden wrench of the steering wheel sent the old
truck into a skid. "No!" she groaned, bracing herself as the truck began going sideways toward the
shallow ditch alongside the road. The two right
wheels landed in the ditch with an impact that rattled
her teeth and loosened her grip from the steering
wheel. She cried out again as she was flung to the
right, her body slamming into the door on the passenger side.

The contraction eased a moment later. Panting,
Kathleen crawled up the slanting seat and wedged
herself behind the steering wheel. The motor had
died, and anxiously she put in the clutch and slid
the shift into neutral, praying she could get the engine started again. She turned the key, and once
again the truck coughed into life.

But the wheels spun uselessly in the icy ditch,
unable to find traction. She tried rocking the truck

back and forth, putting it first in reverse, then in low gear, but it didn't work. She was stuck.

Tiredly, she leaned her head on the steering wheel. She was only a quarter of a mile from the house, but it might as well have been twenty miles in this weather. The wind was stronger, visibility almost zero. Her situation had gone from bad to worse. She should have stayed at the house. In trying to save her baby, she had almost certainly taken away its only chance for survival.

He should either have left his mother's house the day before, or remained until the roads were clear. Hindsight was, indeed, very sharp, unlike the current visibility. His four-wheel-drive Jeep Cherokee was surefooted on the icy road, but that didn't eliminate the need to see where he was going.

Making a mistake made Derek Taliferro angry, especially when it was such a stupid mistake. Yesterday's weather bulletins had warned that conditions could worsen, so he had decided to make the drive back to Dallas right away. But Marcie had wanted him to stay until Christmas morning, and he loved his mother very much, so in the end he'd stayed. His strong mouth softened as he allowed himself to think briefly of her. She was a strong woman, raising him single-handedly and never letting him think she'd have it any other way. He'd been elated when she had met Whit Campbell, a strong, laconic rancher from Oklahoma, and tumbled head over heels in love. That had been...Lord, ten years ago. It didn't seem that long. Marcie and Whit still acted like newlyweds.

Derek liked visiting the ranch, just across the state line in Oklahoma, and escaping the pressures of the hospital for a while. That was one reason he'd allowed Marcie to talk him into staying longer than his common sense told him he should. But this morning the urge to get back to Dallas had also overridden his common sense. He should have stayed put until the weather cleared, but he wanted to be back at the hospital by tomorrow. His tiny patients needed him.

The job was compelling, and he never tired of it. He had known he wanted to be a doctor from the time he was fifteen, but at first he'd thought about being an obstetrician. Gradually his interest had become more focused, and by the time he was midway through medical school his goal was set. He specialized in neonatal care, in those tiny babies who came into the world with less of a chance than they should have had. Some of them were simply premature and needed a protective environment in which to gain weight. Others, who were far too early, had to fight for every breath as their underdeveloped systems tried to mature. Every day was a battle won. Then there were those who needed his surgical skills after nature had gone awry, and still others who were beyond help. Every time he was finally able to send a baby home with its parents, he was filled with an intense satisfaction that showed no signs of lessening. It was also why he was now creeping, almost blindly, through a blizzard instead of waiting for better weather. He wanted to get back to the hospital.

The snow completely covered the road; he'd been following the fence lines, and hoping he was still on track. Hell, for all he knew, he was driving across someone's pasture. This was idiocy. He swore under his breath, holding the Cherokee steady against the gusting, howling, swirling wind. When he got to the next town—*if* he got to the next town—he was going to stop, even if he had to spend the night in an all-night grocery…provided there was an all-night grocery. Anything was better than driving blindly in this white hell.

It was so bad that he almost missed seeing the bulk of an old pickup truck, which had slid into a ditch and was now resting at an angle. In one sense seeing the old truck was good news: at least he was still on the road. He started to go on, thinking that whoever had been driving the truck would have sought more adequate shelter long ago, but a quick uneasy feeling made him brake carefully, then shift into reverse and back up until he was alongside the snow-covered bulk. It would only take a minute to check.

The snow had turned into icy, wind-driven pellets that stung his face as he opened the door and got out, hunching his broad shoulders against the wind that tried to knock him off his feet. It was only a few steps to the truck, but he had to fight for every inch. Quickly he grabbed the door handle and wrenched it open, wanting to verify that the truck was empty so he could get back into the Cherokee's warm interior. He was startled by the small scream from the woman who lay on the seat and then jerked upright in alarm when the door was opened so suddenly.

"I just want to help," he said quickly, to keep from frightening her more than he already had.

Kathleen gasped, panting at the pain that had her in its grips. The contractions had been intensifying and were only a few minutes apart now. She would never have been able to make it to the clinic in time. She felt the numbing blast of cold, saw the big man who stood in the truck's open door; but just for the moment she couldn't reply, couldn't do anything except concentrate on the pain. She wrapped her arms around her tight belly, whimpering.

Derek realized at a glance what was happening. The woman was completely white, her green eyes vivid in her pale, desperate face as she held her swollen belly. A strong sense of protectiveness surged through him.

"It's all right, sweetheart," he murmured soothingly, reaching into the truck and lifting her out in his strong arms. "You and the baby will be just fine. I'll take care of everything."

She was still whimpering, locked in the grip of the contraction. Derek carried her to the Cherokee, sheltering her from the brutal wind as much as he could. His mind was already on the coming birth. He hadn't delivered a baby since he'd been an intern, but he'd been on hand many times when the newborn was expected to have difficulties.

He managed to open the passenger door with her still in his arms, and gently deposited her on the seat before hurrying around to vault in on his own side. "How far apart are the contractions?" he asked, wiping her face with his hands. She lay slumped against the seat now, breathing deeply at the cessation of pain, her eyelids closed.

Her eyes opened at his touch, the wary eyes of a wild animal in a trap. "Th-th-th-three minutes," she said, her teeth chattering from the cold. "Maybe less."

"How far is the hospital?"

"Clinic," she corrected, still breathing hard. She swallowed and wet her lips. "Fifteen miles."

"We won't make it," he said with awful certainty. "Is there anyplace around here where we can shelter? A house, a restaurant, anything?"

She lifted her hand. "My house...back there. Quarter mile."

Derek's experienced eyes took note of the signs. She was exhausted. Labor was tiring enough, without being alone and terrified, too. Stress had taken its toll. He needed to get her warm and comfortable as soon as possible. Her eyes closed again.

He decided not to chance turning the truck around and getting off the road; instead he put the Cherokee in reverse, guiding himself by the fence line beside him, because he couldn't see a damned thing out the back window. "Tell me when I get to your driveway," he ordered, and her eyes fluttered open in response.

A minute or so later another contraction curled her in the seat. Derek glanced at his watch. Just a little over two minutes since the last one. The baby certainly wasn't waiting for better weather.

A rusted mailbox on a leaning fence post caught his attention. "Is this your driveway?" he asked.

She lifted her head, and he could see that her white teeth were sunk into her bottom lip to hold back her groans. She managed a short nod, and he shifted into low gear, turning onto the faint trail by the mailbox and praying for time.

Chapter 2

"The back door's open," Kathleen whispered, and he nodded as he steered the Cherokee as close to the steps as he could.

"Don't try to get out on your own," he ordered as she reached for the door handle. "I'll come around and get you."

Kathleen subsided against the seat, her face pale and taut. She didn't know this man, didn't know whether she should trust him, but she had no choice but to accept his help. She was more frightened than she'd ever been in her life. The pain was worse than she'd expected, and added to it was the numbing fear for her child's life. Whoever the man was, right now she was grateful for his company.

He got out of the Cherokee, bending his head

against the wind as he circled the front of the vehicle. He was a big man, tall and strong; he'd handled her weight easily, but his grasp had been gentle. As he opened the passenger door, Kathleen started to swing her legs around so she could slide out, but again he stopped her by scooping her up in his arms.

"Put your face against my shoulder," he instructed, raising his voice so she could hear him over the howling wind. She nodded and buried her face against his coat, and he turned so that his back blocked the wind from her as he carried her the few feet to the back door. He fumbled for the doorknob and managed to turn it, and the wind did the rest, catching the door and slamming it back against the wall with a resounding crack. A small blizzard of snow entered with them.

Swiftly he carried her through the small, time-worn ranch house until he reached the living room, where the fire still burned low in the fireplace. She felt as though hours had passed, but in reality it had been only about an hour since she had fought her way to the truck.

Still with that powerful, controlled gentleness, he placed her on the sagging old couch. "I've got to get my bag, but I'll be right back," he promised, smoothing her hair back from her face. "Don't try to get up; stay right here."

She nodded, so tired that she couldn't imagine going anywhere. Why did he want his luggage right now? Couldn't it wait?

Another contraction. She curled up on the couch,

giving gasping little cries at the fierceness of the pain. Before it ended he was beside her again, his voice soothing but authoritative as he told her to take quick, short breaths, to pant like a dog. Dimly she remembered reading instructions for breathing during labor, and the same description had been used. She tried to do as he said, concentrating on her breathing, and it did seem to help. Perhaps it just took her mind off the pain, but right then she was willing to do anything.

When the contraction had eased and she slumped exhausted on the couch, he said, "Do you have extra wood for the fire? The electricity is off."

She managed a wan smile. "I know. It went off this morning. I brought extra wood in yesterday, when I heard the weather report; it's in the wash room, just off the kitchen."

"You should have gone to the clinic yesterday," he said crisply as he got to his feet.

She was tired and frightened, but fire still flashed in her green eyes as she glared up at him. "I would have, if I'd known the baby was going to come early."

That got his attention; his black brows snapped together over his high-bridged nose. "You're not full term? How early are you?"

"Almost a month." Her hand went to her stomach in an unconscious gesture of helpless concern.

"Any chance your due date was miscalculated?"

"No," she whispered, her head falling back. She

knew exactly when she'd gotten pregnant, and the memory made her go cold.

He gave her a crooked smile, and for the first time she noticed how beautiful he was, in a strong, masculine way that was almost unearthly. Kathleen had gotten into the habit of not looking directly at men, or she would have seen it before. Even now, something in his golden brown eyes made her feel more relaxed. "This is your lucky day, sweetheart," he said gently, still smiling at her as he took off his thick shearling coat and rolled up his sleeves. "You just got stranded with a doctor."

For a moment the words didn't make sense; then her mouth opened in silent disbelief. "You're a doctor?"

He lifted his right hand as if taking an oath. "Licensed and sworn."

Relief filled her like a warm tide rushing through her body, and she gave a small laugh that was half sob. "Are you any good at delivering babies?"

"Babies are my business," he said, giving her another of those bright, tender smiles. "So stop worrying and try to rest while I get things arranged in here. When you have another contraction, remember how to breathe. I won't be long."

She watched as he brought in more wood and built up the fire until it was blazing wildly, adding warmth to the chilled room. Through the pain of another contraction, she watched as he carried in the mattress from her bed and dumped it on the floor in front of the fire. With swift, sure movements he put a clean sheet on it, then folded towels over the sheet.

He rose to his feet with powerful grace and approached her. "Now, let's get you more comfortable," he said as he removed her coat. "By the way, my name is Derek Taliferro."

"Kathleen Fields," she replied in kind.

"Is there a Mr. Fields?" he asked, his calm face hiding his intense interest in her as he began taking off her boots.

Bitterness filled Kathleen's face, a bitterness so deep it hurt to see. "There's one somewhere," she muttered. "But we aren't married any longer."

He was silent as he removed her thick socks, under which she also wore leotards that she'd put on when she realized she would have to try to get to the clinic. He helped her to her feet and unzipped her serviceable corduroy jumper, lifting it over her head and leaving her standing in the turtleneck sweater and leotards.

"I can do the rest," she said uneasily. "Just let me go into the bedroom for a nightgown."

He laughed, the sound deep and rich. "All right, if you think you can manage."

"Of course I can manage." She had been managing much more than that since Larry Fields had walked out.

But she had barely taken two steps when another contraction bent her double, a contraction so powerful that it was all she could do to gasp for breath. Involuntary tears stung her eyes. She felt his arms around her; then he lifted her and a moment later placed her on the mattress. Swiftly he stripped off her leotards and underwear, and draped a sheet over her; then he held her hand and coached her breathing until the contraction eased.

"Rest for a minute now," he soothed. "I'm going to wash my hands so I can examine you. I'll be right back."

Kathleen lay tiredly on the mattress, staring up at the water-stained ceiling with swimming eyes. The heat from the fire flickered against her cheeks, bringing a rosy glow to her complexion. She was so tired; she felt as if she could sleep for the rest of the day, but there wouldn't be any rest until the baby was born. Her hands clenched into fists as anxiety rose in her again. The baby had to be all right. It had to be.

Then he was back, kneeling at the foot of the mattress and lifting the sheet that covered her. Real color climbed into her face, and she turned her head to stare into the fire. She had never really been comfortable with intimacy, and even her visits to the doctor had been torturous occasions for her. To have this man, this stranger, touch her and look at her...

Derek glanced up and saw her flushed face and expression of acute embarrassment, and a smile flickered around his mouth as amused tenderness welled up in him. How wary she was of him, despite being forced to put her welfare in his hands! And rather shy, like a wild creature that wasn't accustomed to others and didn't quite trust them. She was frightened, too, for her child, and of the ordeal she faced. Because of that, he was immensely gentle as he examined her.

"You aren't fully dilated," he murmured. "The baby isn't in such a hurry, after all. Go with your contractions, but don't push. I'll tell you when to push. How long ago did the contractions start?"

"My back was hurting all last night," she said tiredly, her eyes closing. "The first real contraction was at about ten o'clock this morning."

He glanced at his watch. She had been in labor a little over five hours, and it would probably last another hour or so. Not a long labor, especially for a first pregnancy. "When did your water break?"

He wasn't hurting her, and her embarrassment was fading. She even felt drowsy. "Umm…about one-thirty." Now she felt his hands on her stomach; firm, careful touches as he tried to determine the baby's position. Her warm drowsiness splintered as another contraction seized her, but when she breathed as he'd instructed somehow it didn't seem as painful.

When she rested again, he placed his stethoscope against her stomach and listened to the baby's heartbeat. "It's a strong, steady hearbeat," he reassured her. He wasn't worried about the baby's heart, but about its lungs. He prayed they would be mature enough to handle the chore of breathing, because he didn't have the equipment here to handle the situation if they couldn't. Some eight-month babies did just fine; others needed help. He looked out the win-

dow. It was snowing harder than ever, in a blinding
sheet that blocked out the rest of the world but filled
the house with a strange, white light. There was no
way he could summon emergency help, and no way
it could get here, even if the phones were working.

The minutes slipped away, marked by contractions that gradually grew stronger and closer together. He kept the fire built up, so the baby
wouldn't be chilled when it finally made its appearance, and Kathleen's hair grew damp with sweat.
She tugged at the neck of her turtleneck sweater.
"It's so hot," she breathed. She felt as if she
couldn't stand the confining fabric a minute longer.

"A nightgown wouldn't be much of an improve-
ment," Derek said, and got one of his clean shirts
from his luggage. She didn't make any protest when
he removed her sweater and bra and slipped the thin,
soft shirt around her. It was light, and much too big,
and it felt wonderful after the smothering heat of the
wool sweater. He rolled up the sleeves and fastened
the buttons over her breasts, then dampened a wash-
cloth in cool water and bathed her face.

It wouldn't be too much longer. He checked again
to make certain he had everything he needed at
hand. He had already sterilized his instruments and
laid everything out on a gauze-covered tray.

"Well, sweetheart, are you about ready to get this
show on the road?" he asked as he examined her
again.

The contractions were almost continuous now.

She took a deep breath during a momentary lull. "Is it time?" she gasped.

"You're fully dilated now, but don't push until I tell you. Pant. That's right. Don't push, don't push."

She wanted to push. She desperately needed to push. Her body arched on the mattress, a monstrous pressure building in her, but his deep voice remained calm and controlled, somehow controlling her. She panted, and somehow, she didn't push. The wave of pain receded, the pressure eased, and for a moment she rested. Then it began again.

It couldn't last much longer; she couldn't bear it much longer. Tears seeped from her eyes.

"Here we go," he said with satisfaction. "I can see the head. You're crowning, sweetheart; it won't be but another minute. Let me make a little incision so you won't be torn—"

Kathleen barely heard him, barely felt him. The pressure was unbearable, blocking out everything else. "Push, sweetheart," he said, his tone suddenly authoritative.

She pushed. Dimly, she was astounded that her body was capable of exerting such pressure. She gave a thin cry, but barely heard it. Her world consisted only of a powerful force that squeezed her in its fist, that and the man who knelt at her spread knees, his calm voice telling her what to do.

Then, abruptly, the pressure eased, and she sank back, gasping for breath. He said, "I have the baby's head in my hand. My Lord, what a head of hair! Just rest a minute, sweetheart."

She heard a funny sound, and alarm brought her up on her elbows. "What's wrong?" she asked frantically. "What are you doing?"

"I'm suctioning out its mouth and nose," he said. "Just lie back; everything's all right." Then a thin, wavering wail rose, gaining in strength with every second, and he laughed. "That's right, tell us about it," he encouraged. "Push, sweetheart; our baby isn't too happy with the situation."

She pushed, straining, and suddenly she felt a rush, then a great sense of relief. Derek laughed again as he held a tiny but furious scrap of humanity in his hands. "I don't blame you a bit," he told the squalling infant, whose cries sounded ridiculously like those of a mewling kitten. "I wouldn't want to leave your soft, warm mommy, either, but you'll be wrapped up and cuddled in just a minute."

"What is it?" Kathleen whispered, falling back on the mattress.

"A beautiful little girl. She has more hair than any three babies should have."

"Is she all right?"

"She's perfect. She's tiny, but listen to her cry! Her lungs are working just fine."

"Can I hold her?"

"In just a minute. I'm almost finished here." The umbilical cord had gone limp, so he swiftly clamped and cut it, then lifted the squalling baby into her mother's anxious arms. Kathleen looked dazed, her eyes filling with tears as she examined her tiny daughter.

"Put her to your breast," Derek instructed softly, knowing that would calm the infant, but Kathleen didn't seem to hear him. He unbuttoned her shirt himself and pushed it aside to bare one full breast, then guided the baby's mouth to the rich-looking nipple. Still the baby squalled, its tiny body trembling; he'd have to do more than just give it a hint. "Come on, honey," he coaxed, reached down to stroke the baby's cheek just beside her mouth. She turned her head reflexively, and he guided the nipple into her mouth. She squalled one more time, then suddenly seemed to realize what she was supposed to do, and the tiny mouth closed on her mother's breast.

Kathleen jumped. She hadn't even reacted to his touch on her breast, he realized, and looked closely at her. She was pale, with shadows under her eyes, and her dark hair was wet with perspiration. She was truly exhausted, not just from the physical difficulty of labor and giving birth, but from the hours of anxiety she'd suffered through. Yet there was something glowing in her face and eyes as she looked at her baby, and it lingered when she slowly looked up at him.

"We did it," she murmured, and smiled.

Derek looked down at her, at the love shining from her face like a beacon, and the attraction he'd felt for her from the start suddenly solidified inside him with a painful twist. Something about her made him want to hold her close, protect her from whatever had put that wary, distrustful look in her eyes.

He wanted her to look at him with her face full of love.

Stunned, he sank back on his heels. It had finally happened, when he had least expected it and had even stopped looking for it, and with a woman who was merely tolerating his presence due to the circumstances. It wasn't just that she had other things on her mind right now; he could tell that Kathleen Fields wanted nothing to do with a man, any man. And yet the thunderbolt had hit him anyway, just as his mother had always warned him it would.

Teaching Kathleen to love wouldn't be easy, but Derek looked at her, and at the baby in her arms, and knew he wouldn't give up.

Chapter 3

Kathleen couldn't remember ever being so tired before; her body was leaden with exhaustion, while her mind seemed to float, disconnected from the physical world. Only the baby in her arms seemed real. She was vaguely aware of the things Derek was doing to her, of the incredible confidence and gentleness of his hands, but it was as if he were doing them to someone else. Even the painful prick of the sutures he set didn't rouse her, nor did his firm massaging of her stomach. She simply lay there, too tired to care. When she was finally clean and wearing a gown, and the linen on the mattress had been changed, she sighed and went to sleep with the suddenness of a light being turned off.

She had no idea how long it was before he woke

her, to lift her carefully to a sitting position and prop her against him while the baby nursed. He was literally holding both her and the baby, his strong arms supporting them. Her head lay on his broad shoulder, and she didn't have the strength to lift it. "I'm sorry," she murmured. "I can't seem to sit up."

"It's all right, sweetheart," he said, his deep voice reaching inside her and soothing all her vague worries. "You worked hard; you deserve to be a little lazy now."

"Is the baby all right?" she managed to mumble.

"She's eating like a pig," he said, his chuckle hiding his worry, and Kathleen went back to sleep as soon as he eased her back onto the mattress. She didn't even feel him lift the baby from her and refasten her gown.

Derek sat for a long time, cradling the baby in his arms. She was dangerously underweight, but she seemed remarkably strong for her size. She was breathing on her own and managing to suckle, which had been his two biggest worries, but she was still too tiny. He guessed her weight at about four pounds, too small for her to be able to regulate her own temperature because she simply didn't have the body fat necessary. Because of that, he had wrapped her warmly and kept the fire in the fireplace hotter than was comfortable.

His calm, golden brown eyes glowed as he looked down at her tiny face, dominated by the vague, huge blue eyes of the newborn. Premature infants had both an aged and a curiously ageless look to them, their doll-like faces lacking cuddly baby fat, which revealed their facial structure in a fragile gauntness. Even so, he could tell she was going to be a beauty, with her mother's features and even the same thick, black hair.

Every one of his tiny, frail patients got to him, but this stubborn little fighter had reached into his heart. Maybe it was because he could look at her and see her mother in her, because Kathleen was a fighter, too. She had to be; it wasn't easy to go through a pregnancy alone, as she obviously had. And when she had gone into labor too early, instead of remaining here where *she* would be safer, she had risked her own life in an effort to get to the clinic where her baby could have medical care.

He couldn't help wondering about the absent Mr. Fields, and for the first time in his life he felt jealousy burning him, because the unknown man had been, at least for a while, the recipient of Kathleen's love. Derek also wondered what had happened to put that wariness in her eyes and build the walls in her mind. He knew they were there; he could sense them. They made him want to put his arms around her and rock her, comfort her, but he knew she wouldn't welcome his closeness.

The baby squeaked, and he looked down to see that her eyes were open and she was looking at him with the intensely focused expression of someone with bad eyesight. He chuckled and cuddled her closer. "What is it, honey?" he crooned. "Hungry again?" Because her stomach was so small, she needed far more frequent feedings than a normal newborn.

He glanced over at Kathleen, who was still sleeping heavily. An idea began to form. One of Derek's characteristics, and one that had often made his mother feel as if she were dealing with an irresistible force rather than a child, was his ability to set long-term goals and let nothing sway him from his course. When he wanted something, he went after it. And now he wanted Kathleen. He had been instantly attracted to her, his interest sparked by the mysterious but undeniable chemical reaction that kept animals mating and procreating; humans were no exception, and his own libido was healthy. Her pregnancy hadn't weakened his attraction, but rather strengthened it in a primitive way.

Then, during the process of labor and giving birth, the attraction had changed, had been transmitted into an emotional force as well as a physical one. They had been a team, despite Kathleen's reserve. The baby had become his; he was responsible for her life, her welfare. She had exited her mother's warm body into his hands. He had seen her, held her, laughed at her furious squalling, and put her to her mother's breast. She was, undeniably, *his*. Now his goal was to make the baby's mother his, too. He wanted Kathleen to look at him with the same fiercely tender love she'd shown to her child. He wanted to father the next infant that grew inside her. He wanted to make her laugh, to ease the distrust in her eyes, to make her face shine with happiness.

No doubt about it, he'd have to marry her.

The baby squeaked again, more demandingly. "All right, we'll wake Mommy up," he promised. "You'll help with my plan, won't you? Between the two of us, we'll take such good care of her that she'll forget she was ever unhappy."

He woke Kathleen before the baby began to squall in earnest, and carefully propped her in a sitting position so she could nurse the child. She was still groggy, but seemed more alert than she had before. She held the baby to her breast, stroking the satiny cheek with one finger as she stared down at her daughter. "What time is it?" she asked dreamily.

He shifted his position so he could see his wristwatch. "Almost nine."

"Is that all? I feel as if I've been asleep for hours."

He laughed. "You have, sweetheart. You were worn out."

Kathleen's clear green eyes turned up to him. "Is she doing all right?"

The baby chose that moment to slurp as the nipple momentarily slipped from her lips. Frantically the tiny rosebud mouth sought the beading nipple again, and when she found it she made a squeaky little grunting noise. The two adults laughed, looking down at her.

"She's strong for her size," Derek said, reaching down to lift the miniscule hand that lay on Kathleen's ivory, blue-veined breast. It was such a tiny hand, the palm no bigger than a dime, but the fingernails were perfectly formed and a nice pink color. Sweat trickled at his temple, and he could see a fine sheen on Kathleen's chest, but at least the baby was warm enough.

Kathleen tried to sit up away from him, her eyes sharpening as she considered his reply, but her body protested the movement, and with a quiet moan she sank back against his muscled chest. "What do you mean, she's strong for her size? Is she doing all right or not?"

"She needs an incubator," he said, wrapping his arm around Kathleen and supporting her soft weight. "That's why I'm keeping it so hot in here. She's too small for her body to regulate its own temperature."

Kathleen's face was suddenly white and tense. She had thought everything was fine, despite the baby being a month early. The sudden knowledge that the baby was still in a precarious position stunned her.

"Don't worry," Derek soothed, cradling her close to him. "As long as we keep her nice and warm, she shouldn't have any trouble. I'll keep a close watch on her tonight, and as soon as the weather clears we'll get her to a cozy incubator." He studied the fragile little hand for a moment longer, then tenderly replaced it on Kathleen's breast. "What are you going to name her?"

"Sara Marisa," Kathleen murmured. "Sara is—

was—my mother's name. But I'm going to call her
Risa. It means 'laughter.'"

Derek's face went still, and his eyes darkened
with barely contained emotion as he looked at the
baby. "How are you spelling it? S-a-r-a or S-a-r-
a-h?"

"S-a-r-a."

It was still the same name, the name that had become synonymous, in his mind, with love. He had
first seen mind-shattering, irrevocable love in Sarah
Matthews's face when he had been fifteen, and he
had known then that he would never settle for anything less. That was what he wanted to feel, what
he wanted to give, what he wanted in return. Sarah's
love was a powerful, immense thing, spilling over
into the lives of everyone near her, because she gave
it so unselfishly. It was because of her that he was
a doctor now, because of her that he had been able
to finish college at an accelerated pace, because of
her that he had a warm, loving extended family
when before there had been only himself and his
mother. Now this new life was leading him into the
sort of love he'd waited for, so it was only fitting
that she should be named Sara. He smiled when he
thought of Sara holding her namesake. She and her
husband, Rome, could be the baby's godparents,
though they'd probably have to share the honor with
Max and Claire Conroy, two other very special
friends and part of the extended family. He knew
how they would all take to Kathleen and the baby,
but he wondered how Kathleen would feel, sur-

rounded by all those loving strangers. Anxious?
Threatened?

It would take time to teach Kathleen to love him,
and all the people who were close to him, but he
had all the time in the world. He had the rest of his
life.

The baby was asleep now, and gently he took her
from Kathleen's arms. "Risa," he murmured, trying
her name on his tongue. Yes, the two of them together would overwhelm Kathleen with love.

Kathleen dozed on and off the rest of the night,
and every time she woke she saw Derek with her
daughter in his arms. The picture of the tall, strong
man holding the frail infant with such tender concern gave her a feeling she couldn't identify, as if
something expanded in her chest. He didn't let down
his guard for a minute all night, but kept vigil over
the child, kept the room uncomfortably warm, and
held Kathleen so she could nurse her whenever that
funny, indignant little squeak told them the baby
was getting hungry. Sometime during the night he
removed his shirt, and when she woke the next time
she was stunned by the primitive beauty of the picture he made, sitting crosslegged before the fire, the
powerful muscles of his damp torso gleaming as he
cuddled the sleeping baby to him.

It struck her then that he wasn't like other men,
but she was too sleepy and too tired to pursue the
thought. Her entire body ached, and she was in the
grip of a powerful lassitude that kept her thoughts

and movements down to a minimum. Tomorrow would be time enough to think.

It stopped snowing around dawn, and the wild, whistling wind died away. It was the pale silence that woke her for good, and she gingerly eased herself into a sitting position, wincing at the pain in her lower body. Derek laid the baby on the mattress and reached out a strong arm to help her.

"I have to go—" she began, stopping abruptly as she wondered how she could phrase the urgent need to a stranger.

"It's about time," he said equably, carefully lifting her in his arms.

Her face turned scarlet as he carried her down the dark, narrow hallway. "I don't need any help!" she protested.

He set her on her feet outside the bathroom door and held her until her legs stopped wobbling. "I put a couple of candles in here last night," he said. "I'll light them, then get out of your way, but I'll be just outside the door if you need me."

She realized that he didn't intend to embarrass her, but neither was he going to let her do more than he deemed wise. There was a calm implacability in his face that told her he wouldn't hesitate to come to her aid if she became too weak to take care of herself. It was difficult to remember that he was a doctor, used to bodies of all sizes and shapes. He just didn't seem like any doctor she'd ever met before.

To her relief, her strength was returning, and she

didn't need his help. When she left the bathroom, she walked down the hall under her own power, though he kept a steadying hand under her arm just in case. The baby was still sleeping peacefully on the mattress, and Kathleen looked down at her daughter with a powerful surge of adoration that shook her.

"She's so beautiful," she whispered. "Is she doing okay?"

"She's doing fine, but she needs an incubator until she gains about a pound and a half. The way she's been nursing, that might take only a couple of weeks."

"A couple of weeks!" Kathleen echoed, aghast. "She needs hospital care for a couple of weeks?"

His eyes were steady. "Yes."

Kathleen turned away, her fists knotting. There was no way she could pay what two weeks in a hospital would cost, yet she couldn't see that she had a choice. Risa's life was still a fragile thing, and she would do anything, anything at all, to keep her child alive.

"Does the clinic that you were going to have the facilities to care for her?" he asked.

Another problem. She swallowed. "No. I...I don't have any medical insurance. I was going to have her there, then come home afterward."

"Don't worry about it," he said. "I'll think of something. Now, sweetheart, lie down and let me take a look at you. I want to make sure *you're* doing all right."

It had been bad enough the day before, when she was in labor, but it was worse now. It had been a medical emergency then; now it wasn't. But, again, she had the feeling he would do exactly as he intended, regardless of any objections she raised, so she stared fixedly at the fire as he examined her and firmly kneaded her abdomen.

"You have good muscle tone," he said approvingly. "You'd have had a lot harder time if you hadn't been as strong as you are."

If she was strong, it was the strength given by years of working a small grubby ranch, then long hours of waiting on tables. Spas and gyms were outside her experience.

"What do we do now?" she asked. "Wait?"

"Nope. You're doing well enough to travel, and we can't afford to sit around until the phones are fixed. I'm going to start the Jeep and get it warm, and then I'm taking both you and the baby to a hospital."

She felt instant panic. "You want to take the baby *out?*"

"We have to. We'll keep her warm."

"We can keep her warm here."

"She needs a hospital. She's doing all right now, but things can change in the blink of an eye with a preemie. I'm not going to take that chance with her life."

Kathleen couldn't control a mother's natural fear of exposing her fragile child to the elements. There was no telling which roads were closed, or how long it would take them to reach a hospital. What if they ran off the road again and got in a wreck?

Seeing her panic build, Derek reached out and firmly took her hand. "I won't let anything happen," he said calmly, as if he had read her thoughts. "Get dressed while I start the Jeep and fix something for breakfast. Aren't you hungry? You haven't eaten a bite since I found you yesterday."

Only then did she realize how empty she was; it was odd, how even the thought of hunger had been pushed from her mind by all that happened. She changed in her icy bedroom, hurriedly pulling on first one pair of pants after another, and growing more and more frustrated as she found that they were too small. Finally she settled on one of the first pairs of maternity pants she had bought, when she had been outgrowing her jeans. Her own body was unfamiliar to her. It felt strange not to have a swollen, cumbersome stomach, strange to actually look down and see her toes. She had to move carefully, but she could put on socks and shoes without twisting into awkward contortions. Still, she didn't have her former slenderness, and it was disconcerting.

After pulling on a white cotton shirt and layering a flannel shirt over it, she pulled a brush through her tangled hair and left the bedroom, too cold to linger and worry about her looks. Wryly, she admitted that he had successfully distracted her from her arguments; she had done exactly as he'd ordered.

When she entered the kitchen, he looked up from his capable preparations of soup and sandwiches to smile at her. "Feel strange not wearing maternity clothes?"

"I am wearing maternity clothes," she said, a faint, very feminine despair in her eyes and voice. "What feels strange is being able to see my feet." Changing the subject, she asked, "Is it terribly cold outside?"

"It's about twenty degrees, but the sky is clearing."

"What hospital are you taking us to?"

"I've thought about that. I want Risa in my hospital in Dallas."

"Dallas! But that's—"

"I can oversee her care there," Derek interrupted calmly.

"It's too far away," Kathleen said, standing straight. Her green eyes were full of bitter acknowledgement. "And I won't be able to pay. Just take us to a charity hospital."

"Don't worry about paying. I told you I'd take care of you."

"It's still charity, but I'd rather owe a hospital than you."

"You won't owe me." He turned from the old wood stove, and suddenly she felt the full force of his golden brown gaze, fierce and compelling, bending her to his will. "Not if you marry me."

Chapter 4

The words resounded in her head like the ringing of a bell. "Marry you?"

"That's right."

"But...*why?*"

"You'll marry me so Risa can have the care she needs. I'll marry you so I can have Risa. You're not in love with someone, are you?" Numbly she shook her head. "I didn't think so. I guess I fell in love with your daughter the minute she came out of you, into my hands. I want to be her father."

"I don't want to get married again, ever!"

"Not even for Risa? If you marry me, you won't have to worry about money again. I'll sign a pre-nuptial agreement, if you'd like; I'll provide for her, put her through college."

"You can't marry me just because you want my baby. Get married to someone else and have your own children."

"I want Risa," he said with that calm, frightening implacability. Alarm began to fill her as she realized that he never swerved from the course he had set for himself.

"Think, Kathleen. She needs help now, and children need a lot of support through the years. Am I such a monster that you can't stand the thought of being married to me?"

"But you're a stranger! I don't know you and you don't know me. How can you even think of marrying me?"

"I know that you loved your child enough to risk your own life trying to get to the clinic. I know you've had some bad luck in your life, but that you're strong, and you don't give up. We delivered a baby together; how can we be strangers now?"

"I don't know anything about your life."

He shrugged his broad shoulders. "I have a fairly uncomplicated life. I'm a doctor, I live in an apartment, and I'm not a social lion. I'm great with kids, and I won't mistreat you."

"I never thought you would," she said quietly. She had been mistreated, and she knew that Derek was as different from her ex-husband as day was from night. But she simply didn't want another man in her life at all, ever. "What if you fall in love with someone else? Wouldn't that tear Risa's life apart? I'd never give up custody of her!"

"I won't fall in love with anybody else." His voice rang with utter certainty. He just stood there, watching her, but his eyes were working their power on her. Incredibly, she could feel herself weakening inside. As his wife, she wouldn't have the bitter, day after day after day struggle simply to survive. Risa would have the hospital care she needed, and afterward she would have all the advantages Kathleen couldn't give her.

"I couldn't…I couldn't have sex with you," she finally said in desperation, because it was her last defense.

"I wouldn't want you to." Before she could decide if she should feel relieved or insulted, he continued, "When we sleep together, I want you to think of it as making love, not having sex. Sex is cheap and easy. Making love means caring and commitment."

"And you think we'll have that?"

"In time." He gave her a completely peaceful smile, as if he sensed her weakening and knew he would have things his way.

Her throat grew tight as she thought about having sex. She didn't know what making love was, and she didn't know if she would ever *want* to know. "Things…have happened to me," she said hoarsely. "I may not ever—"

"In time, sweetheart. You will, in time."

His very certainty frightened her, because there was something about him that abruptly made her just as certain that, at some point in the future, she would indeed want him to make love to her. The idea was alien to her, making her feel as if her entire life had suddenly been rerouted onto another track. She had had everything planned in her mind: she would raise Risa, totally devoted to her only child, and take pleasure in watching her grow. But there was no room for a man in her plans. Larry Fields had done her a tremendous favor by leaving her, even if he had left her broke and pregnant. But now, here was this man who looked like a warrior angel, taking over her life and shaping it along other lines.

Desperately she tried again. "We're too different! You're a doctor, and I barely finished high school. I've lived on this scrubby little ranch my entire life. I've never been anywhere or done anything; you'd be bored to death by me within a month!"

Amusement sparkled in his amber eyes as he walked over to her. "You're talking rubbish," he said gently, his hand sliding under her heavy hair to clasp her nape. Before she could react he had bent and firmly pressed his mouth to hers in a warm, strangely intimate kiss; then he released her and moved away before she could become alarmed. She stood there staring at him, her vivid green eyes huge and confused.

"Say yes, then let's eat," he commanded, his eyes still sparkling.

"Yes." Her voice sounded dazed, even to herself.

"That's a good girl." He put his warm hand on her elbow and led her to the table, then carefully got her seated. She was uncomfortable, but was not in such pain that it killed her appetite. Hungrily they ate chicken noodle soup and toasted cheese sandwiches, washed down with good strong coffee. It wasn't normal breakfast fare, but after not eating for so long, she was delighted with it. Then he insisted that she sit still while he cleaned up the kitchen, something that had never happened to her before. She felt pampered, and dazed by all that had happened and she had agreed to.

"I'll pack a few of your clothes and nightgowns, but you won't need much," he said. "Where are the baby's things?"

"In the bottom drawer of my dresser, but some of her clothes are in the truck. I didn't think to get them yesterday when you stopped."

"We'll pick them up on the way. Come into the living room with the baby while I get everything loaded."

She held the sleeping child while he swiftly packed and carried the things out. When he had finished, he brought a tiny, crocheted baby cap that he'd found in the drawer, and put it on Risa's downy head to help keep her warm. Then he wrapped her snugly in several blankets, helped Kathleen into her heavy coat, put the baby in Kathleen's arms, and lifted both of them into his.

"I can walk," she protested, her heart giving a huge leap at being in his arms again. He had kissed her....

"No going up or down steps just yet," he explained. "And no climbing into the Jeep. Keep Risa's face covered."

He was remarkably strong, carrying her with no evident difficulty. His strides were sure as he waded through the snow, avoiding the path he'd already made because it had become icy. Kathleen blinked at the stark whiteness of the landscape. The wind had blown the snow into enormous drifts that almost obliterated the fence line and had piled against the sides of the house and barn. But the air was still and crisp now, the fog of her breath gushing straight out in front of her.

He had turned the heater in the Jeep on high, and it was uncomfortably warm for her. "I'll have to take off this coat," she muttered.

"Wait until we've stopped to get the things out of your truck or you'll get chilled with the door open."

She watched as he went back inside to bank the fires in the fireplace and the wood stove, and to lock the doors. She had lived in this house her entire life, but suddenly she wondered if she'd ever see it again, and if she cared. Her life here hadn't been happy.

Her confusion and hesitancy faded as if they had never been. This place wasn't what she wanted for Risa. For her daughter, she wanted so much more than what she had had. She didn't want Risa to wear patched and faded clothes, to marry out of desperation, or to miss out on the pleasures of life because all her free time was spent on chores.

Derek was taking her away from this, but she

wouldn't rely on him. She had made the mistake of relying on a man once before, and she wouldn't do it again. Kathleen decided that as soon as she had recovered from giving birth, and Risa was stronger, she would get a job, save her money, work to better herself. If Derek ever walked away from her as Larry had done, she wouldn't be left stone broke and without the means to support herself. Risa would never have to go hungry or cold.

Five hours later, Kathleen was lying on a snowy-white hospital bed, watching the color television attached to the wall. Her private room was almost luxurious, with a full bath and a pair of comfortable recliners, small oil paintings on the wall, and fresh flowers on her bedside table. The snowstorms hadn't reached as far south as Dallas, and from the window she could see a blue sky only occasionally studded with clouds.

Risa had been whisked away to the neonatal unit, with people jumping to obey Derek's orders. Kathleen herself had been examined by a cheerful obstetrician named Monica Sudley and pronounced in excellent condition. "But I never expected anything different," Dr. Sudley had said casually. "Not with Dr. Taliferro taking care of you."

Dr. Taliferro. Her mind had accepted him as a doctor, but somehow she hadn't really understood it until she had seen him here, in his own milieu, where his deep voice took on a crisp tone of command, and everyone scrambled to satisfy him. She had only seen him wearing jeans and boots and a casual shirt, with his heavy shearling coat, but after arriving at the hospital he had showered and shaved, then changed into the fresh clothes he kept in his office for just such situations. He had seen to Risa, then visited Kathleen to reassure her that the trip hadn't harmed the infant in any way.

He had been the same, yet somehow different. Perhaps it was only the clothes, the dark slacks, white shirt and blue-striped tie, as well as the lab coat he wore over them and the stethoscope around his neck. It was typical doctor's garb, but the effect was jarring. She couldn't help remembering the firelight flickering on his gleaming, muscled shoulders, or the hard, chiseled purity of his profile as he looked down at the child in his arms.

It was also hard to accept the fact that she had agreed to marry him.

Every few hours she put on a robe and walked to the neonatal unit, where Risa was taken out of the incubator and given to her to be fed. The sight of the other frail babies, some of them much smaller than Risa, shook her. They were enclosed in their little glass cubicles with various tubes running into their tiny naked bodies, while little knit caps covered their heads. Thank God Risa was strong enough to nurse!

The first time she fed her daughter, she was led to a rocking chair in a small room away from the other babies, and Risa was brought to her.

"So you're the mother of this little honey," the

young nurse said as she laid Risa in Kathleen's eager arms. "She's adorable. I've never seen so much hair on a newborn, and look how long it is! Dr. Taliferro had us scrambling like we were having an air raid until we had her all comfy. Did he really deliver her?"

Faint color burned along Kathleen's cheekbones. Somehow it seemed too intimate to discuss, even though giving birth was an everyday occurrence to the staff. But the young nurse was looking at her with bright, expectant eyes, so she said uncomfortably, "Yes. My truck slid off the road during the blizzard. Derek came by and found me."

"Ohmigod, talk about romantic!"

"Having a baby?" Kathleen asked skeptically.

"Honey, digging ditches would be romantic if Dr. Taliferro helped! Isn't he something? All the babies know whenever he's the one holding them. They never get scared or cry with him. Sometimes he stays here all night with a critical baby, holding it and talking to it, watching it every minute, and a lot of his babies make it when no one else gave them much of a chance."

The nurse seemed to have a case of hero worship for Derek, or maybe it was more than that. He was incredibly good-looking, and a hospital was a hothouse for romances. It made Kathleen uneasy; why was she even thinking of marrying a man who would constantly be pursued and tempted?

"Have you worked in this unit for long?" she asked, trying to change the subject.

"A little over a year. I love it. These little tykes need all the help they can get, and, of course, I'd have walked barefoot over hot coals to get to work with Dr. Taliferro. Hospitals and clinics from all over the nation were fighting to get him."

"Why? Isn't he too young to have built a reputation yet?" She didn't know how old he was, but guessed he was no older than his midthirties, perhaps even younger.

"He's younger than most of them, but he finished college when he was nineteen. He graduated from med school at the top of his class, interned at one of the nation's best trauma centers, then studied neonatal medicine with George Oliver, who's also one of the best. He's thirty-two, I think."

It was odd to learn so much about her future husband from a stranger, and odder still to find he was considered a medical genius, one of those rare doctors whose very name on the staff listing gave a hospital instant credibility. To hide her expression, she looked down at Risa and gently stroked the baby's cheek. "He sat up all night holding Risa," she heard herself say in a strange voice.

The nurse smiled. "He would. And he's still on the floor now, when he should be home sleeping. But that's Dr. Taliferro for you; he puts the babies before himself."

When Kathleen was back in her room, she kept thinking of the things the nurse had told her, and of the things Derek had said to her. He wanted Risa, he'd said. Was that reason enough to marry a woman he didn't love, when he could marry any woman he wanted and have his own children? Of course, he'd also said that eventually he expected to have a normal marriage with her, meaning he intended to sleep with her, so she had to assume he also intended to have children with her. But why was he so certain he'd never fall in love with someone and want out of the marriage?

"Problems?"

The deep, quiet voice startled her, and she looked up to find Derek standing just inside the door, watching her. She'd been so engrossed in her thoughts that she hadn't heard him.

"No, no problems. I was just…thinking."

"Worrying, you mean. Forget about all your second thoughts," he said with disquieting perception. "Just trust me, and let me handle everything. I've made arrangements for us to be married as soon as you're released from the hospital."

"So soon?" she gasped.

"Is there any reason to wait? You'll need a place to live, so you might as well live with me."

"But what about blood tests—"

"The lab here will handle them. When you're released, we'll get our marriage license and go straight to a judge who's an old friend of mine. My apartment is near here, so it'll be convenient for you to come back and forth to feed Risa until she's released. We can use the time to get a nursery set up for her."

She felt helpless. As he'd said, he had handled everything.

Chapter 5

Kathleen felt as if she'd been swept up by a tornado, and this one was named Derek. Everything went the way he directed. He even had a dress for her to wear for the wedding, a lovely blue-green silk that darkened her eyes to emerald, as well as a scrumptious black fake-fur coat, shoes, underwear, even makeup. A hairdresser came to the hospital that morning and fixed her hair in a chic, upswept style. Yes, he had everything under control. It was almost frightening.

He kept his warm hand firmly on her waist as they got the marriage license, then went to the judge's chamber to be married. There, Kathleen got another surprise: the chamber was crowded with people, all

of whom seemed ridiculously delighted that Derek
was marrying a woman he didn't love.

His mother and stepfather were there; dazedly,
Kathleen wondered what his mother must think of
all this. But Marcie, as she had insisted Kathleen
call her, was beaming with delight as she hugged
Kathleen. There were two other couples, two teenagers, and three younger children. One of the couples consisted of a tall, hard-looking man with gray-
ing black hair and a wand-slender woman with
almost silver-white hair and glowing green eyes. Derek introduced them as Rome and Sarah Matthews,
very good friends of his, but something in his voice
hinted at a deeper relationship. Sarah's face was incredibly tender as she hugged him, then Kathleen.

The other couple was Max and Claire Conroy,
and again Kathleen got the feeling that Derek meant
something special to them. Max was aristocratic and
incredibly handsome, with gilded hair and turquoise
eyes, while Claire was quieter and more understated,
but her soft brown eyes didn't miss a thing. The
three youngsters belong to the Conroys, while the
two teenagers were Rome and Sarah's children.

Everyone was ecstatic that Derek was marrying,
and Marcie couldn't wait to get to the hospital to
visit her new grandchild. She scolded Derek se-
verely for not contacting her immediately, but
stopped in midtirade when he leaned down and
kissed her cheek, smiling at her in that serene way
of his. "I know. You had a good reason," she
sighed.

"Yes, Mother."

"You'd think I'd eventually learn."

He grinned. "Yes, Mother."

The women all wore corsages, and Sarah pressed an arrangement of orchids into Kathleen's hands. Kathleen held the fragile flowers in shaking fingers as she and Derek stood before the judge, whose quiet voice filled the silent chamber as he spoke the traditional words about love and honor. She could feel the heat of Derek's body beside her, like a warm wall she could lean against if she became tired. They made the proper responses, and Derek was sliding a gold band set with an emerald surrounded by small, glittering diamonds on her finger. She blinked at it in surprise, then looked up at him just as the judge pronounced them man and wife, and Derek leaned down to kiss her.

She had expected the sort of brief, warm kiss he had given her before. She wasn't prepared for the way he molded her lips with his, or the passion evident in the way his tongue probed her mouth. She quivered, her hands going up to grab his shoulders in an effort to steady herself. His hard arms pressed her to him for a moment, then slowly released her as he lifted his head. Purely male satisfaction was gleaming in his eyes, and she knew he'd felt her surprised response to him.

Then everyone was surrounding them, laughing and shaking his hand, and there was a lot of kissing and hugging. Even the judge got hugged and kissed.

Half an hour later Derek called a halt to the festivities. "We'll have a real celebration later," he promised. "Right now, I'm taking Kathleen home to rest. We have to be back at the hospital in a couple of hours to feed Risa, so she doesn't have a lot of time to put her feet up."

"I'm fine," she felt obliged to protest, though in truth she would have appreciated the chance to rest.

Derek gave her a stern look, and she felt inexplicably guilty. Sarah laughed. "You might as well do what he says," the older woman said in gentle amusement. "You can't get around him."

Five minutes later Kathleen was sitting in the Jeep as he expertly threaded his way through the Dallas traffic. "I like your friends," she finally said, just to break the silence. She couldn't believe she'd done it; she had actually married him! "What do they do?"

"Rome is president and CEO of Spencer-Nyle Corporation. Sarah owns Tools and Dyes, a handcraft store. Two stores now, since she just opened another one. Max was a vice president at Spencer-Nyle with Rome, but about five years ago he started his own consulting business. Claire owns a bookstore."

His friends were obviously very successful, and she wondered again why he had married her, because she wasn't successful at all. How would she ever fit in? "And your mother?" she asked quietly.

"Mother helps Whit run his ranch, just across the Oklahoma border. I'd spent Christmas with them, and was on the way back to Dallas when I found you," he explained.

She didn't have anything else to ask him, so silence reigned again until they reached his apartment. "We'll look for something bigger in a few weeks, after your doctor releases you," he said as they left the elevator. "I've shoved things around and made closet space, but feel free to tell me to rearrange anything else you'd like moved."

"Why should I change anything?"

"To accommodate you and Risa. I'm not a bachelor any longer. I'm a husband and a father. We're a family; this is your home as much as mine."

He said it so simply, as if he were impervious to all the doubts that assailed her. She stood to the side as he unlocked the door, but before she could move to enter the apartment he turned back to her and swept her up in his arms, then carried her across the threshold. The gesture startled her, but then, everything he'd done that day had startled her. Everything he'd done from the moment she met him had startled her.

"Would you like a nap?" he asked, standing in the foyer with her still in his arms, as if awaiting directions.

"No, just sitting down for a while will do it." She managed a smile for him. "I had a baby, not major surgery, and you said yourself that I'm strong. Why should I act like a wilting lily when I'm not?"

He cleared his throat as he carefully placed her on her feet. "Actually, I said that you have great muscle tone. I don't believe I was admiring your strength.''

Her pulse leaped. He was doing that to her more and more often, saying little things that made it plain he found her desirable, or stealing some of those quick kisses. Five days earlier she would never have found those small advances anything but repulsive, but already a secret thrill warmed her whenever he said or did anything. She was changing rapidly under his intense coddling, and, to her surprise, she liked the changes.

"What are you thinking?" he asked, tapping her nose with a fingertip. "You're staring at me, but you aren't seeing me."

"I was thinking how much you spoil me," she replied honestly. "And how unlike me it is to let you do it."

"Why shouldn't you let me spoil you?" He helped her off with her coat and hung it in the small foyer closet.

"I've never been spoiled before. I've always had to look out for myself, because no one else really cared, not even my parents. I can't figure out why you should be so kind, or what you're getting out of our deal. You've done all this, but basically we're still strangers. What do you want from me?"

A faint smile touched his chiseled lips as he held out his hand. "Come with me."

"Where?"

"To the bedroom. I want to show you something."

Lifting her brows in curiosity at his manner, Kathleen put her hand in his and let him lead her to the bedroom. She looked around. It was a cheerful, spacious room, decorated in blue and white and with a king-size bed. The sliding closet doors were mirrored, and he positioned her in front of the mirrors with himself behind her.

Putting his hands on her shoulders, he said, "Look in the mirror and tell me what you see."

"Us."

"Is that all? Look at yourself, and tell me what I got out of our deal."

She looked in the mirror and shrugged. "A woman." Humor suddenly sparked in her eyes. "With great muscle tone."

He chuckled. "Hallelujah, yes. But that's only part of it. That's not to say I'm not turned on by your fantastic legs and gorgeous breasts, because I am, but what really gets me is what I see in your face."

He'd done it again. She felt her entire body grow warm as her eyes met his in the mirror. "My face?"

One arm slid around her waist, pulling her back to lean against him, while his other hand rose to stroke her face. "Your wonderful green eyes," he murmured. "Frightened and brave at the same time. I sometimes see hurt in your eyes, as if you're remembering things you don't want to talk about, but you don't let it get you down. You don't ask me for anything, so I have to guess at what you need, and maybe I overdo it. I see pleasure when I hold you

or kiss you. I see love for Risa, and compassion for
the other babies. I've turned your life upside down,
but you haven't let it get to you; you've just gone
along with me and kept your head above water.
You're a survivor, Kath. A strong, valiant, loving
survivor. That's what I got out of the deal. As well
as a great body, of course, and a beautiful baby
girl.''

The eyes he had described were wide as Kathleen
heard all those characteristics attributed to herself.
He smiled and let his fingers touch her lips. ''Did I
forget to mention what a kissable mouth you have?
How sweet and soft it is?''

Her mouth suddenly felt swollen, and her lips
moved against his fingers. ''I get the picture,'' she
breathed, her heart pounding at her aggressiveness.
''You married me for my body.''

''And what a body it is.'' He bent his head to
nuzzle her ear, while his hands drifted to her breasts
and gently cupped them. ''While we're being so
honest, why did you marry me? Other than to give
Risa all the advantages of being a doctor's daughter.''

''That was it,'' she said, barely able to speak. She
was stunned by his touch to her breasts, stunned and
scared and shocked, because she was aware of a
sense of pleasure. Never before had she enjoyed
having a man touch her so intimately. But her
breasts were sensitive now, ripe and full of milk,
and his light touch seared through her like a lightning bolt.

"Forget about what I can give Risa," he murmured. "Wasn't part of your reason for marrying me because of what I can give you?"

"I...I can live without luxury." Her voice was low and strained, and her eyelids were becoming so heavy she could barely hold them open. Her mind wasn't on what she was saying. The pleasure was so intense it was interfering with her breathing, making it fast and heavy. Frantically she tried to tell herself it was only because she *was* nursing Risa that her breasts were so warm and sensitive, and that, being a doctor, he knew it and how to exploit it. He wasn't even touching her nipples, but lightly stroking around them. She thought she would die if he touched her nipples.

"You look gorgeous in this dress, but let's get you out of it and into something more comfortable," he whispered, and his hands left her breasts. She stood pliantly, dazed with pleasure, as he unzipped the lovely dress and slipped it off her shoulders, then pushed it down over her hips to let it fall at her feet. She wore a slip under it, and she waited in a haze for him to remove it, too, but instead he lifted her in his arms and placed her on the bed, moving slowly, as if trying not to startle her. Her heart was pounding, but her body felt liquid with pleasure. She had just had a baby; he knew she couldn't let him do *that*...didn't he? But he was a doctor; perhaps he knew more than she did. No, it would hurt too much.

Perhaps he had something else in mind. She

thought of his hands on her naked skin, of feeling his big, muscled body naked against her, and a strange excitement made her nerves throb. Slowly the thought filled her mind that she trusted him, truly trusted him, and that was why she wasn't afraid. No matter what, Derek would never hurt her.

His eyelashes were half-lowered over his eyes, giving him a sensually sleepy look as he slipped her shoes off and let them drop to the floor. Kathleen watched him in helpless fascination, her breath stilling in her lungs when he reached up under her slip and began pulling her panty hose down. "Lift your hips," he instructed in a husky voice, and she obeyed willingly. When the nylon was bunched around her knees, he bent and pressed a kiss to her bare thighs before returning to his pleasant task and removing the garment.

Her skin felt hot, and the bed linens were cool beneath her. She had never *felt* so much before, as if the nerve endings in her skin had multiplied and become incredibly sensitive. Her limbs felt heavy and boneless, and she couldn't move, even when his hands stroked her thighs and pleasure shivered through her. "Derek," she whispered, vaguely surprised to find that she could barely speak; she had slurred his name, as if it were too much effort to talk.

"Hmm?" He was bent over her, the warmth of his body soothing her as he lifted her with one arm and stripped the cover back on the bed, then settled her between the sheets. His mouth feathered over her breasts, barely touching the silk that covered them.

Incredible waves of relaxation were sweeping over her. "You can't make love to me," she managed to whisper. "Not yet."

"I know, sweetheart," he murmured, his deep voice low and hypnotic. "Go to sleep. We have plenty of time."

Her lashes fluttered down, and with a slow, deep sigh she went to sleep. Derek straightened, looking down at her. His body throbbed with the need for sexual relief, but a faint, tender smile curved his lips as he watched her. She had called it "sex" before, but this time she had said "make love." She was losing her wariness, though she still seemed to have no idea why he had married her. Did she think she was so totally without charm or appeal? Did she truly think he'd married her only because of Risa? He'd done his best to convince her that he was attracted to her, but the final argument would have to wait about five weeks longer.

Her thick lashes made dark fans on her cheeks, just as Risa's did. He wanted to lie down beside her and hold her while she slept. He'd known she was tired; since Risa's birth, Kathleen had been sleeping a great deal, as if she had been pushing herself far too hard for far too long. Her body was insisting on catching up on its healing rest now that she no longer had such a pressing need to do everything herself.

The telephone in the living room rang, but he'd

had the foresight to unplug the phone by the bed, so Kathleen slept on undisturbed. Quickly he left the room, closing the door behind him, and picked up the other extension.

"Derek, is she asleep yet?" Sarah's warm voice held a certain amusement, as if she had known he would somehow have gotten Kathleen to take a nap by now.

He grinned. Sarah knew him even better than his mother, better than anyone else in the world, except perhaps Claire. Claire saw into people, but she was so quiet it was easy to underestimate her perception.

"She didn't think she needed a nap, but she went to sleep as soon as she lay down."

"Somehow, I never doubted it. Anyway, I've had an idea. Now that I've opened up the other store, I need to hire someone else. Do you think Kathleen would be interested? Erica is going to manage the new store, so I thought Kathleen could work with me, and she'd be able to have the baby with her."

Leave it to Sarah to notice that Kathleen needed a friend, as well as the measure of independence the job would give her while she adjusted to being his wife.

"She'll probably jump at it, but it'll be a couple of weeks before she's able to drive, and at least that long before Risa will be strong enough."

"Then I'll hold the job for her," Sarah said serenely.

"I'm going to remind you of this the next time

you accuse me of 'managing' people," he informed her, smiling.

"But hadn't you already thought of it?"

His smile grew. "Of course."

Chapter 6

The day they brought Risa home from the hospital, Kathleen could barely tolerate having the baby out of her sight for a moment. Risa was thirteen days old, and now weighed a grand total of five pounds and six ounces, which was still two ounces short of the five and a half pounds a baby normally had to weigh before Derek would allow it to be released from the neonatal unit, but, as he'd noted before, she was strong. Her cheeks had attained a newborn's plumpness, and she was nursing vigorously, with about four hours between each feeding.

Derek drove them home, then left the Cherokee with Kathleen so she would have a way of getting around if she needed anything, a gesture that eased a worry she hadn't known she had until he gave her the keys. The hospital was only a few blocks away, and the January day was mild, so he walked back.

She spent the day playing with Risa when the baby was awake, and watching her while she slept. Late that afternoon, Kathleen realized with a start that she hadn't given a thought to what she would prepare for dinner, and guilt filled her. Derek had been a saint, coddling her beyond all reason, letting her devote all her time to Risa, doing all the household chores himself, but Risa's homecoming marked a change in the status quo. It had been two weeks since Risa's birth, and Kathleen felt better than she had in years. She was rested, her appetite was better; there was no reason to let Derek continue to wait on her as if she was an invalid. He had given everything, and she had given nothing, not even her attention.

She rolled Risa's bassinet, which she and Derek had bought only the day before, into the kitchen so she could watch Risa while she prepared dinner. The baby slept peacefully, with the knuckles of one fist shoved into her mouth, undisturbed by the rattling of pots and pans. It was the first time Kathleen had cooked, so she had to hunt for everything, and it took her twice as long to do anything than it normally would have. She was relieved when Derek didn't come home at his usual time, since she was running behind schedule, but when half an hour had passed she became concerned. It wasn't like him to be late without calling her himself or having a nurse call to let her know that one of the babies needed

him. As short a time as they had been married, she
had already learned that about him. Derek was always considerate.

Derek was…incredible.

She wanted to give him something, even if it was
just a hot meal waiting for him when he came home.
She looked at the steaming food, ready to be served,
but he wasn't there. She could keep it warming on
the stove, but it wouldn't be the same.

Then she heard his key in the door, and she was
filled with relief. She hurried out of the kitchen to
greet him, her face alight with pleasure.

"I was worried," she said in a rush, then was
afraid he would think she was complaining, so she
changed what she had been about to say. "Believe
it or not, I actually cooked dinner. But I couldn't
find anything, and it took me forever to do. I was
afraid you'd be home before everything was finished, because I wanted to surprise you."

His eyes were warm as he put his arm around her
shoulders and hugged her to him for a kiss. He
kissed her a lot, sometimes with carefully restrained
passion, and she had stopped being shocked by her
own pleasure in his touch.

"I'm more than surprised, I'm downright grateful," he said, kissing her again. "I'm also starving.
Where's Risa?"

"In the kitchen, where I could watch her sleep."

"I wondered if you'd spend the day hanging over
her bassinet."

"Actually, yes."

His arm was around her waist as they walked into the kitchen. Risa was still asleep, so he didn't disturb her by picking her up. He set the table while Kathleen served the food, then they ate leisurely, one of the few times they'd had a chance to do so. Kathleen knew she was a good cook, and it gave her a great deal of satisfaction to watch Derek eat with evident enjoyment.

When they had finished, he helped her clean up, then, as sort of an afterthought, took a set of car keys out of his pocket and gave them to her. She took them, frowning at him in puzzlement. "I already have keys to the Cherokee."

"These aren't for the Jeep," he explained calmly, going into the living room and sitting down to read the newspaper. "They're for your car. I picked it up on the way home this afternoon."

Her car? She didn't own a car, just the old truck. The truth burst in her mind like a sunrise, robbing her of breath. "I can't take a car from you," she said, her voice strained.

He looked up from the newspaper, his black brows rising in a question. "Is there a problem? If you don't want the car, I'll drive it, and you can have the Jeep. I can't continue walking to the hospital, so buying a car seemed like the logical thing to do."

She felt like screaming. He'd hemmed her in with logic. He was right, of course, but that only made her feel more helpless. She'd felt so proud of preparing dinner for him, the first time she'd contributed anything to their marriage, while he'd stopped on the way home and bought a *car* for her! She felt like an insatiable sponge, soaking up everything he had to give and demanding more just by her very existence, her presence in his life.

Licking her lips, she said, "I'm sorry. I'm just…stunned. No one ever bought…I don't know what to say."

He appeared to give it thought, but his eyes were twinkling. "I suppose you could do what anyone else would do: jump up and down, squeal, laugh, throw your arms around my neck and kiss me until I beg for mercy."

Her heart jumped wildly. He was as splendid as a pagan god, powerfully built and powerfully male; that wasn't a twinkle in his eyes, after all, but a hard, heated gleam, and he was looking at her the way men have looked at women since the beginning of time. Her mouth went suddenly dry, and she had to lick her lips again.

"Is that what you want me to do?" she whispered.

He carefully put the newspaper aside. "You can skip the jumping and squealing, if you want. I won't mind if you go straight to the kissing part."

She didn't remember moving, but somehow she found herself on his lap, her arms around his strong neck, her mouth under his. He had kissed her so often in the week they'd been married that she'd become used to it, expected it, enjoyed it. In a way his kisses reassured her that she would be able to have something to give, even if it were only physical ease. She couldn't even do that completely, at the present, but at least the potential was there. If he wanted her to kiss him, she was more than willing.

His arms closed around her, holding her to his strong chest as he deepened the kiss, his tongue moving to touch hers. Kathleen felt very brave and bold; she had no idea that her kisses were rather timid and untutored, or that he was both touched and highly aroused by her innocence. He kissed her slowly, thoroughly, teaching her how to use her tongue and how to accept his, holding himself under tight control lest he alarm her.

Finally she turned her head away, gasping for breath, and he smiled because she had forgotten to breathe. "Are you ready to beg for mercy?" she panted, color high in her face.

"I don't know anyone named Mercy," he muttered, turning her face back to his for another taste of her mouth. "Why would I beg for a woman I don't even know?"

Her chuckle was muted by his lips as he turned passion to teasing, kissing her all over her face with loud smacking noises. Then he hoisted her to her feet and got to his. "Wake up the tiny tyrant so I can show you which car is yours," he said, grinning.

Kathleen threw an anxious look at the sleeping baby. "Should we take her out in the cold?"

"Do you want to leave her here by herself? Unless you want to try the key in every car in the parking lot, you have to know which one is yours.

It won't take a minute; just wrap her up and keep her head covered. It isn't that cold outside, anyway.''

"Are you certain it won't hurt her?"

He gave her a very level look, and without another word she turned to get a jacket for herself and a blanket for Risa. She felt like kicking herself. Did he think she didn't trust him to know what would harm the baby and what wouldn't? He was a doctor, for heaven's sake! He'd taken care of her and Risa from the moment they'd met. She'd really made a mess of it again, kissing him as if she could eat him up one minute, then practically insulting him the next.

When she returned with the blanket, he'd already picked Risa up, waking her, and he was crooning to her. Risa watched him with a ridiculously serious expression, her tiny face intent as she stared up at him, her hands waving erratically. To Kathleen's surprise, the baby was working her rosebud mouth as if trying to mimic Derek's actions. She seemed totally fascinated by the man holding her.

"Here's the blanket."

He took it and deftly wrapped Risa in it, covering her head. The baby began fussing, and Derek chuckled. "We'd better hurry. She won't tolerate this for long; she wants to see what's going on."

They hurried down to the parking lot, and Derek led her to a white Oldsmobile Calais. Kathleen had to swallow her gasp. It was a new car, not a used one, as she'd expected. It was sleek and sporty looking, with a soft dove-grey interior and every optional convenience she could think of. Tears burned her eyes. "I...I don't know what to say," she whispered as she stared at it in shock.

"Say you love it, promise me that you'll always wear your seat belt, and we'll take the baby back inside before she works herself into a tantrum. She doesn't like this blanket over her face one bit." Risa's fussing was indeed rising in volume.

"I love it," she said, dazed.

He laughed and put his arm around her waist as the fussing bundle in his arms began to wail furiously. They hurried back inside, and he lifted the blanket to reveal Risa's red, tightly screwed-up face. "Stop that," he said gently, touching her cheek. She gave a few more wails, then hiccuped twice and settled down, once more intently staring up at his face.

He was perfect. Everything he did only compounded the imbalance in the deal she'd made with him. He not only took care of everything, gave her everything, but he was better at taking care of Risa. The parents of his tiny patients all thought he ranked right up there with angels, and all the nurses were in love with him. He could have had anyone, but instead he'd chosen to saddle himself with a...a *hick* who didn't know anything but how to work a ranch, and a child who wasn't his. Kathleen felt like a parasite. If nothing else, she could begin to repay him for the car, but to do that she'd have to get a job.

She took a deep breath and broached the subject as soon as he'd laid Risa down. Kathleen didn't believe in putting things off. She'd learned the hard way that they didn't go away; it was better to meet trouble head-on. "I'm going to start looking for a job."

"If you feel well enough," he said absently as he tucked a light blanket around the baby. "You might want to call Sarah; she mentioned something about needing more help in one of her stores."

She'd been braced for objections, but his matter-of-fact acceptance made her wonder why she'd thought he wouldn't like the idea. Then she realized she had expected him to act as Larry would have; Larry hadn't wanted her to do anything except work like a slave on the ranch, and wait on him hand and foot. If she'd gone out and gotten a job, she might have been able to get out from under his thumb before he'd finished bleeding her dry. Derek wasn't like that. Derek wanted her to be happy.

It was an astounding revelation. Kathleen couldn't remember anyone ever going out of their way to give her any sort of happiness. Yet since Derek had appeared in her life, everything he'd done had been with her happiness and well-being in mind.

She thought about his suggestion, and she liked it. She wasn't trained to do anything except be a waitress, but she did know how to operate a cash register; working in a crafts store sounded interesting. She made up her mind to call Sarah Matthews the next day.

When they went to bed that night, Derek practically had to drag Kathleen out of the nursery.

"Maybe I should sleep in here," she said worriedly. "What if she cries and I can't hear her?"

Sleeping in the same bed with her without touching her had been one of the worst tortures a man had ever devised for himself, but Derek wasn't about to give it up. Besides, he was ready to advance his plan a step, which wouldn't work if Kathleen wasn't in bed with him. He'd anticipated all her first-night-with-a-new-baby jitters, and set about soothing them. "I bought a baby-alarm system," he said, and placed a small black speaker by Risa's crib. "The other speaker will be by our bed. We'll be able to hear if she cries."

"But she needs to be kept warm—"

"We'll leave the heat turned up, but close the vents in our room." As he talked, he was leading her to the bedroom. He'd already closed the heat vents, and the room was noticeably cooler than the rest of the apartment. Anticipation made his heart beat faster. For over a week he'd let her get used to his presence in the bed; he even knew why she tolerated it. She thought she *owed* it to him. But now he was going to get her used to his touch as well as his presence, and he meant more than those kisses that were driving him wild. He wanted her so much he ached with it, and tonight he would take another step toward his goal.

She crawled into bed and pulled the covers up over her. Derek turned out the light, then dropped his pajama bottoms to the floor and, blissfully nude, got in beside her. He normally slept nude, but had worn the aggravating pajamas since their marriage, and it was a relief to shed them.

The cold room would do the rest. She would seek out his warmth during the night, and when she woke up, she would be in his arms. A smile crossed his face as he thought of it.

The baby alarm worked. A little after one, Kathleen woke at the first tentative wail. She felt deliciously warm, and groaned at the idea of getting up. She was so comfortable, with her head on Derek's shoulder and his arms around her so tightly—

Her eyes flew open, and she sat up in bed. "I'm sorry," she blurted.

He yawned sleepily. "For what?"

"I was all over you!"

"Hell, sweetheart, I enjoyed it! Would you listen to that little terror scream," he said in admiration, changing the subject. Yawning again, he reached out to turn on the lamp, then got out of bed. Kathleen's entire body jerked in shock. He was naked! Gloriously naked. Beautifully naked. Her mouth went dry, and her full breasts tightened until they began to ache.

He held out his hand to her. "Come on, sweetheart. Let's see about our daughter."

Still in shock, she put her hand in his as he gave her a slow, wicked smile that totally robbed her of breath.

Chapter 7

That smile remained in her mind the next morning as she drove carefully to Sarah Matthews's store, following the directions she'd gotten from Sarah only an hour before. Risa slept snugly in her car seat, having survived the first night in her crib, as well as being tended by her gorgeous, naked daddy. Kathleen had been too stunned to do anything but sit in the rocking chair and hold Risa to her breast. Derek had done everything else. And after Risa was asleep again, Kathleen had gone docilely back to bed again, and let him gather her close to his warm, muscular *naked* body…and enjoyed it.

Enjoyed seemed like too mild a description for the way her thoughts and emotions had rioted. Part of her had wanted to touch him, taste him, run her hands all over his magnificent body. Another part of her had panicked; deep in her mind she still hadn't recovered from the brutal, contemptuous way that Larry had humiliated her before walking out.

She didn't want to think about that; she shoved the memory from her mind, and found the blank space it left promptly filled by Derek's sensual, knowing smile. *That was it!* Knowing! He'd known exactly how she had felt!

She found the cozy crafts store easily enough, despite her lack of total attention to where she was going. There was ample parking, but she carefully parked her spotless new car well away from everyone else, then gathered Risa and the ton of paraphernalia babies required into her arms and entered the store.

There were several customers browsing and chatting with Sarah, as well as each other, but when Kathleen came in a glowing smile lit Sarah's face, and she came right over to take the baby from her arms. "What a darling," she whispered, examining the sleeping infant. "She's beautiful. Missy and Jed will spoil her rotten, just like Derek spoiled them when they were little. I brought Jed's old playpen and set it up in the back, where I used to keep my kids, if you want to put all Risa's stuff back there."

Kathleen carried the bulging diaper bag into the back room, which was a section of the store stocked with doll supplies, as well as a cozy area with several rocking chairs, where Sarah's customers could sit and chat if they wanted. It was the most popular area of the store, and warmer than the front section. A sturdy playpen had been set up next to the rocking chairs, and Kathleen looked at it in bewilderment.

"You drove home to get the playpen after I called you this morning? Who watched the store?"

Sarah laughed, her warm green eyes twinkling. "Actually, I've had the playpen set up for several days. I called Derek the day you were married and told him I needed help here, if he thought you'd be interested."

"He didn't tell me until last night," Kathleen said, wondering if she should be angry at his manipulation, and also wondering if it would do any good.

"Of course not. I knew he'd wait until Risa was home and you were feeling better. But don't let the playpen pressure you into thinking you have to take the job if you don't want it."

Kathleen took a deep breath. "I'd like to take the job. I don't have any training for anything except being a waitress and doing ranch work, but I can work a cash register."

Sarah beamed at her. "Then it's settled. When can you start?"

Kathleen looked around the warm, homey store. This would be a good place to work, even though she hated the idea of leaving Risa during the day. She would have to find a day-care center or a babysitter nearby, so she could nurse the baby during lunch. She supposed Risa would have to get used to a bottle for supplemental feedings, though it made her want to cry to think about it. "I'll have to find someone to keep Risa before I can start," she said reluctantly.

Sarah blinked in surprise. "Why? My babies grew up in this store. That way I could keep them with me. Just bring Risa with you; you'll have more helping hands than you can count. Whenever you feel strong enough to start work—"

"I'm strong enough now," Kathleen said. "After working on a ranch my entire life, I'm as strong as a packhorse."

"What does Derek think about this?" Sarah asked, then laughed at herself. "Never mind. He wouldn't have told you about the job if he didn't think you were well enough to handle it. It isn't hard work; the only physical labor is putting up stock, and Jed usually manhandles the boxes for me."

Kathleen searched her memory for a picture of Jed, because she knew he'd been at her wedding. "Is Jed the tall, black-haired boy?"

"Yes. My baby's almost six feet tall. It's ridiculous how fast they grow up. Enjoy every moment with Risa, because her babyhood won't last long." Sarah smiled down at the sleeping bundle in her arms, then leaned over and gently deposited Risa in the playpen. "She's gorgeous. Derek must be insufferably proud of her."

It hit Kathleen like a slap that everyone must think Risa was truly Derek's daughter, which would explain why he had hustled Kathleen into such a hasty marriage. Why wouldn't they think it? Risa's hair was the same inky shade as Derek's, as well as her own. She didn't know what to say, yet she knew she had to say something. She couldn't let his friends think he was the type of man who would abandon a woman who was pregnant with his child, not when he had been so good to her, given her so much. In the end, she just blurted it out. "Risa isn't Derek's. I mean, I'd never met him until the day she was born."

But Sarah only smiled her serene smile. "I know; Derek told us. But she's his now, just like you are."

The idea of belonging to, or with, anyone was alien to Kathleen, because she'd never known the closeness. At least, she hadn't until Risa had been born, and then she had felt an instant and overpowering sense of possession. It was different with Derek. He was a man…very much so. The image of his bare, powerful body flashed into her mind, and she felt herself grow warm. He had taken her over completely, so in that respect she did belong to him. The odd thing was that she had just sprung to his defense, unwilling to let his friends think anything bad about him. She had felt the need to protect him, as if he belonged to her, and that sense of mutual possession was confusing.

She pushed her thoughts away, concentrating on learning about the shop with the same intensity she'd learned how to be a waitress. As Sarah had said, it wasn't hard work, for which Kathleen was grateful, because she found that she did tire easily. For the most part Risa slept contentedly, whimpering only when she needed changing or was hungry, and occasionally looking around with vague, innocent eyes. It seemed that all the customers knew Derek, and there was a lot of oohing and aahing over the baby.

In the middle of the afternoon, when school was out, Sarah's teenagers came in, with Jed dwarfing his older sister in a protective manner. Missy, who was startlingly lovely, with her father's black eyes and black hair, nevertheless had Sarah's fragile bone structure. When she saw Kathleen, she rushed to her and hugged her as if they were long-lost friends, then breathlessly demanded to know where the baby was. Laughing, Kathleen pointed to the playpen, and Missy descended on Risa, who was just waking from another nap.

Jed watched his sister, and there was something fierce in his own black eyes. "She's crazy about little kids," he said in a rumbly voice, without any adolescent squeak. "She'll be pushing you and Derek out the door every night just so she can babysit." Then he turned and said, "Hi, Mom," as he enveloped Sarah in his muscled arms.

But there was a small frown in Sarah's eyes as she looked up at her son. "What's wrong? You're angry about something." He was too much like his father for her ever to mistake his moods.

"A pipsqueak punk has been hassling Miss," he said bluntly.

"There's nothing to it!" Missy insisted, approaching them with Risa cuddled to her shoulder.

"He hasn't really said anything. He just keeps asking me out."

"Do you want to go?" Sarah asked calmly.

"No!" Missy's answer was too swift, denying her casual attitude. "I just don't want to make any big deal about it; I'd be too embarrassed."

"I'll talk to Rome," Sarah said.

"Oh, Mom!"

"I can handle it," Jed said, his voice deadly calm. He reached out and tickled Risa's chin, then deftly scooped her out of Missy's arms.

"Give her back!" Missy said, breathing fire.

They wandered into the back room, still arguing over who would get to hold the baby, and Sarah shook her head. "Teenagers. Just wait," she said with a smile for Kathleen. "Your turn will come."

"Jed's very protective, isn't he?"

"He's just like Rome, but he isn't old enough yet to know how to control all that intensity."

Ten minutes later Missy returned, having regained possession of Risa. Jed had settled down in the back room, watching the portable televison and doing his homework at the same time. "Mom, please don't say anything to Dad about that guy," she began earnestly. "You know how Dad is. You almost couldn't talk him into letting me date, and I was *fifteen!*"

"What guy?" a deep voice asked calmly, and they all whirled to face the newcomer.

"Derek!" Missy said in relief, reaching to give

him a hug which he returned, cradling her head against his shoulder for a moment.

Kathleen couldn't say anything; she just stared at him with her tongue glued to the roof of her mouth. The light wind had ruffled his black hair, and with his naturally dark complexion it gave him a raffish look that almost literally stopped her heart. His broad shoulders strained the light jacket he wore, his only concession to the January weather.

Sarah was frowning at him. "Why didn't the bell ring when you came in?"

"Because I reached up and caught it," he answered calmly as he slid his arm around Kathleen's waist and drew her to him. His golden eyes went back to Missy. "What guy?"

"Some scuzzball keeps pestering me to go out with him," she explained. "Jed's gone all macho, and Mom is threatening to tell Dad, and if she does he'll *never* let me date anyone again."

Derek lifted his eyebrows. "Is this scuzzball dangerous?"

An uncertain look flitted over Missy's delicate features. "I don't know," she admitted in a small voice. "Do you think Dad should know?"

"Of course. Why would he blame you for something that isn't your fault? Unless he wants to blame you for being a traffic-stopper."

She blushed, then laughed. "All right. I guess he'll let me go to the prom…if I can get a date."

"No boyfriend?" Kathleen asked, having finally found her tongue. Talking to Missy seemed safe enough, though her attention was splintered by the heat of Derek's body against her side.

Missy shrugged. "No one special. They all seem so *young*." With that scathing denunciation of her peer group, she allowed Derek to take Risa from her and went to join Jed.

"You're off from work early." Kathleen finally managed to talk to him, since he had released her when he lifted the baby to his shoulder.

"I'm on call. We have a mother trying to go into labor three months early. If they can't get it stopped, I'll have to be there when the baby is born. I decided to take a break while I can, and see my women."

She felt a pang at the thought that she might not be sleeping with him that night, and even a little jealousy that it was Risa who was cuddled so lovingly on that broad shoulder. Well, he'd made it plain from the start that it was Risa he wanted. Why should she be jealous? Did she want Derek to demand more from her than she could give?

Maybe she just wanted him to demand *any*thing from her, so she would know *what* to give.

"What time do you leave work?" he asked as he checked his watch.

Kathleen looked at Sarah. They hadn't even talked about hours. It had been more like visiting with friends than working, anyway. "Go on," Sarah said, smiling. "You've been on your feet a lot today, and the kids are here to help. See you in the morning at nine. Wait, let me get a key for you." She fetched an extra key from the bottom of the cash register, and Kathleen put it in her purse.

Derek got the blanket and diaper bag from the playpen and wrapped Risa snugly in the blanket. Predictably, she began fussing when her face was covered, and he grinned. "We have to go," he told Sarah as he ushered Kathleen out the door. "Having her face covered makes her mad."

Quickly he carried the baby to the car and strapped her into her seat; she settled down as soon as he whisked the blanket from her face. Then he came around to Kathleen's side and bent down to kiss her. "Be careful on the way home," he said, then kissed her again. "I'll pick up dinner. What do you like? Chinese? Mexican?"

She'd never eaten Chinese food, but she liked tacos. "Mexican?"

He straightened. "I'll get the food and come straight home." Then he closed her door and walked to the Cherokee without looking back.

Kathleen licked her lips as she started the car, savoring the taste of his mouth. She could feel an unfamiliar tightening inside, and her breasts were aching. She glanced at Risa. "Aren't you hungry?"

A tiny fist waved jerkily back and forth as the baby tried to find her mouth with it. She was monumentally unconcerned with her mother's agitation.

Derek was less than half an hour behind her, but they had scarcely sat down to the spicy meal when his beeper went off. Without hesitation he went to the phone and called the hospital. "All right. I'm on my way."

He barely stopped to snag his jacket on the way out. "Don't wait up for me," he called over his shoulder; then the door closed, and Kathleen sat there with refried beans lumping in her mouth, suddenly tasteless.

The hours passed slowly as she waited for him to come home. Risa was fed and put to bed; then Kathleen tried to become interested in television. When that failed, she tried to read. That was also a dismal failure, and she was furious at herself. She was used to being alone, and had never found it oppressive before. Had she become so dependent on him that she couldn't function without his presence?

At last, disgusted, she went to bed, and her body was tired enough that she went to sleep despite her restless thoughts. When Risa's first hungry cries woke her at one-thirty, the other side of the bed was still empty.

But when she entered the nursery she jumped in surprise, because Derek was sitting in the rocking chair holding the baby while she cried, his hand rubbing her tiny back. There was a terrible emptiness in his eyes that made her hurt, but she sensed that he got some comfort from holding Risa.

"The baby died," he said in a toneless voice. "I did everything I could, but he didn't make it. He wouldn't have had much of a chance even if he'd gone full term; his heart was hopelessly malformed. Damn it to hell and back, I still had to try."

She touched his shoulder. "I know," she whispered.

He looked down at the furious baby, then caught Kathleen's wrist and drew her down on his lap. Holding her against his chest, he unbuttoned her nightgown and bared her breast, then let her take Risa and guide the child's mouth to her nipple. The outraged wails stopped immediately. Derek looked down at the vigorously suckling infant and gathered both mother and child closer to his body, then leaned his head back and closed his eyes.

Kathleen let her head rest on his shoulder, her own eyes closing as she soaked up his warmth and nearness. He needed her. For the first time, he needed her. She knew that any warm body would have done for him right now, but the warm body was hers, and she'd be there as long as her touch gave him comfort. Or maybe it was Risa who gave him comfort, Risa whom he couldn't bear to release. She was a healthy, thriving baby now, gaining weight every day. He had seen death, and now he needed to see life, the precious life of a baby he'd helped into the world.

Kathleen had to bite her lip. Why hadn't he come to their bed? To her? Why didn't he need *her?*

Chapter 8

Four weeks later, Kathleen could feel a secret smile tugging at her lips as she unlocked the front door and carried Risa inside to her crib. The baby grunted and waved her fists, then broke into a quick, open-mouthed smile as Kathleen tickled her chin. Even Risa was happy, but Kathleen thought her daughter was smiling at the world in general, while *she* had a very personal reason.

The obstetrician had given her a clean bill of health earlier in the day, and since then she hadn't been able to stop grinning. These past four weeks had been almost impossible to bear as she fretted the days away, impatient for the time when she could truly become Derek's wife. He was a healthy, virile man; she'd seen the evidence of it every day, because he had no modesty around her. She couldn't say that she'd gotten used to seeing him nude; her heart still jumped, her pulse still speeded up, she still grew very warm and distracted by all that muscled masculinity. She was even...fascinated.

Marital relations with Larry hadn't been a joy. She had always felt used and even repulsed by his quick, callous handling; she hadn't been a person to him, but a convenience. Instinctively, she knew that making love with Derek would be different, and she wanted to experience it. She wanted to give him the physical ease and enjoyment of her body, a deeply personal gift from her to the man who had completely changed her life. Derek was the strongest, most loving and giving man she could imagine, but because he was so strong it sometimes seemed as if he didn't need anything from her, and being able to give him something in return had become an obsession with her. At last she could give him her body, and sexual fulfillment.

He knew of her appointment; he'd reminded her of it that morning. When he came home, he would ask her what the doctor had said. Then his golden eyes would take on that warm intensity she'd seen in them sometimes, and when they went to bed he would take her in his powerful arms, where she felt so safe and secure, and he would make her truly his wife, in fact as well as in name....

Risa's tiny hands batted against Kathleen's arm, jerking her from her exciting fantasy. ''If I give you a bath and feed you now, will you be a good girl and sleep a long time tonight?'' she whispered to her daughter, smiling down at her gorgeous offspring. How she was growing! She weighed eight pounds now, and was developing dimples and creases all over her wriggling little body. Since she had begun smiling, Missy and Jed were in a constant state of warfare to see who could get her to flash that adorable, smooth-gummed grin, but she smiled most often for Derek.

Kathleen checked her wristwatch. Derek had called the store while she'd been at the doctor's office and left a message with Sarah that he would be a few hours late, so she had time to get Risa settled for the night—she hoped—and prepare dinner before he'd be home. Would candles be too obvious, or would it be a discreet way of letting him know what the doctor's verdict had been? She'd never prepared a romantic dinner before, and she wondered if she would make a fool of herself. After all, Derek was a doctor; there were no physical mysteries for him, and how could there be romance without some mystery?

Her hands shook as she prepared Risa's bath. How could there be romance between them anyway? It was payment of a debt, part of the deal they'd made. He was probably expecting it. The only mystery involved was why she was letting herself get into such a lather over it.

Risa liked her bath and with the truly contrary nature of all children, chose that night to want to play. Kathleen didn't have the heart to hurry her, because she enjoyed seeing those little legs kick. How different things might have been if it hadn't been for Derek! She might never have known the joy of watching her child splash happily in the bathwater.

But finally the baby tired, and after she was dried and dressed she nursed hungrily, then fell asleep at Kathleen's breast. Smiling, Kathleen put her in the crib and covered her with a light blanket. Now it was time for her own bath, so she would be clean and sweet-smelling in case Derek came home in an impatient mood, ready to end his period of celibacy.

She bathed, then prepared dinner and left it warming in the oven until she heard Derek's key in the lock, then hurried to pour their drinks and serve the food while he hung up his coat and washed. Everything was ready when he joined her at the table.

As always, he drew her to him for a kiss; she had hoped he would deepen the kiss into passion, but instead he lifted the warm pressure of his mouth and looked around. "Is Risa already asleep?" He sounded disappointed.

"Yes, she went to sleep right after the bath." She felt disappointed, too. Why hadn't he kissed her longer, or asked immediately what the doctor had said? Oh, he had to know everything was okay, but she still would have liked for him to be a little eager.

Over dinner, he told her about the emergency that had kept him at the hospital. Just when she had decided that her visit to the doctor had slipped his mind and was wondering how to mention it, he asked casually, "Did the doctor release you from her care?"

She felt her heartbeat speed up. She cleared her throat, but her voice was still a little husky as she answered. "Yes. She said I'm back to normal, and in good health."

"Good."

That was it. He didn't mention it again, but acted as if it were any other evening. He didn't grab her and take her off to bed, and a sense of letdown kept her quiet as they read the newspaper and watched television. He was absorbed in a hockey game, which she didn't understand. Football and baseball were more her style. Finally she put down the newspaper she'd been reading and tried one more time. "I think I'll go to bed."

He checked his watch. "All right. I'm going to watch a little more of the game. I'll be there in half an hour."

She waited tensely in the dark, unable to relax. Evidently he didn't need her sexually as much as she'd been counting on. She pressed her hands over her eyes; had she been fooling herself all along? Maybe he had someone else to take care of his physical needs. As soon as the thought formed, she dismissed it. Derek. He had sworn fidelity in their marriage vows, and Derek Taliferro was a man who kept his word.

Finally she heard the shower running, and a few minutes later he entered the bedroom. She could feel the damp heat of his body as he slid between the sheets, and she turned on her side to face him.

"Derek?"

"Hmm?"

"Are you tired?"

"I'm tense more than tired." She could see him staring through the darkness at the ceiling. "It's hard to unwind after a touchy situation like we had this afternoon."

Kathleen moved closer to him, her hands going out to touch his chest. The crisp curls against her palm gave her a funny, warm feeling. Her head found the hollow of his shoulder, and the clean, masculine scent of his skin surrounded her. His arms went around her, the way they had every night for the past four weeks. It was going to be all right, she told herself, and waited.

But he didn't do anything other than hold her, and finally she decided he was waiting for her to give him the go-ahead. Clearing her throat, she whispered, "I...the doctor said it's okay for me to...you know. If you want to, that is," she added hastily.

Slowly Derek reached out and switched on the lamp, then lifted himself onto his elbow and looked down at her. There was a strange expression in his eyes, one she couldn't read. "What about you?" he asked in that even tone that sometimes gave her chills. "Do *you* want to 'you know'?"

"I want to please you." She could feel her throat closing up under his steady gaze. "We made a deal...and I owe you so much it's the least I—"

"You don't owe me a damn thing," he interrupted in a harsh voice she barely recognized as his. Moving abruptly, he rolled away from her and got out of bed, standing there glaring down at her with golden eyes molten with fury. She had never seen Derek angry before, she realized dimly through her shock, and now he wasn't just angry, he was raging. Being Derek, he controlled his rage, but it was there nonetheless.

"Before we got married, I told you we wouldn't make love without caring and commitment; I never said a damned word about keeping a deal or paying a debt. Thanks, sweetheart, but I don't need charity." He grabbed a blanket and slammed out of the bedroom, leaving Kathleen lying in bed staring at the spot where he'd stood.

She shook her head, trying to deal with what had just happened. How had it blown up in her face like that? She had just been trying to give back some of the tenderness he'd given her, but he hadn't wanted her. She began to shake, lying there in the bed that gradually became cool without his body to keep it warm, but it wasn't just the temperature that chilled her. His absence chilled her; she had come to rely on him so much that now she felt lost without him.

She had been fooling herself all along. She didn't have anything to give him, not even sex. He didn't need her at all, despite his words about caring and commitment. She *did* care about him, and she was committed to making their marriage work, but he still didn't want her, not the way she wanted him

to. But then, why should he? He was extraordinary
in every way, while she was worse than ordinary;
she had been, and still was, unwanted.

Her hands knotted into fists as she lay there, trying to control her convulsive shaking. Her parents
hadn't wanted her; they had been middle-aged when
she was born, and her presence had almost embarrassed them. They hadn't been demonstrative people, anyway, and they'd had no idea what to do with
a curious, lively child. Gradually the child had
learned not to make noise or trouble, but she had
been so starved for love that she'd married the first
man who had asked her, and gone from bad to
worse, because Larry hadn't wanted her either.
Larry had wanted to live off her and the ranch she'd
inherited, and in the end he'd bled the ranch to
death, then left her because she'd had nothing else
to give him.

It looked as if she didn't have anything to give
Derek, either, except Risa, but it was Risa he'd
wanted, anyway.

Derek lay on the sofa, his jaw clenched and his
body burning as he stared through the darkness.
Damn, he wanted her so much he hurt, but it was
like being punched in the gut for her to tell him he
could use her body because she "owed" him! All
these weeks he'd done everything he could to pam-
per her and make her love him, but sometimes he
felt as if he were butting his head against a stone

wall. She accepted him, but that was it, and he wanted more than mere acceptance…so much more.

She watched him constantly, with wary green eyes, as if trying to gauge his mood and anticipate his needs, but it was more the attention of a servant trying to please than that of a wife. He didn't need a servant, but he desperately needed Kathleen to be his wife. He needed her to touch him with the fierce want and love he could sense were bottled up inside her, if she would only let them out. What had happened to her that she suppressed the affectionate side of her nature with everyone except Risa? He'd tried to tell her how much she meant to him without putting a lot of pressure on her, and he'd tried to show her, but still she held back from him.

Maybe he should take what she'd offered. Maybe emotional intimacy would follow physical intimacy. God knew his body craved the pleasure and release of lovemaking; at least he could have that. But she had told him, when he'd asked her to marry him, that things had happened to her, and she might never be able to accept lovemaking again; when he calmed down, he realized that she had come a long way to even be able to offer him the use of her body.

It just wasn't enough. He wanted to erase the shadows from her eyes, to watch her smile bloom for him. He wanted her slim body twisting beneath him in spasms of pleasure; he wanted to hear her chanting love words to him; he wanted her laughter and tenderness and trust. God, how he wanted her trust! But most of all, he wanted her love, with the desperate thirst of a man stranded in the desert.

Everything had always come so easily for him, including women. He'd scarcely reached his teens before older girls, and even women, had begun noticing him. It was probably poetic justice that he had fallen in love with a woman who protected her emotions behind a wall so high he couldn't find a way over it. He had always known what to do in any situation, how to get people to do what he wanted, but with Kathleen he was stymied. Wryly he admitted to himself that his emotions were probably clouding his normally clear insight, but he couldn't detach himself from the problem. He wanted her with a force and heat that obscured all other details.

He was so wrapped up in his rage and frustration that he didn't hear her enter the room. The first he knew of her presence was when her hand touched his shoulder briefly, then hurriedly withdrew, as if she were afraid to touch him. Startled, he turned his head to look at her as she knelt beside the sofa; the darkness hid her expression, but not the strain in her low voice.

"I'm sorry," she whispered. "I didn't mean to embarrass you. I know I'm not anything special, but I thought you might want to…" Her voice fumbled to a halt as she tried and failed to find the phrasing she wanted. Finally she gave up and simply continued. "I swear I won't put you in that position again. I'm not much good at it, anyway. Larry said I was lousy.…" Again her voice died away, and the pale oval of her face turned to the side as if she couldn't face him, even in the darkness.

It was the first time she'd mentioned her ex-husband voluntarily, and his name brought Derek up on his elbow, galvanized by this abrupt opportunity to learn what had happened between Kathleen and the man. "What happened?" His voice was full of raw, rough demand, and Kathleen was too vulnerable at the moment to deny it.

"He married me for the ranch, so he could live off it without having to work." Her words were almost prosaic, but her voice shook a little in betrayal of that false calm. "He didn't want me, either; I don't guess anyone ever has, not even my folks. But Larry used me whenever he had the urge and couldn't get to town; he said I might as well be some use, because even though I was lousy in bed, I was still better than nothing. Then finally he couldn't get any more money out of the ranch, and he filed for divorce so he could move on to something better. The last time I saw him, he...he used me again. I tried to stop him, but he was drunk and mean, and he hurt me. He said it was a goodbye present, because no man would ever be interested in me. He was right, wasn't he?"

Slowly, shakily, she rose to her feet and stood beside him in the darkness. "I just wanted to do something for you," she whispered. "You've done so much, given me so much, and I don't have anything to give you except that. I'd give you my life if you needed it. Anyway, I won't let loving you the

way I do embarrass you again. I guess all you want
from me is to be left alone.''

Then she was gone, walking silently back into the
bedroom, and Derek lay on his cold, lonely sofa, his
heart pounding at what she'd said.

Now he knew what to do.

Chapter 9

Kathleen had had years of practice in hiding her emotions behind a blank face, and that was what she did the next day at work. She talked to the customers as usual, played with Risa and chatted with Sarah, with whom she had developed a warm friendship. Being friends with Sarah wasn't difficult; the older woman was serene and truly kind. Within a few days Kathleen had easily been able to see why her children adored her and her big, fierce husband looked at her as if the entire world spun around her.

But Sarah was also keenly intuitive, and by lunchtime she was watching Kathleen in a thoughtful manner. Knowing those perceptive eyes were on her made Kathleen withdraw further inside her shell, because she couldn't let herself think about what a terrible mess she'd made of things.

She couldn't believe what she'd said. It horrified her that she had actually blurted out to him that she loved him, after he had made it so painfully plain that he wasn't interested in her even for sex. She hadn't meant to, but she had only just discovered it herself, and she'd still been reeling from the shock. The hardest thing she'd ever done had been to leave the bedroom that morning; she had steeled herself to face him, only to discover that he had already left for the hospital. Now she had to steel herself all over again, but her nerves were raw, and she knew she couldn't do it if she kept replaying the mortifying scene in her mind.

Sarah placed a stack of embroidery kits on the counter and looked Kathleen in the eye. "You can tell me it's not any of my business if you want," she said quietly, "but maybe it would help to talk about it. Has something happened? You've been so…*sad* all day long."

Only Sarah would have described Kathleen's mood as sad, but after a moment of surprise she realized that was exactly how she felt. She had ruined everything, and a choking sadness weighed on her shoulders, because she loved him so much and had nothing to give him, nothing he wanted. Old habits ran deep, and she had just opened her mouth to deny her mood when her throat closed. She had received nothing but kindness and friendship from

Sarah; she couldn't lie to her. Tears stung her eyes, and she quickly looked away to hide them.

"Kathleen," Sarah murmured, reaching across the counter to take Kathleen's hands and fold them in hers. "Friends are for talking to; I don't know what I'd have done all these years without my friends. Derek helped me through one of the hardest times of my life, even though he was just a boy then. I would do anything for him…and for you, if you'll only tell me what's wrong."

"I love him," Kathleen croaked, and the tears overflowed.

Sarah looked perplexed. "Of course you do. Why is that a problem?"

"He doesn't love me." Hastily she withdrew one of her hands and wiped her cheeks. "He only tolerates me."

Sarah's green eyes widened. "*Tolerates* you? He adores you!"

"You don't understand," Kathleen said, shaking her head in despair. "You think he married me because he loves me, but he doesn't. He only married me because of Risa, because it was the only way he could get her."

"Derek loves children," Sarah admitted. "He loves all children, but he doesn't marry all their mothers. He may have told you that for reasons of his own, and you may have believed it because it was something you wanted to believe, but *I* don't believe it for one minute. Surely you've noticed by now how he *manages* things; if something doesn't suit him, he works things around until it's just the way he wants it. He talked you into marrying him by using the only argument he thought you'd listen to, but Risa wasn't his main objective; you were."

"You wouldn't say that if you had seen him last night," Kathleen said in bitter hurt. She stared at Sarah, wondering if she should complete her humiliation by admitting everything, only to find that, once she had begun talking, it was more difficult to stop than to go on. "I told him that the doctor had released me—" She drew a deep breath. "I tried to get him to make love to me, and he b-b-blew up like a volcano. He was so angry it scared me."

Sarah's eyes were huge. "Derek? *Derek* lost his temper?"

She nodded miserably. "He doesn't want me, Sarah; he never has. He just wanted Risa. He's practically perfect; all the nurses at the hospital would lie down and let him walk on them if he wanted. He's strong and kind, and he'd done everything he could to take care of us; I owe him so much I can never begin to repay him. I just wanted to give him s-s-sex, if nothing else, but he doesn't even want that from me. Why should he? He can have any woman he wants."

Sarah folded her arms and gave Kathleen a long, level stare. "Exactly," she said forcefully.

Kathleen blinked. "What?"

"I agree with you. Derek can have any woman he wants. He chose you."

"But he *doesn't* want me!"

"In all the years I've known him, I've never seen or heard of Derek losing his temper. Until now," Sarah said. "If he lost his temper with you, it's because you touch him more deeply than anyone else has before. Few people ever cross Derek, but when they do, he never loses his temper or even raises his voice. He doesn't have to; one look from him can shrivel you. His control is phenomenal, but he doesn't have that control with you. You can hurt him; you can make him angry. Believe me, he loves you so much it might frighten you if you knew how he feels. That may be the reason he fed you that line about wanting to marry you so he could have Risa. Risa is adorable, but Derek could have any number of his own children, if children were what he wanted."

"Then why wouldn't he make love to me last night?" Kathleen cried.

"What did he say?"

"He said he didn't need my ch-ch-charity."

"Of course he doesn't. Of all the things Derek would want from you, that wouldn't even be on the list. He wouldn't want gratitude, either. What else did he say?"

Kathleen stopped, thinking, and suddenly it was as if a door opened. "He said something about caring and commitment, but he wasn't…I didn't think he meant…" Her voice trailed off, and she stared at Sarah.

Sarah gave a very unladylike snort. "Kathleen, you crawl into bed with him tonight and tell him you *love* him, not how grateful you are or how much you owe him. Believe me, Derek will take things from there. He must be slipping, or he'd have handled things better last night. But then, he's never been in love before, so his own emotions are in the way right now.''

Sarah's absolute certainty lifted Kathleen out of the doldrums, and for the first time she began to hope. Was it true? Could he possibly love her? She had never been loved before, and it scared her to think that this strong, perfect, gorgeous man could feel the same way about her that she felt about him. She shivered at the thought of putting Sarah's plan into action, because she would be putting her heart, her entire life, on the line, and it would be more than she could bear if he rejected her again.

Her heart was pounding so violently as she drove home that afternoon that she felt sick, and she forced herself to breathe deeply. Risa began fussing, and she gave the child a harried look. ''Please, not tonight,'' she begged in an undertone. ''You were so good last night, let's try for an encore, all right?''

But Risa continued fussing, and gradually worked herself into a real fit. Kathleen was only a few blocks from the apartment house, so she kept driving, but her nerves frayed at the effort it took her to ignore her child's crying for even that short time. When she pulled into the parking lot and cut off the motor, she felt a painful sense of relief as she unbuckled Risa from her seat and lifted the baby to her shoulder.

"There, there," she crooned, patting the tiny back. "Mommy's here. Were you feeling lonesome?" Risa subsided to hiccups and an occasional wail as Kathleen gathered everything in her arms and trudged up to the apartment. She had a sinking feeling Risa wasn't going to have a good night.

Just as she reached the door, it opened and Derek stood there. "You're early," she said weakly.

She couldn't read his expression as he reached out to take the baby. "I heard her fussing as you came down the hall," he said, ignoring Kathleen's comment as he put the baby on one shoulder and relieved Kathleen of the diaper bag. "Why don't you take a bath and relax while I get her settled; then we'll have a quiet dinner and talk."

She stepped into the apartment and blinked her eyes in astonishment. What was going on? There was a Christmas tree standing in the corner decorated with strands of tinsel and hand-painted ornaments, while the multicolored lights blinked serenely. There were piles of gift-wrapped boxes under the tree, and fresh pine boughs lent their scent to the air, while glowing white candles decorated the table. An album of Christmas music was on the stereo, sleigh bells dancing in her ears.

The apartment had been perfectly normal when she had left that morning. She put her hand to her cheek. "But this is February," she protested, her voice blank with astonishment.

"This is Christmas," Derek said firmly. "The month doesn't matter. Go on, take your shower."

Then they would talk. The thought both frightened and thrilled her, because she didn't know what to expect. He must have spent most of the day doing this, which meant he had someone covering for him at the hospital. And where had he found a Christmas tree in February? It was a real tree, not an artificial one, so he must have cut it down himself. And what was in those boxes under the tree? He couldn't possibly have found a tree out in the country somewhere, too. It just wasn't possible. Yet it was done.

Despite his instructions to relax, she hurried through her shower, unable to tolerate any delay. When she entered the nursery, Derek had finished bathing Risa and was dressing her. Risa had settled down and was waving her fists around while she gave the little half cooing, half squeaking noises she had recently learned to make. Kathleen waited until she was finished, then took the baby to nurse her. As she settled herself in the rocking chair she looked at Derek uncertainly, wondering if he intended to remain in the room. Evidently he did, because he propped himself against the wall, his warm, golden eyes on her. Slowly she undid her robe and bared her breast, putting Risa to it. The baby's hungry little mouth clamped down on her nipple with comical greed, and for a moment she forgot everything but the baby and this special closeness. Quiet filled the small room, except for the sounds Risa made as she nursed.

Kathleen kept her eyes down, cuddling the baby to her and rocking long after the tugging on her breast had ceased. Derek moved away from the wall, and at last she had to look at him as he leaned down and, with the gentle pressure of one finger, released her nipple from the baby's mouth. "She's asleep," he murmured, and put the baby in her crib. Then he turned back to Kathleen, hot need in his eyes as they moved over her bare chest, and she blushed as she quickly drew the robe around her again.

"Dinner," he said in a strained voice.

Afterward, she was never certain how she managed to eat, but Derek put a plate in front of her and told her to eat, and somehow she did. He waited until they had finished before taking her hand and leading her into the living room, where that impossible Christmas tree still blinked its cheerful lights. She looked at the nostalgic scene, and her throat was suddenly thick with tears. She could never remember truly celebrating Christmas before; it just hadn't been a part of her family's tradition. But she could remember looking at pictures of a family gathered around just such a tree, with love shining in everyone's faces as they laughed and opened gifts, and she could remember the painful longing she had felt for that kind of closeness.

She cleared her throat. "Where did you manage to find a tree?"

He gave her a mildly surprised look, as if wondering why she would think finding a Christmas tree would be difficult for him. "I have a friend who grows them," he explained in that calm manner of his.

"But…why?" Helplessly, she gestured at the entire room.

"Because I thought this was what we needed. Why should Christmas be restricted to one certain time, when we need it all the time? It's about giving, isn't it? Giving and loving."

Gently he pushed her down to the floor in front of the tree, then sat down beside her and reached for the closest present, a small box gaily wrapped in scarlet, with a trailing gold ribbon. He placed it in her lap, and Kathleen stared down at it through a veil of hot tears that suddenly obscured her vision. "You've already given me so much," she whispered. "Please, Derek, I don't want to take anything else. I can never begin to repay—"

"I don't want to hear another word about repaying me," he interrupted, putting his arm around her and drawing her close to his side. "Love doesn't need repaying, because nothing can match it except love, and that's all I've ever wanted from you."

Her breath caught, and she stared up at him with liquid green eyes. "I love you so much it hurts," she said on a choked-back sob.

"Shhh, sweetheart," he murmured, kissing her forehead. "Don't cry. I love you and you love me; why should that make you cry?"

"Because I'm not good at loving. How could you possibly love me? Even my parents didn't love me!"

"That's their loss. How could I *not* love you? The first time I saw you, there in that old truck with your

arms folded around your stomach to protect your
baby, staring at me with those frightened but un-
beaten green eyes, I went down for the count. It took
me a little while to realize what had happened, but
when I put Risa in your arms and you looked at her
with your face lit with so much love that it hurt to
look at you, I knew. I wanted that love turned on
me, too. Your love is so fierce and strong, sweetheart; it's concentrated from being bottled up inside
you all those years. Not many people can love like
that, and I wanted it all for myself.''

"But you didn't know me!"

"I knew enough," he said quietly, looking at the
tree, his eyes calm with a deep inner knowledge few
people ever attained. "I know what I want. I want
you, Kathleen, the real you. I don't want you tip-
toeing around, afraid of doing something in a different way from how I would have done it. I want
you to laugh with me, yell at me, throw things at
me when I make you mad. I want the fire in you,
as well as the love, and I think I'll lose my mind if
you don't love me enough to give it to me. The last
thing I've ever wanted is gratitude."

She turned the small box over and over in her
hands. "If loving is giving, why haven't you let me
give anything to you? I've felt so *useless*."

"You're not useless," he said fiercely. "My heart
wouldn't beat without you. Does that sound useless?"

"No," she whispered.

He put one finger under her chin and tilted her

face up, smiling down into her eyes. "I love you," he said. "Now you say the words back to me."

"I love you." Her heart was pounding again, but not because it was difficult to say the words; she barely noticed them. It was the words he'd said that set the bells to ringing. Then she realized bells really were ringing; the stereo was now playing a lilting song about Christmas bells. A smile tilted her lips as she looked at the twinkling lights. "Did you really do this just for me?"

"Umm, yes," he said, bending his head to nuzzle her ear and the curve of her jaw. "You gave me the most wonderful Christmas of my life; I got you and our pretty Christmas baby all at one time. I thought I should give you a Christmas in return, to show you how much you mean to me. Open your present."

With trembling fingers she removed the wrapping paper and opened the small box. An exquisite gold locket in the shape of a heart gleamed richly on its white satin bed. She picked it up, the delicate links of the chain sliding over her fingers like golden rain.

"Open it," Derek whispered. She used her nail to open it, and found that it wasn't just a simple two-sided locket. There was more than one layer to it. There was room for two pictures; then she lifted a finely wrought divider section and found places for two more. "Our picture will go in the first section," he said. "Risa's will go in the side opposite ours, and our future children will go in the second section."

She turned the locket over. On the back was engraved, *You already have my heart; this is just a symbol of it—Your loving husband, Derek.*

Tears blurred her eyes again as she clasped the locket in her hands and lifted it to her lips.

He put another, larger, present in her lap. "Open this one," he urged gently.

There was a small white card uppermost in the box when she opened it. She had to wipe the tears from her eyes before she could read the inscription: *Even during the night, the sun is shining somewhere. Even during the coldest winter, somewhere there are bluebirds. This is my bluebird to you, sweetheart, so you'll always have your bluebird no matter how cold the winter.* Inside the box was a white enamel music box, with a small porcelain bluebird perched on top, its tiny head tilted upward as if ready to sing, the little black eyes bright and cheerful. When she lifted the top, the music box began to play a gay, tinkling tune that sounded like bird song.

"Open this one," Derek said, putting another box in her lap and wiping her tears away with his hand.

He piled box after box in her lap, barely giving her time to see one present before making her open another. He gave her a bracelet with their names engraved on it, a thickly luxurious sweater, silk underwear that made her blush, bunny-rabbit house shoes that made her laugh, perfume, earrings, record albums and books, and finally a creamy satin-and-lace nightgown that made her breath catch with its seductive loveliness.

"That's for *my* enjoyment," he said in a deep voice, looking at her in a way that made her pulse speed up.

Daringly, she lifted her head, stopping with her lips only inches from his. "And for mine," she whispered, almost painfully eager to taste his mouth, to know the feel of his body on hers. She hadn't known love could feel like this, like a powerful river flooding her body with heat and sensation and incredible longing.

"And yours," he agreed, taking her mouth with slow, burning expertise. Her lips parted for him automatically, and his tongue did a love dance with hers. She whimpered, her hands going up to cling behind his neck as blood began to pound in her ears. She felt warm, so warm she couldn't stand it, and the world seemed to be tilting. Then she felt the carpet under her, and Derek over her. His powerful body crushed her against the floor, but it wasn't painful. His mouth never left hers as he opened her robe and spread it wide, his hands returning to stroke slowly over her bare curves.

Never in her imagination or her dreams had she thought loving could be as wildly ecstatic as Derek showed her it could. He was slow, enthralled by her silken flesh under his hands, the taste of her in his mouth, the restless pressure of her legs around his hips as she arched mindlessly against him, begging for something she didn't fully understand. Her innocence in that respect was as erotic to him as her full, love-stung lips or the entranced look in her green eyes. He took his time with her despite his own agonizing tension and need, soothing her whenever some new sensation startled her. Her rich, lovely breasts were his, her curving hips were his, her silken loins were his.

She cried out, her body surging against his as he finally entered her with exquisite care, making her his wife in flesh as well as heart. They loved each other there on the carpet, surrounded by the presents he'd given her and the strewn, gaily-colored paper that had wrapped them. The candles burned with their serene white flame, and the joyously colored lights on the tree cast their glow on the man and woman, twined together in the silent aftermath of love.

Derek got to his feet and lifted Kathleen in his muscled arms. "I love you," she whispered, lacing kisses across his throat.

Her naked body gleamed like ivory, with the lights casting transparent jewels across her skin. He looked down at her with an expression that both frightened and exalted her, the look of a strong man who loves so much that he's helpless before it. "My God, I love you," he said in a shaking voice, then glanced around the living room. "I meant to wait; I wanted you to wear the gown I bought you, and I wanted you to be comfortable in our bed."

"I'm comfortable wherever you are," she assured him with glowing eyes, and he cradled her tightly to him as he carried her to their room. Most of his presents to her remained on the living room floor, but two were clutched in his hands: the heart-shaped locket, and the bluebird music box. The winter was cold, but not her heart. She would always have her bluebird and the memory of her first real Christmas to keep her warm while her bluebird sang her lover's song to her.

A Note from Linda Howard

In my family it takes us three days to properly celebrate Christmas. My husband, Gary, and I both come from large families, and when it's taken into account that some branches of our families have lived in this area for at least a hundred and fifty years, that gives us an enormous extended family of aunts, uncles, cousins, nieces, nephews, in-laws, and out-laws, as well as kissing cousins of various degrees. It takes a while to see that many people.

Gary and I begin small, with our own immediate family: Mike, Donna, Tammy, Jeff and Mark. Seven people isn't bad; this is our quiet time. From there, though, it quickly becomes something resembling either a three-ring circus or a riot.

Then we move on to our parents' houses. Christmas with my parents involves only three generations under one roof, and even though it's an army, it's a small one. The toddlers are thoroughly petted and spoiled, and everyone keeps an eye out because the babies could get lost in the sea of discarded wrapping paper.

At Gary's parents' we have our four-generation Christmas celebration. Forget about chairs; just find a bare spot on the floor to sit and don't dare get up. Bribe people to bring things to you. If a trip to the bathroom is necessary, you've lost your place to sit. Kids are everywhere, like puppies, their excited laughter adding to the din of conversation. We all eat so much we just want to lie down, but there isn't room. Actually, we start munching on the extra goodies like stuffed dates and the shrimp ball as soon as we get there. I usually don't get hungry again until about the twenty-seventh.

Just thinking about it makes me smile. Merry Christmas.

* * * * *

Dear Reader,

Christmas is a difficult time for me, because it was my mother's birthday, and every year the holiday reminds me that she's no longer with us. But the holiday was *her* favorite, and she went all out with the special foods and the decorating, with huge piles of gifts gaily wrapped and stacked under the tree.

Decorating the tree was always a family affair, one we always begged her to do early, but she had her timetable and stuck to it. The tree went up a week before Christmas, and not any earlier than that. First the house had to be cleaned, and sometimes we would spray snow stencils on the picture window before the tree went up, and drape garlands around the mantel. Sprigs of fresh pine would be brought in and placed on top of the mantel, with candles arranged among the pine. The scent alone was enough to send thrills through six children who had been looking forward to this day for a year.

Then the tree would be brought in. Sometimes it was a real tree, sometimes it was artificial. Yes, we had one of those tacky silver aluminum trees that are now worth a fortune, though it was eventually discarded and a more real-looking fake tree took its place. All the decorations were brought down from the attic, and the boxes filled the living room. It was like unwrapping old friends, because most of the ornaments were the ones we used every year, and they were distinctive. The lights went on first, of course, but we never seemed to have much trouble with them. Lights did *not* misbehave with my mother! Bulbs seldom blew, cords didn't get tangled; she had good Christmas light karma.

Every day, more brightly wrapped packages would appear under the tree, and with six kids she knew better than to put names on the boxes! Instead she would number the gifts. She had a master list hidden away that told which number was assigned to which child, but we never managed to find it. The name tags didn't go on until Christmas Eve. Talk about anticipation!

Bowls of fruit and candy were set out, and for two weeks we were in snack heaven. The little plastic spice gum tree was all decked out with spice gum balls stuck on its little spikes; the red ones went first. And we always cooked a fruitcake, which tasted nothing like the fruitcakes that everyone groans over. It took all day to do it, with all of us chopping and mixing and packing, but when the thing was finished, it was the most popular treat in the house. All our visitors always asked for a slice of that fruitcake. Not being a baker, I've never tried to duplicate the achievement, but I know she didn't put rum in it, and it was packed with at least twice as much fruit as normal. She didn't use the sour or bitter stuff, either, just the sweetest fruits. A tiny thin slice was so rich and filling, one was all you could eat. Your stomach cried "uncle" even though your mouth was watering for more.

When the big day finally arrived, the house was filled to overflowing. It was *fun*. We played and opened gifts and ate. We were together. We were family. When it comes down to it, the heart of life is the family.

I hope your holidays are as special as ours always were.

Sincerely,

Dyida Howard

THE GIFT OF JOY
Joan Hohl

Chapter 1

Seated in a cramped booth in a small roadside diner, outside an even smaller New Mexico town, near the Colorado state line, Mason Conyers spied the notice of sale while perusing the local newspaper. Having just polished off a breakfast of sunny-side-up eggs, home fries, sausages and toast, he had taken a deep swallow of black coffee and flipped back the paper to the Properties For Sale section. The notice seemed to jump out and shout at him.

Rereading the particulars, Mason—Mace to his friends and enemies alike—dug a pencil stub from his shirt pocket and circled the ad. If the place proved to be halfway near as good as advertised, he mused, it could be close to what he had spent some weeks looking for.

Sliding out of the cracked vinyl seat, Mace rose and arched his back to loosen the muscle kinks caused by folding his six-foot-four-inch frame into a space he felt better suited to young children or rather small adults.

Standing next to the booth, Mace drained the coffee from the mug before shrugging into his sheepskin jacket. Plucking his pearl-gray Stetson from the opposite seat, he settled it at an angle over the wavy shock of gray-streaked mink-brown hair tumbling onto his forehead and ambled to the cash register to pay the check.

The redheaded, thirty-something waitress working the counter sashayed to the register. Taking his money, she eyeballed his rangy muscular length with overt appreciation. "Stranger to these parts?" she asked, avid interest alive and hopeful in her pale blue eyes.

"I've been through before, a time or two," Mace said, his eyes, a shade darker brown than his hair, sparkling with tired amusement.

"Stayin' around a while?" The hope had seeped from her eyes to her voice.

Mace controlled a cynical twitch at the corners of his mouth and gave a quick shake of his head. "Not this time." Touching his fingers to his hat brim, he curved his lips into a polite smile. "Mornin', ma'am." Turning away, he strolled to the door, stepped outside and drew a deep breath of the crisp early-morning September air.

Damn, the woman must have taken a bath in the

perfume she was wearing, he thought. He inhaled again to wash the cloying smell from his senses and replace it with the clean scent of sage and dew-drenched earth.

The freshness wouldn't last long, Mace knew. The day ahead promised to be hot and dry, as the entire, seemingly endless summer had been. The earth lay sear, exhausted...but lately, the nights and early mornings held the tantalizing coolness of approaching autumn.

Shrugging off the memory of the smell, and the woman, Mace loped across the gravel lot. He stopped at the dust-and-mud-spattered Bronco with an attached horse trailer, which he had parked in the shade.

Pausing alongside the slotted window in the front of the horse carrier, he smacked his palm against the conveyance in a familiar greeting. "Stand easy, Horse, we've got some traveling to do," he murmured in soothing tones before moving on to the attached vehicle.

Slipping behind the wheel, he slid aviator sunglasses onto the bridge of his nose, fired the engine and drove the Bronco out of the shade and into the hot glare of cresting New Mexican sunshine.

From the parking lot, Mace swung the vehicle onto the road heading north. He had a destination. A definite place to go, a particular person to see, a parcel of land to look at.

The ad had been sketchy, at best. Few details had been given, just enough to whet the appetite...at least, enough to whet Mason's appetite. But then Mace had a gnawing hunger, a hunger for land, a wide expanse of land, the peace and quiet it could afford.

He'd put in fifteen years of service to his country wearing the badge of U.S. marshal. After putting duty first, even to the detriment of his personal life and ultimately his brief and contentious marriage, Mace was tired…tired of serving papers, tired of chasing bail jumpers, tired of escorting disgruntled extradicted criminals, tired of it all.

Over two weeks back, Mace had given formal notice of retirement to his superior…thus his country.

His notice served, Mace was still on the hunt. His target: a place of his own. Instead of collaring bad-asses, Mace was looking forward to corralling horses…his horses.

In effect, Mace was tracking a long-held dream.

The notice of sale in the paper, now on the seat beside him, was the third to catch his interest. Mace fervently hoped the advertised ranch turned out to be more prepossessing than the previous two had.

Even fewer instructions had been included in the ad; merely the name of a town in Colorado Mace had never heard of, but fortunately indicating its location in the Great Plains region, a telephone number and a name.

Emma Hartman.

Mace rolled the name around in his mind.

Emma. The old-fashioned name conjured an image of a woman past middle years. Perhaps she was a widow, plump, eyes bright, cheeks flushed from whipping together steaming pies redolent with the mouthwatering aromas of apples baked in cinnamon and sugar.

It was a comforting image to bear Mace company during the long drive north.

Another dud. Grimacing at the thought, Emma stood on the porch steps, one hand jammed into a pocket of her designer jeans, the other hand shading her dark blue eyes as she watched the plume of dust billowing in the wake of the battered truck bouncing its way along the private rutted dirt road to the mile distant highway.

She didn't turn around at the sound of the screen door shutting behind her.

"Not too promising, was he?"

Emma shook her head, sighed. "Not at all promising." She slanted a wry smile of acceptance over her shoulder at the housekeeper she had, for all intents and purposes, inherited with the property. "Although I wouldn't have believed it possible, he was even worse than the three others that were here last week." The older woman's expression was grim, but her optimism remained steadfast. "It's early days yet, Emma. You'll see, someone with the sense to appreciate the potential of the property will come along."

"Oh, Mr. Jenkins had the sense to appreciate the potential of the place," Emma said, flashing near-perfect teeth in a quick grin. "He just lacked the cents…and many dollars, necessary for purchase of same.''

The housekeeper, Nancy Powel, gave a solemn nod. ''I figured that…just from the looks of him, the condition of that ancient truck he drove. 'Course, a body can't always tell a person's financial worth by appearance, but…'' She shrugged. ''Mr. Jenkins had the look of a man hopin' to find an almost free pot of gold at the end of your rainbow.'' She retreated back inside the house, the door slamming behind her, as if to punctuate her declaration.

Emma laughed in appreciation of Nancy's unique way of expressing herself.

It had been that way ever since Emma arrived at the ranch the week before.

Had it really only been a week? Emma marveled, gazing out over the property she had so unexpectedly inherited. Odd, but, from the day she had driven the rental car into the ranch yard, one week ago, she had experienced the strangest sense of homecoming, of belonging.

Odd? More like weird, she mused, her roaming gaze settling on the large barn, or stables…Emma wasn't yet quite sure which designation was correct.

Whatever, the building, like the other smaller outbuildings, and the low, sprawling ranch house itself, was in excellent repair.

And it was hers, all hers—the house, the stables, the white railed corrals and paddocks, the three-car garage and other assorted outbuildings, in addition to the spacious acres and acres of land.

Why the realization should instill an intense thrill of ownership eluded Emma. She had always thought herself a city girl, through and through. And, so far as ownership went, she already owned an elegantly restored town house in Philadelphia, the city of her birth.

So, what was the appeal? Emma asked herself. The fabled wide-open spaces, defined by the soaring snow-capped Rockies in the background to the west? The expanse of unbelievably blue sky in the daytime, and a bizillion stars against black velvet at night? The earthy scent of land and nature on the air, instead of industrial and auto fumes?

All of the above, Emma acknowledged. But there was more to it than that, an indefinable something she couldn't quite put her mental finger on.

The strange sense of belonging nagged at the back of Emma's mind. How could she feel that she belonged here, on this particular piece of prime ranch property, when she had never been here before, never even visited?

Emma frowned in consternation.

It should feel alien to her. The lack of paving—streets, roads, sidewalks—by itself should make her feel lost, out of her element.

Oh, sure, the small town a couple of miles away boasted sidewalks and intersecting streets that were paved, as was the road leading to the town, she conceded. But the paving did not begin right outside her door, the curbing lined with parked cars, the streets beyond alive with vehicular activity throughout the day and most of the night as they were outside her place in Philly.

The near absolute quiet alone should seem, if not alien, then strange, disorienting at the very least. And yet, the only strange note appeared to be the lack of strangeness.

Oh, most certainly, she had needed a break from the hurry-scurry of big city living, needed more a break from her hectic routine. Emma acknowledged she'd needed a complete change of scene, of schedule, possibly even of companions.

But she was definitely not burned-out, as one of those co-worker/companions had suggested.

Of course she wasn't, Emma assured herself, with a quick shake of her head. She loved the pace of the city, loved her work, loved being the top-selling agent in the realty firm she worked for, loved having the edge.

So, okay, she admitted to herself with grudging reluctance, squinting into the westering sunlight. Perhaps, in her dedicated drive to hone her professional edge, maybe—just maybe—she had drifted too close to her psychological edge, but that didn't mean she was burned-out.

She was simply a little tired, that's all. Hell, she had a right to be tired, Emma allowed. Her sales for the firm's past fiscal year had been astronomical, her commission exorbitant, and the subsequent effusive commendations from her superiors personally satisfying.

To top it all off, it had been a bear of a summer

back east. Philly had sweltered under an unrelenting sun, with precious little relief from the meager amount of rainfall. The weather had taken a toll on everyone, Emma included.

Dammit, she had earned the right to be tired; had earned the right to take a break, have a rest, get away from it all, if only for a little while, she reflected.

All of which was why she had cashed in her three years worth of accrued vacation time, deciding to jet to Colorado and handle the sale of the ranch herself. She *was* a real estate agent, for goodness' sake. Why hand over the property, and pay a hefty commission, to a stranger?

It all made perfect sense to Emma, sound economic and psychological sense, and had nothing whatever to do with work-related burnout.

Satisfied with her rationalizations, Emma turned, calling to the housekeeper, "Nancy, I'm going for a walk."

The older woman materialized at the door and pushed it open, a carrot in one hand, a battered hat in the other. "Can't stay away from that mare, can you?" she said, her smile wry. "You'll want this." She held out the carrot. "And you'll need this." She held out the hat.

"Thanks." Laughing, Emma accepted both. "Perhaps I'll take her for a short run."

"I kinda thought you might," Nancy said in her best Western drawl. "Don't get lost," she cautioned. "There's pot roast for supper."

"I won't...I love pot roast." Chuckling, Emma plopped the disreputable Stetson on her head and stepped down to the hard-packed ground. She strode toward the stables, empty except for the solitary mare that had not been sold along with the other ranch stock.

The mare, a gleaming chestnut called Glory, had been expressly named as part of Emma's inheritance. Emma had fallen in love with the beautiful animal on first sight. A thoroughbred, the horse was sleek, with a narrow head, dainty ankles and a gentle disposition.

There was a hollow, deserted air permeating the inside of the stables. The normal smell redolent of hay and horses seemed diminished by the absence of the former equine residents. The tall, wide double doors were open, and a soft whinny of entreaty greeted Emma the moment she crossed the threshold into the shaded interior.

"Lonesome, are you?" she murmured, moving to the stall nearest the stable entrance. Glory stood close to the stall door, neck extended, dark eyes wide, ears pricked. "Missing your stable mates?"

Glory bobbed her long head, as if in agreement, and gave a gentle nudge at Emma's shoulder.

Laughing softly, Emma raised her hand holding the carrot. "Here only a week, and already you know that I never come to visit you empty-handed."

While the horse made quick, crunching work of the carrot with her big teeth, Emma whispered sweet nothings and stroked her long satiny neck.

"You are a beauty," she murmured. "I'd love having hair the exact color of your coat, but the closest I can come to it is when the sunlight sparks red highlights in my own black mane."

Chomping away on the carrot, Glory angled her head, as if to check out Emma's hair color for herself.

Emma laughed. "You're not only beautiful, you're smart. I wish I could take you home with me." She sighed. "But, with my schedule, I'd hardly ever get to see or ride you. Besides, it would probably cost the earth to board you. So..." She paused to swallow a sudden tightness in her throat. "I'm afraid I'll have to sell you as well as the ranch."

Glory nickered and shook her head, almost as if she understood and objected.

"Don't worry, sweetheart, I'll be very particular and selective in choosing a new owner for you," she assured the animal, accepting as a given Glory's instinctive comprehension. "I won't sell you to just any old geezer who comes along." She patted the mare's neck. A grim smile curving her soft lips, she repeated Nancy's description of the prospective buyer. "Like that geezer who was here earlier, looking for a pot of gold at the end of my rainbow."

As if in complete agreement with the houskeeper's assessment, Glory snorted and again bobbed her narrow head. The carrot consumed, the horse danced in place.

"Ready for some exercise now, are you?"

The long head bobbed once more.

"So am I." Pivoting, Emma headed for the tack room. "Give me a minute to get your gear, and we'll be off."

Emma had to laugh to herself as she strode away. If her friends and co-workers could hear her now, conversing with a horse, for goodness' sake, they'd very likely conclude that she was off...off her rocker.

It had been a while since Emma had had the time to indulge her girlhood passion for horseback riding. After arriving at the ranch, her approach to Glory and the discipline had been tentative and uncertain at first. But, after nearly a week of daily outings in the saddle, her confidence had grown, both in herself and the horse.

After a brief shake-out canter, Emma reined Glory into a gentle walk. Talking to the animal, as if to another person, to which Glory responded with head shakes and snorts, they ambled along with no particular destination in mind.

Still, she didn't go far. Unfamiliar with the terrain, Emma prudently kept the ranch house in sight.

The landscape fascinated her. It was so utterly different than what she was accustomed to.

Used to tall buildings rising to the sky above her head, and cement and macadam beneath her feet, Emma was enthralled by the awesome beauty of nature surrounding her, most especially the thrilling sight of the Rockies, their jagged spires soaring into the heavens, not unlike a rambling, majestic cathedral. Their appearance was both inspiring and humbling.

Although it was not yet officially autumn by the calendar, a brisk breeze appeared to harbinger the cooler weather lurking in the wings of the waning summer. The dry, tired-looking grasses, trees and other plant life were just beginning to reveal a haze of changing color. Nancy had said that before too long, the aspens would be a blaze of shimmering gold.

Her imagination caught, Emma found herself hoping she would still be there to see it. Stranger still, she supposed, since she had never taken the time to make the relatively short trip to the Pennsylvania Pocono mountains to see the brilliant display of russets, golds and reds, which drew the tourists in their throngs each and every autumn.

Sighing with a sense of contentment she hadn't felt in years, Emma brought Glory to a halt. With her right hand easy on the reins, her left hand resting on her thigh, she stood in the stirrups and sent a quick look over the landscape to make sure she could still see the ranch house. She groaned aloud at the unmistakable sight that met her gaze.

A plume of dust billowed in the distance, heralding a vehicle traversing the dirt road to the house.

"Damn, looks like we have a visitor," she muttered, unconsciously tightening her grip on the reins as she settled back into the saddle. "I hope it's not that old geezer, Jenkins, returning to say he has changed his mind, and is now prepared to meet my price.''

A shudder rippled through Emma at the recent, unpleasant memory of the crotchety old man, the gleam in his washed-out eyes as he stared hungrily at Glory.

''The horse comes with the property,'' he had said in a sly, calculating tone. ''Don't she?''

Though that had been Emma's original intent, she changed her mind on the spot. ''Uh, no. She doesn't.''

He laughed, nastily. ''Then you're a damned fool.''

That was his first mistake; Emma didn't respond well to being called a fool...by anyone, most especially by this down-at-heel, unpleasant excuse for a man.

''Perhaps,'' she said, her tone repressive. ''Nevertheless, that's the deal.''

His voice took on a surly edge. ''You're asking that kind of money for the place and the horse don't come with it?'' He curled his lip in a sneer, revealing unsightly yellow teeth with several gaps. ''You ain't gonna get it, girly.''

That was his second mistake; Emma detested the demeaning designation of ''girly.'' Using a trick she had learned from her often arrogant employer, she lifted one raven's wing eyebrow in a high arch. ''We'll see.''

''You betcha, honey.'' The geezer added insult to insult with a snicker. ''A couple'a months of trying to palm this place off at the price you're askin' and, more'n likely, you'll be downright desperate to hand this place and the nag over to me, and at my price, which will be even lower by then.''

That absolutely did it for Emma. Drawing herself up to her full height of five feet three inches, she glared into his, to her thinking, shifty eyes. ''In your dreams, sir,'' she enunciated, in the deadly cold voice she reserved for deadbeats and hot-eyed, sweaty-handed males, who envisioned themselves her would-be lovers. ''There's your truck, and the road.'' She made a quick hand gesture. ''I suggest you make use of both.''

Though he had shot her glowering looks, and muttered unintelligible words Emma had been grateful she couldn't quite catch, he had slouched his way to the beat-up truck and tore up the already rutted dirt road to the highway.

Emma had thought that was the end of it.

Now, dismay trembled through her as she watched the trail of billowing dust move closer to the house. Tension tightened her hand on the reins, her thighs clamped to Glory's sides. If that man had returned to further harass her, she'd…

The horse reacted to her tension by dancing sideways. The unexpected jolt of movement brought her to her senses, reactivated her common sense.

''Steady, steady,'' she murmured in soothing tones, loosening her death grip on the reins, relaxing her thighs.

Glory stilled, but flicked her head back to fix

Emma with one big, wild-eyed look. In that moment, Emma imagined the animal had divined her thoughts and fears concerning Mr. Jenkins and shared them.

"It's all right," she said, reaching forward to stroke the animal's arched and quivering neck. "I won't sell you to him, ever. I promise."

Once again, to Emma's amazement, Glory seemed to comprehend, and immediately settled down. While, intellectually, she knew the horse had merely responded to the ease of her tension, the crooning tenor of her voice, she also felt certain that a bond had been forged between them. Which, she recollected, was not all that unusual between some humans and animals.

With a final pat to the sleek neck, Emma straightened in the saddle, and lightly flicked the reins to set Glory into motion. "I suppose we'd better go investigate," she said, directing the horse for home. "And, if our visitor does turn out to be Mr. Jenkins—we'll send the old geezer packing."

Turned out, the visitor was definitely not Mr. Jenkins, and decidedly not an old geezer.

Chapter 2

The woman didn't look anything like he had pictured her. Then, again, she wasn't Emma Hartman, either.

After informing him that Ms. Hartman had gone for a ride, and was expected back shortly, the woman who had introduced herself as Nancy Powel, the housekeeper, had asked if he cared to wait.

Mace cared to wait.

Taking a careful sip of the strong hot coffee Nancy Powel had offered him, along with an invitation to make himself comfortable at the long, solid wood kitchen table, Mace studied the woman seated opposite him over the rim of the solid stoneware mug.

In late middle age, the woman was tall, angular,

close to gaunt, with a no-nonsense look about her. Her steel-gray hair was scraped back in a tight bun. Her steel-framed glasses magnified steely-gray eyes. And Mace would have risked a ten-spot bet that she possessed a will of steel to match.

"You from around these parts?"

Mace swallowed another sip of coffee before answering. "No, ma'am." He shook his head; the unruly swath of hair flopped onto his forehead. "Texas, originally. New Mexico the past fifteen years or so."

"I figured."

Mace arched a brow. "Figured what?"

"That you were a Texan." She grinned. The softening change in her appearance was startling. "You've got the look of the mythical tall, lean and tough Texan."

In the act of taking another sip of coffee, Mace choked on a burst of laughter, damn near spewing the fragrant brew all over himself and her spotless kitchen table and floor.

"Mythical, huh?" he said, swiping a big work-roughened hand over his tearing eyes. "That's a load of, uh, donkey dust, and you know it."

"Sure." Her steely eyes glittered with amusement. "But the greenhorns eat it for breakfast, lunch and supper."

His dark brows converged near the bridge of his nose. "Was this a dude ranch?"

"Sure was." Nancy chuckled. "For a spell, leastways. Back about ten or so years, the former owner, rest his soul, a recluse by inclination, took the notion that he could do with some company for a spell." She gave a hearty laugh. "The spell didn't last too long. The company like to drive him up the corral fence." She flashed the face-softening grin. "He decided to breed horses, instead."

"My intention, as well," Mace confided, returning her friendly grin.

"With one horse?" Nancy jerked her head in the direction of the yard, and the trailer.

Mace smiled, nodded, informed. "The stud."

"Hmmm." She hummed. "Good stock?"

"Quarter horse." He grinned, showing off his straight, white teeth. "From a Morgan sire."

"That'll do for a start," she said, rising with an agility belying her accumulated years. "But first you need the land, right?"

"Right," Mace agreed, mouth watering in appreciation of the aromas emanating from the oversize oven in the industrial-size stove. "Which is why I'm here." Hungry for land, and food, he thought. Aloud, he asked, "You think Ms. Hartman will be getting back anytime soon?"

"Sure." Moving to the stove, she slid the glass pot from the modern coffeemaker. "Refill...before I dump this to ready a fresh pot for supper?"

"Okay. Why waste it." Mace drew another deep breath, savoring the smell of... "Whatever it is you're cooking for supper, it smells good enough to eat."

"Well, I should hope so." She laughed. Turning

from the countertop, she set his refilled cup in front of him, and raised thinning gray brows. "Would you like to stay for supper, and decide for yourself?"

Would he like to stay for supper? Only as much as a parched man would like a cool glass of water, Mace thought, fighting the urge to readily accept.

"I don't want to intrude," he said, hoping she'd brush aside his show of hesitancy.

She leveled a steely, get-real look at him. "If it was an intrusion, I wouldn't have asked you."

"Well, I am kinda hungry, since I haven't eaten since breakfast early this morning. And it surely does smell awfully good." Mace offered his most charming smile. "I'd like to stay— If you're certain Ms. Hartman won't mind."

"Don't know why she would," she said, shrugging. "Other than a few no-account window-wishers lookin' to buy prime property at bargain basement prices, we haven't had any company since she got here."

"Got here?" Mace frowned. "From where?"

"Philadelphia."

Mace swiveled on the straight-back wood chair to the sound of the new voice. He peered through the screening, but all he could see was the smallish figure of a woman standing on the roof-shaded porch outside the door.

"There you are, Emma, and about time, too," Nancy said in a gently scolding voice. "Supper's almost ready."

The door was pushed in, the woman crossed the

threshold, stopped, pulled off her hat and stared at Mace. "You belong to the Bronco, the trailer and that horse doing his laps in the corral as if he owned it?"

Mace got to his feet, slowly, to give himself time to catch the breath a clear look at her had stolen from his his body...his suddenly alerted, overheated body.

"Yes, ma'am," he answered, shoving the words from his rapidly drying throat.

"I told him to put the horse in the corral, and give him feed, Emma," Nancy said. "The animal had traveled a fair piece in that trailer...needed to eat and stretch his legs, move around a bit."

"Hmm."

What in hell did "Hmm" mean? Mace wondered, his gaze riveted to her closed expression.

She slanted a wry look to the housekeeper, only to find Nancy had turned back to finish her coffee-making. "I suppose it's all right." She shifted her gaze back to him.

For a moment...a forever moment, they stood there, unmoving and silent, staring, taking each other's measure.

From Mace's perspective, on a scale of one to ten, Ms. Emma Hartman measured in at a twenty. She sure as sunrise didn't fit the picture he'd drawn in his mind. Rather than middle-aged, plump and rosy-cheeked, Emma was breath-catching, heart-thump-ing, flat-out beautiful.

With his heart thumping right along, Mace

mapped the delectable terrain of her exquisite face and body with his slow, meandering gaze.

Somewhere in the mid-twenties, slender but not near skinny, she stood five foot two, maybe three, Mace judged, every inch of her sheathed in creamy skin with the look of warm satin. In figure hugging, obviously expensive designer jeans, her legs appeared long and neatly tapered, her butt tight, rounded. Her waist was narrow, one might say tiny, gently expanding upward to a slightish chest, proudly presenting to the discerning eye two small but firm and jutting, tip-tilted breasts.

Once past her breasts—a feat of self-discipline— Mace skimmed his now-hungry gaze up her smooth throat to come to rest on her lovely face, her fantasy-inspiring mouth.

In that instant, sweet, hot desire ran a marathon through his system. Mace wanted Emma's mouth. God, how he wanted her mouth…more than food, more than drink, more, even, at that instant than he wanted land.

The noise made by the oven door being opened ended the forever moment.

Mace drew a deep breath.

So did Emma.

He wished to hell she hadn't. The quick upward lift of her breasts drained the rampaging desire in his system, painfully tightening parts south in his anatomy.

Emma narrowed her eyes and opened her luscious lips, most likely to sear a strip off his hide with an acid-laced tongue, but Nancy, who appeared unaware of the electrical charge in the atmosphere, beat her into speech.

"This is Mace Conyers, Emma," the housekeeper said, turning away from the stove, a placid smile on her face. "He read the notice of sale you put in that Taos newspaper. He's looking for a place to breed horses." She smiled a nudge at Mace.

Duly prompted, he extended his right hand. "A pleasure, Ms. Hartman," he said, still tingling from the effects of the heated, uncomfortable pleasure.

"Mace?" she asked, arching a brow.

"Short for Mason," he explained, refusing to lower the hand she had as yet not taken.

"Hmm," she repeated the hum, finally sliding her palm against his.

Sparks. Mace felt them, as if her touch had drawn the electrical charge and gathered it together into one blast, jolting from her palm to his hand to every quivering nerve ending in his body.

Damn it felt good…but with the potential to shock the ladies, and embarrass him.

"I invited Mace to stay for supper," Nancy said with casual unconcern. "You don't mind, do you?"

Oh, she minded, Mace thought, identifying the flare of annoyance in her gorgeous blue eyes. Ms. Emma Hartman minded like blazes having him stay to supper.

"No, of course not," she answered, arranging her expression into a bland mask for the housekeeper.

"I knew you wouldn't." Nancy's smile was serene, but her steely eyes sparkled with secret amusement. "So, let's get this show on the road. I'll dish up the pot roast, as soon as the table's set."

Mace recognized a cue when he heard one. So, apparently, did Emma. They spoke in unison.

"I'll do it," she offered.

"Anything I can do to help?" he asked.

Nancy galvanized them into action, directing the activity from her position at the stove with the innate authority of the fabled matriarch, ending with, "You might want to shut the kitchen door, too. The air's gettin' downright chilly, and this room'll cool off quick now that the oven's off."

In no time at all, the solid door was shut, place settings and accessories were laid out, the aromatic coffee was brewing, the steaming meal was on the table and Nancy, hands clasped, head bowed, was saying grace over the pot roast.

Mace was giving thanks, too, for the house-keeper's kind invitation, for the food and for the simple fact that he was at last sitting down, his still semiaroused state concealed beneath the solid wood table.

It was the best pot roast he had ever tasted, by far, and he didn't hesitate in his praise to Nancy, nor in standing and offering to lend a hand to her with the dishes and cleaning up when she rose from the table.

"You can give Emma a hand with that," she said, crossing to the doorway to the living room. "Ever since she arrived, Emma has insisted that, so long

as I do the cooking, she'll do the clearing away.''
Grinning, she exited the kitchen, quipping over her
shoulder, ''Works for me…gives me a chance to
catch up on my favorite news program.''

''You really don't need to help, Mr. Conyers.''
Emma had to struggle to keep her tone steady, her
expression mild—no way could she have achieved
pleasant.

''Mace,'' the annoying man replied. ''And I do
need to help, need to, and want to.''

''Whatever.'' She shrugged and tried to ignore
him. Which was a joke in itself.

Want. Emma ground her back teeth, and fairly
threw the stainless-steel utensils into the plastic basket.

Who cared what he wanted. It was her kitchen,
and her wants came first. And she wanted him out
of the room, as far away from her as possible, and
not shadowing her every move back and forth between the table and the dishwasher.

He was too close, entirely too close, too disturbing, too sexily alluring, and much too damn big.

Mason Conyers dwarfed her.

Literally.

Though she had somehow managed to conceal it,
Emma had felt intimidated from the minute he had
jackknifed to his feet, to his full height, when she'd
stepped into the house.

From her five-foot-three perspective, the man appeared an absolute giant. Tall…very tall, lean,

corded muscles evident on his forearms below the
turned-back sleeves of his soft washed-out blue
denim shirt, faded jeans riding low on his hips below
his narrow waist, hugging the considerable length of
his straight legs, Mason Conyers was one intimidat-
ing—and magnetically attractive—sight to behold.

But, to Emma, his height and form posed only
half the problem. The other half centered on the
symmetric arrangement of his chiseled, rough-hewn,
mature and utterly masculine features, topped by unruly and overlong silky, wavy hair, the exact color
of Ms. Big Bucks Whomever's expensive mink
coat…in this case constructed from aging minks, as
his hair was liberally streaked with strands of silver-
gray.

And his eyes. Emma suppressed a delicate shudder. Bracketed by squint or laughter lines, possibly
both, his eyes were an exact match in color to his
hair, sans the gray, and were the most all-seeing,
piercing orbs she had ever had the misfortune to
stare into.

Deeper grooves scored his face from the lower
curve of his nostrils to the corners of his thin-lipped
yet sensuous mouth. She guessed his age at between
thirty-five and forty.

To Emma's rattled and fevered imagination, Mason Conyers epitomized the legendary man of the
West—tall, rangy, tough, soft-spoken, experienced
as hell and good-looking as all get-out.

Merely to glance at him had an effect on Emma
similar to a fisted blow to the midsection.

It was not a sensation she appreciated.

"See that, done in half the time."

His laconic remark yanked Emma from the fruitless railings of her thought processes. Done? Blinking, she glanced around the neat kitchen. Darned if it wasn't done.

Now what? Emma slid a sidelong look at the man propped lazily against the kitchen counter less than a foot from her. Get rid of him, she decided, that's what.

"Er...Mr. Conyers..." she began.

"Mace," he interrupted her, in a deep, soft, tremble-inducing tone. "May I have a look at the ranch now?"

Emma shot a glance at the window, relief shivering through her at the pinky-lavender evidence of approaching twilight on the mountain-jagged horizon.

"I'm afraid it will have to be another time," she said, crossing the room, to put some distance between them, and to show him the door. "It's too dark now to..."

"Time enough to examine the structural soundness of the stables and the other outbuildings," he again rudely, if gently, cut her off. "And all the time needed to go through the house after dark."

After dark? The words exploded in her mind like a bomb. No thanks, no way, no how, was she showing him through the house, the bedrooms, after dark, not even with Nancy right there to keep a steely eye on them.

Fortunately Emma possessed the perfect excuse of protocol to refuse him access to both grounds and living quarters. She didn't hesitate in using it.

"Mr. Conyers," she said, in her most cool and professional tone of repression. "It is a requirement for a prospective buyer of real estate to make an appointment to view the property offered for sale."

"I did make an appointment."

That stopped her cold...for a second.

"When?" She demanded when the second had elapsed, knowing damn well she had made no appointment with him.

"While you were out riding," he answered, an irritating smile playing on his sculpted mouth. "I phoned here as soon as I arrived in town—expressly to make an appointment to inspect the place. Nancy told me to come on out."

"Oh." Emma stifled a sigh. "I see."

"So, then." The playing smile quirked the corners of his lips. "You want to show me around... while there's still some light left?"

Want to? No, Emma thought. She didn't want to show him a thing. But, unfortunately, she despaired, she was caught within the boundaries of that old and overused saying: to wit—between a rock and a hard place.

Her options zilch, she stepped to the door and yanked it open, inviting, less than happily, "I'd be happy to show you around...Mr. Conyers."

"Mace." Blatant laughter danced on his tone and in his gleaming eyes.

Like hell, she thought.

"You'll need a jacket." Emma raised her eyebrows, and made a point of glancing around the room. "You don't have one."

"It's in the Bronco. I'll get it along the way," he said, moving aside to give her access to the coat hooks attached to the wall next to the door.

"Thank you," she said through gritted teeth, grabbing her banded-waist-length, stylish suede jacket hanging on a hook next to an unfamiliar pearl-gray Stetson before preceding his too tall, too lean, too attractive and virile-looking form out of the house.

When he stepped onto the porch, he was wearing the Stetson at a rakish angle on his head...which explained why the hat was unfamiliar to her.

The breeze had kicked up and turned chilly with sunset. Grateful for his suggestion, but unwilling to admit to it, Emma pulled up the zipper and huddled inside the meager warmth provided by the light-weight suede garment.

Chagrin tightened her lips as, making a detour to his vehicle, Mason removed and shrugged into a jacket that was also suede, but thigh-length and sheepskin lined. It made her shiver, it looked so toasty warm.

From the Bronco, he moved not to one of the buildings, as she had expected him to do, but to the corral. A soft murmur brought the animal to the fence.

"So, fella," he said in a soft croon, raising a hand

to the animal's quivering muzzle, "feeling better now that you've run out the road kinks?"

Dancing in place, the powerful-looking stallion snorted into Mason Conyers hand.

"I should have brought a carrot." Emma sighed, silently chiding herself for getting so bent out of shape about the man, the odd wariness his presence instilled, she had forgotten his horse, as well as a treat for Glory.

Mason Conyers tilted his head to look at her. "More than a carrot, he needs a warm place for the night." He arched a brow. "I was meaning to ask you if I could stable him here for the night—collect him when I come back tomorrow."

A flat-out refusal leaped to her mind...it didn't make it to her tongue.

"It's only for one night, and I'll pay the going stabling fee rate," he added the inducement.

She simply didn't have the heart to refuse to house the animal. "All right," she acquiesced, but she did have the sense to add caution to her agreement. "But you'll have to keep him separate...my horse is a mare."

"Oh, he knows that." He gave her a wry look. "He knows she's in there." He nodded at the stables. "Why do you suppose he was running laps around the corral? He picked up her scent at once."

There was something in his voice, some nuance in his droll tones that brought a flash of warmth to Emma unrelated to the jacket she had zipped, or the collar she had turned up.

Inexplicably uncomfortable, kind of nervy, she moved away from the corral fence, and him. "If you're determined to inspect the buildings, we'd better get at it," she said. "We're rapidly losing the light."

"Yes, ma'am."

Whether from the amusement threaded through his voice, or from his nearness, Emma didn't know, didn't want to know, but she felt every one of her muscles clench when he fell into step beside her. All she did know was that she wanted this damn inspection over with, and Mason Conyers on his way back to town, as soon as possible.

In short order, Emma realized the man knew what he was about. Which meant he knew a lot, an awful lot more about ranches and ranching, than she did.

Really, no great surprise, Emma consoled herself, since she knew next to nothing about any of it.

Eyes narrowed, Mason Conyers piercing gaze crawled over every visible inch of every structure. Every so often, he paused for a closer inspection, knocking against exposed and concealed support beams with one fist.

Having left the stables for last, darkness was swiftly encroaching by the time he moved in a long-legged amble to the large building.

"Since it's nearly dark, wouldn't it be best to save this for another day?" She suggested, clutching at her turned-up jacket collar, and the hope of getting rid of him.

Without slowing his forward motion, he canted

his head to bestow a droll look on her. "The place isn't wired for lights?" He asked, hiking up one mink-hued brow.

"Yes, of course it is," she answered in rough tones of exasperation. "But..."

He silenced her with a casual hand gesture. "Then, please, step inside and flick the switch. If you don't mind?"

Emma minded. Nevertheless, she did as he asked...if not in the least graciously, and expressly to get out of the chill nip on the breeze. Storming by him, she pulled open one of the huge double doors, strode inside and hit the switch with an upward slam of her hand. Immediately, and as inconspicuously as possible, she dropped her arm and rubbed her smarting palm against her side.

Glory whinnied a greeting.

"Hello," Mason Conyers murmured, strolling to the first stall. "What have we here?" Raising a broad, long and slim-fingered hand, he stroked the mare's neck, arched forward over the stall door.

"Glory, my horse," Emma said, emphasizing the "my," while suppressing a reflective shiver instilled by the sight of his hand caressing the mare's coat.

How would it feel to have that strong, long-fingered hand stroke her... Emma applied the brakes to the ridiculous thought. Of all the stupid— Her self-chastisement was interrupted by the sound of Mason's voice.

"—with the ranch?"

"I beg your pardon?" she apologized, hating the

necessity to do so. "But I'm afraid I missed the first part of your question."

His smile conveyed infinite patience.

Emma felt hard-pressed to keep from smacking the faint smile from his lips.

"I asked if the mare comes with the property," he explained, his smile taking on a wry tilt.

Reminded too vividly of the last person—that scruffy-looking old geezer—to ask that exact same question, Emma was only too happy to inform him, "No, she does not."

"Pity," he said, with genuine feeling. "She is a beauty, and should produce handsome, healthy foals."

"Yes." Emma turned away, torn by sudden inner conflict. The suspicious part of her nature rejoiced at her cold decisiveness, while another, softer part of her wished she hadn't been quite so coldly adamant.

"Will you sell her to me?" He asked, turning to face her. "In a separate transaction, of course," he tacked on.

Oh, hell, Emma thought, musing that it must be her day to fall into the realm of clichés, this one being, firmly caught in a cleft stick.

She extricated herself with vagueness. "I really haven't decided exactly what I'm going to do with her."

"Thoroughbred, isn't she?" He slid a quick glance at the mare before returning a shrewd gaze to her.

"Yes." Emma nodded, breath catching at the feeling of being pinned by his drilling stare.

"I'd like to breed her with Horse."

Lost, Emma frowned. "What horse?"

"My horse."

Her mental light clicked on. "Don't tell me, let me guess. You named your horse...Horse?"

"Good guess." He grinned.

The sheer sensual impact of his grin hit Emma with the force of an eighteen-wheeler. Her insides seemed to go into a frenzied conga dance. Her pulse skipped along to the beat. Her heart rate went off the chart. And her rattled mind quoted a line from an old movie: "I'm melting, I'm melting."

Enough, she decided, pivoting to move farther into the cavernous interior. "If you're going to inspect, please do so. I'm chilly and want to get back to the house."

A low sound wafted to her, soft and indistinct. Emma couldn't be positive, of course, but she suspected the sound had come in the form of a chuckle from Mason Conyers. Annoyed, she swung around to confront him...and slammed headlong into his broad chest.

The body collision knocked the breath out of Emma, while allowing sensual awareness in. His jacket was unbuttoned and hanging open. His chest felt rock-hard and warm. The tantalizing scent of citrus-tangy aftershave or cologne and healthy male teased her senses.

For a moment, Emma couldn't think, couldn't move.

A moment was all he needed.

"Chilly, are you?" he asked in an enticing murmur. "Let me warm you."

Her sense and senses undone by the deep, mind-altering sound of his voice, the feel of him, the smell of him, Emma was barely aware of where she was, who she was, never mind the curving of his tall body over her smaller form, and the slight upward movement of his hands.

But, suddenly, she felt herself being enveloped by the warming fleece lining of the front panels of his jacket, and the even more warming, exciting embrace of his arms.

"Wh…what do you think you're doing?" she said in a halting, breathy voice she didn't recognize, yet couldn't control.

"Warming you," he answered, his breath ruffling her hair near her forehead, and her nerves everywhere. "And I don't think I'm doing it…I am doing it."

That wasn't all he was doing. Not by a long shot. Holding her tight, he stepped into the valley of her parted leg stance. His arms crushed her soft curves to the hard angles of his muscular body, making her shockingly, excitingly aware of the denim-concealed, yet obvious, solid length of his erection pressing into the apex of her suddenly weak and quivering thighs.

Emma was no longer chilly. Like a flash fire, heat

suffused her body, hot moisture pooling in the lower, most vulnerable part of her femininity.

"You smell good," he whispered, fanning the fire with his warm breath. "And you're so soft."

You smell good, too, Emma thought, too bereft of breath to speak. And you're so hard.

She burned. Burned. For him. For his hard body…to be joined in sensual union with hers.

The realization jolted her, restored her rational thinking. Was she out of her mind? Emma railed at herself. Loosening the arms she had mindlessly curled around his waist, she slid her hands up his torso and pressed her palms to his chest.

"Let me go," she ordered, managing at least a semblance of commendable authority.

"Why?" Raising one hand, he caught her chin and lifted her head to gaze into her eyes. He rotated his hips, eliciting a gasp from her. Passion flared hot and strong in his dark eyes. "A moment ago, you were trying to draw me inside you, right through our jeans."

Denial would have been both fruitless and a lie. Emma didn't so much as consider it. She added force to the pressure of her hands against his chest, imprinting the feel of him onto her palms.

"I mean it, Conyers," she said in a near snarl. "Let me go, at once."

"I might consider it," he drawled, tightening his one-armed hold on her. "For a price."

"That's blackmail," she protested, outraged.

"Whatever works." He grinned.

The melting process began again, deep inside Emma. Steeling herself against his potent sensual power, she went still, narrowing her eyes into glaring slits of defiance.

He laughed, obviously unimpressed.

"Name your damned price," she hissed, positive his intent was her agreement to sell Glory to him.

"A kiss."

"What?" Startled by what she considered his curveball response, her eyes flew wide-open.

"With your full participation," he amended. "Opened mouths, tangling tongues, the works."

Emma was tempted to lift her hands to his face, rake her nails down the chiseled planes of his cheeks. She was even more tempted to pay the price, taste the promise of ravishment of his seductive mouth.

Madness. This man was a virtual stranger. She couldn't. She wouldn't. Could she? Would she?

Sliding his hand to her bottom, he pulled her to him and thrust his hips against hers.

It terrified Emma…because it felt so good.

"All right, damn you." Sheer frustration—sexual in nature, if she were honest—shimmered on her raised voice. "Do it and get it over with."

"How can I resist such a sweet invitation," he said, slowly lowering his head and slanting his lips over hers.

There was nothing tentative or soft about his kiss. It seared Emma from the first contact of mouth to mouth. His lips were hard, demanding, demoralizing.

Undone, Emma surrendered to the command of his expertise. Coiling her hands around his neck, she clung to him for dear life, and returned the kiss with avid involvement.

Mason had it all his way. Mouths open, tongues tangling, the kiss deepened, went on and on.

Without conscious thought—hell, she had stopped thinking altogether—Emma plunged down the slippery slope of sensuality running rampant.

But, on a subconscious level, her senses were aware of myriad sensations.

Even through the material of her jacket, Emma could feel the tenseness of his muscles, in the hand that cupped her face, the long fingers stroking, sensitizing her skin; in his chest, imprinting against her breasts, the tightly aroused nipples; in his thighs, tight and hard, and the harder part between, moving evocatively against hers.

After a long, very long period of self-imposed sexual denial, Emma's body and senses rejoiced in the reawakening. Drenched in the spicy, male scent of him, the feel of him, the taste of him, she reveled in the sheer masculinity of him, until, mindless with raw desire, yet starved for breath, she tore her lips from the hungry possession of his mouth.

Gasping in short, harsh breaths, Emma stared up at him in mute wonder.

"That wasn't bad," he said, smiling with devastating effect. "For starters."

"Starters!" Emma yelped, wrenching out of his one-armed embrace. "You...you..." She broke off, teeth grinding at his eruption of laughter.

"Yes, me," he said, suddenly all narrow-eyed and serious. "You and me, and the undeniable sexual attraction between us. I meant what I said, Emma," he promised. "That was for starters. There'll be a helluva lot more to come." He had the audacity to grin. "No pun intended."

"Over my dead body," she vowed. "And this tour is over. Stable your horse, then hit the road, Jack." She groaned in silent despair as she stalked away from him.

She had just added trite to cliché. It definitely was not her best day.

Chapter 3

God, that woman's kiss was dynamite.

Feeling bemused, beguiled, maybe even bewitched, Mace stood rock still—and still rock hard—watching Emma's slight form disappear into the darkness.

Damn, he couldn't believe he had come on to Emma that way, that soon, that hard. Never before in his thirty-seven years on this earth had he so swiftly cut through the niceties to get to the nitty-gritty sex stuff.

But then, never before in his life had he reacted with such immediacy to his first sight of a woman...any woman.

Mace released a pent-up breath in a harsh whoosh, feeling again the power-punch he had experienced when Emma had stepped into the kitchen earlier.

It was kinky.

Almost mystical.

Preordained, maybe? Mace mused, his rational mind reaching for understanding.

The sound of the kitchen door slamming behind her brought him to his senses, to the painful realization of the bittersweet discomfort of sexual frustration.

"She's mine," he murmured, savoring the sound, the determined certainty of his self-promise.

Glory snorted.

Mace laughed. "I wasn't referring to you, beautiful, even though I'm hoping Emma will decide to sell you to me," he said, moving to the stall to stroke the mare's long neck. "You're targeted for Horse."

Glory whinnied and shook her head.

"'Fraid so, girl, but look at it this way," he murmured, conversationally, "Together, you and Horse should produce one magnificent foal."

As if in complete understanding of his words, Glory backed away from him.

"Skittish as your owner, are you?" Mace chuckled. "Not to worry," he went on in soothing tones. "Mutual pleasure is the intended purpose. I won't let Horse hurt you, any more than I'd deliberately hurt Emma."

But, first things first, Conyers, Mace told himself. Turning from the stall, he ambled—because, in his aroused condition, he sure as hell couldn't manage a stride—through the open doorway and to the corral.

And the first thing Mace needed to do was get Horse settled for the night. After that, he planned to break the speed limit getting to the unprepossessing motel room he'd rented at a seedy-looking place a few miles from town, and jump under a freezing cold shower.

Mace wasn't even sure he'd bother to shuck out of his clothes first.

Once Emma was inside the house, she engaged the lock, then stood with her back pressed against the door, her pulse thrumming, her breathing erratic.

Never in her twenty-six years had she experienced anything close to the mind and body dissolving sensations Mason Conyers had so effortlessly created inside her.

In her unnerved opinion, the man defined the term powerful masculine potency.

Emma was not a novice to lovemaking, not a virgin. She had bestowed that gift on the man she had, in a weak moment, agreed to marry. Their engagement had endured all of three months. That had been all the time needed for her to realize their union wouldn't work.

They were too much alike, Emma and her fiancé, too self-absorbed, too ambitious, too dedicated to the pursuit of their own careers, too unwilling to compromise. Besides, their lovemaking had been less than earth-shattering, mechanical, almost robotic, completely devoid of anything even remotely related to ecstasy.

That had been almost four years ago. And, although she received and accepted many invitations from a variety of men, Emma, unstirred by their nearness or touch, had not been intimate with any one of them. Why bother? she had figured, when intimacy had proved so overrated.

Until this evening, with Mason Conyers.

Unbearably stirred, Emma shuddered at the mere memory of his devastating kiss, the hot need that kiss had aroused, the feel of his body, pressing into hers, stoking the flame of desire into a blazing inferno.

The memory reactivated the heat. Suddenly feeling she was burning up, Emma unzipped her jacket and quickly shrugged out of it. While hanging up the garment, she recalled the gray Stetson that had hung on the next hook, remembered the rakish look of the hat, set at an angle on Mace's head.

The inner melting had commenced, making Emma feel much too weak, and far too vulnerable.

"Why is it so quiet out there, Emma?" Nancy called, obviously having heard the door slam minutes before. "Isn't Mace with you?"

Blessing the older woman for saving her from the ignominity of melting into a puddle of need on the floor, Emma drew a deep breath, straightened her spine, squared her shoulders and headed for the source of that curious voice.

"No, Mr. Conyers isn't with me," she finally answered in hard-fought tones of unconcern. Strolling into the living room, she worked up a smile…it was damn near painful. "He, er, I decided to put off showing him over the house until he comes back tomorrow to see the land."

"Good idea," Nancy murmured, vaguely, distracted by her obvious interest in the program she was watching on TV. "It's always better to look at a house in the daylight."

"Yes," Emma responded, starting for the sofa, and the novel she had left on the table next to it.

"But you did remember that you gave me the weekend off to visit my sister in Denver, and that I'll be leaving around nine tomorrow morning?" Nancy reminded her.

Emma hadn't remembered, and wasn't exactly thrilled at the reminder, either. But, what could she do? Nancy had appeared so grateful for the three-day weekend off.

"Uh, yes, of course I remembered," she lied, unwilling to disappoint the older woman by asking her to change her plans…just because she, herself, was wary of being alone on the property, in the house, with Mason Conyers.

"Good." Nancy nodded her head, as if to say, "Glad that's settled" and went back to the TV.

Suppressing a sigh, Emma picked up her novel.

Fortunately, for her peace of mind, not to mention her jangled nerves, Emma heard the sound of the

Bronco's engine turning over just as she was reading the same page for the third or fourth time.

Mason Conyers was leaving, she deduced, sighing in relief. Maybe now she could make some sense of what the author of the mystery story had written.

No such luck. She was halfway through the page, and finally getting the gist of the point being made, when a sharp knock sounded on the kitchen door, reverberating through her nervous system.

"Now…who…?" It must have been a pivotal part of the documentary program, because Nancy's voice and frown conveyed annoyance.

"I'll go," Emma offered, knowing full well who it was, and cursing to herself in frustration.

Of course, it was Mason Conyers…who else would it be, she mused. Neighbors didn't often stop by to visit in the evening when they lived miles apart from one another. Come to that, neighbors living smack up against one another in rows of town houses in the city didn't casually drop in to visit in the evenings, either. At any rate, Emma's neighbors gratefully never had.

Still quivering inside in reaction to that scene in the stables, she yanked the door open and glared at him.

"I just thought I'd better tell you," he was quick to say, before she had a chance to blister him with a verbal blast, which she was about to do. "I unhitched the trailer…I hope you don't mind."

Emma actually ground her teeth together. What difference would it make if she did mind…since the deed was done? But, in all honesty, she didn't mind. It was admitting it to him that bugged her.

"No, I don't mind. Good night." She moved to shut the door; he stuck his large, booted foot across the doorjamb. She bared her teeth. "Is there something else?"

"Yes." Firm conviction shimmered on his deep voice. "I want to take an option on the ranch, and—"

"But you haven't even seen it yet," she interrupted in stunned disbelief. "Why—"

He interrupted her. "I don't want to take a chance on the possibility of somebody else getting in a bid before I get back here tomorrow."

"But…no one has even called about an appointment to see the place."

"Don't care." His expression was set in hard lines of determination. "I want the horse, too."

She opened her mouth to remind him that she had not as yet decided what she would do about Glory.

"If you decide to sell her," he quickly tacked on, before she could voice her reminder.

Emma sighed, prepared to agree to just about anything to get his too attractive, too tempting, too unnerving presence out of there. "All right."

"Give me a figure," he said, reaching for his back pocket. "I'll write you a check."

Wanting him gone, five minutes ago, she shook her head. "That won't be necessary. Your option is duly noted." She lowered her glance to his foot. When she returned her gaze to him, the rigid lines of resolution had eased on his face. "Was there something else?"

He grinned. "No...just, good night, Emma." Touching the brim of his Stetson with two fingers, he drew back his foot, spun around and walked away.

Emma was left staring after his tall, loping figure, and fighting the demoralizing, melting sensation reactivated by his devastating grin.

Damn the man.

Emma had her emotional act, and her rampaging hormones, together by the next morning. At least, she assured and reassured herself she had it all together, first as she had applied herself to mucking out Glory's stall before giving her feed and water, then later, as she stood irresolute in the kitchen after waving Nancy on her way.

Her self-assurance was tested midmorning when she spied a telltale plume of dust trailing a vehicle coming at speed up the ranch road.

Certain it was the Bronco creating the cloud of dust, Emma stepped out onto the porch to wait for the would-be buyer of her property. Fooled by the deceptively warm look of the blue sky and bright sunshine, she gasped in shock at the chilling sting in cold air.

"It's still supposed to be summer, already," she mumbled, dashing back inside and up the stairs to her room, to pull on a sweatshirt over her short-sleeved cotton blouse. Dashing back downstairs, she grabbed her suede jacket, the only outer garment she had brought with her from home.

The vehicle came to a noisy stop as Emma again walked out of the house, onto the porch. She groaned aloud at the unwelcome sight of Mr. Jenkins stepping out of the battered truck.

"Mornin', missy," he called in suspicious tones of smug self-satisfaction.

"Good morning, Mr. Jenkins," she responded, feeling duty-bound to be polite, even though the man did look like he hadn't bathed or shaved for several days.

He chuckled—more like cackled, to her way of thinking—and shuffled toward her. "I'm here to make you an offer for that there horse of yours." He indicated the stables with a jerk of his head.

Emma sighed in resignation, wondering what part he hadn't understood of the explanation she had given him less than twenty-fours hours before regarding Glory. "As I told you yesterday, Mr. Jenkins," she said, slowly and distinctly, "I haven't yet made a decision about the mare."

"Yeah, but that was then, and this is now." He produced a sly smile that gave her the willies. "Since then, I had a little talk with my son, and young Billy—he's a junior, you know—he agreed to go halfies with me on your horse. And you ain't heard our offer yet, girly."

Girly. Again. Anger-spurred impatience ripped through Emma, bringing with it an adamant determination to refuse his blasted offer, no matter how high it might be.

"I'm listening, Mr. Jenkins." Emma was rather proud of the even tone she had managed, considering what she'd have preferred to do was yell at him to get the hell off her land. "But, I feel I must tell you," she rushed on, suddenly recalling with infinite relief Mason Conyers's insistence on having an option. "I already have a serious prospective buyer for both the land and the horse."

"How so?" he demanded, bristling like an underfed spaniel defending a bone. "I only left here yesterday afternoon, and I surely didn't spy any suckers tramplin' all over each other to see the place."

Emma did a little bristling herself at his "suckers" remark. "Nevertheless," she said, hanging on for all she was worth to her by now chancy temper. "An option has been taken."

"Yeah, well, you ain't heard our offer yet." Like a proud cock-of-the-barnyard, he puffed up his narrow, bony chest. A smirk curling his lip, he tossed out a figure.

Stunned, Emma stared at him in sheer disbelief for a full thirty seconds. His offer was so pitifully low, it was almost laughable. She wasn't amused.

"Yeah, yeah," he crowed, cackling. "That got your attention, din't it?"

Actually, what it got her was a surge of outraged fury. The man—the excuse for a man—genuinely

believed her to be that stupid…that naive…
that…that much a *girly*.

Emma was so angry she could barely speak, so
damn mad that, had she possessed the physical
strength, she'd have kicked his skinny butt all the
way back to his ramshackle truck.

Well, though she *didn't* possess the physical
strength, she could lay claim to some verbal skill.

"Your offer, sir, is a gross insult to my intelli-
gence," she elucidated clearly and distinctly. Head
up, chin angled, she swept his revolting form with
a look of haughty disdain. "You are not only at-
tempting to legally rob me, you are wasting my
time. So, toddle on back to that pile of junk you
dare call a vehicle, and get off my land…before I
am tempted to call the local law."

"The law?" Jenkins yelled. "What are you goin'
on about? There ain't no call for the law."

Emma was so incensed, she never saw the telltale
plume of dust. She blinked, startled by the roar of
another vehicle coming to a screeching stop less
than five feet away from where she stood.

It was at once obvious that Jenkins hadn't taken
note of the vehicle, either. Face mottled a nasty dark
red, he had taken a threatening step toward her.

Although she abhorred violence, Emma tensed,
prepared to defend herself; she might lack the physical strength to kick his butt back to his truck, but
she could inflict damage to the most vulnerable section of his scrawny anatomy, and wouldn't hesitate
to do so, should he raise a hand to her.

The newly arrived vehicle's door slammed shut. Jenkins stumbled to a halt.

Emma breathed a heartfelt sigh of relief.

"Problems, Ms. Hartman?" His quiet voice underlined with steel, one dark brow arched, Mason Conyers sauntered to a stop less than two feet from her.

"A minor one," Emma answered, wanting to downplay the incident now that she had backup support. She flicked a hand at the older man. "Mr. Jenkins here insists I consider a ridiculously low offer for Glory."

"It ain't low," Jenkins muttered, without conviction.

Mace spared a brief, cool glance at the older man, then returned his steady gaze to Emma. "How low?"

She quoted the figure.

Amusement flashed in his dark eyes, and his eyebrows rose a notch. "I thought an option had been taken on the mare...and the land."

"That's correct. As you know, I did receive—" Emma began, only to be cut off by Jenkins' irritating voice.

"What option?" he objected in whiny tones. "I was here yesterday afternoon, and there was no talk of any option then. Who'd had time 'nough to look the place over?"

"I did." Mace again favored the older man with a direct, cool look.

"Well, who the hell are you, anyways?" Jenkins demanded, all bluster and bluff.

Mace smiled.

Emma shivered at the sight of that slight, chilling movement of his firm lips.

Jenkins visibly paled.

Reaching for his back jeans pocket, Mace removed a billfold and flipped it open, revealing official-looking identification. "Mason Conyers, United States marshal."

Emma blinked. Mace was a lawman?

Jenkins went from pale to bone-white. "I don't want no trouble with the law!" he yelped, shuffling back, away from Mace. "You can have the nag."

"Big of you," Mace drawled. "Now, I suggest you haul your rump out of here—" his voice lost the drawl and gained a jagged edge "—And don't bother Ms. Hartman again."

Jenkins was already on the move. "Yes, sir, Marshal. I mean, no, I won't."

Without a backward look, he went hotfooting it to the truck, jumped in and took off at a speed that raised a cloud of dust and small pebbles in his wake.

Choking and coughing as the billowing cloud enveloped her, Emma spun on her heel and dashed for the house to get out of the rain of dust.

Mace was right behind her as she raced inside. Laughing softly, he shut the door and leaned back against it.

Aggravated by the entire fiasco, Emma paused in

the act of brushing the fine coating of dust from her jacket and tossed a narrow-eyed look at him.

"What's so damned funny about getting a shower of dust?" she demanded, shuddering as she swiped her tongue over her gritty teeth.

"A little dust won't hurt you," he observed in a tone as dry as the topic. "Besides, I wasn't laughing at that." Moving to her, he raised a hand to gently brush the stuff from her hair, her cheeks.

"What then?" Emma asked, taking a cautious step back.

He smiled at her wary retreat, and took the step to bring him closer again. "The whole scene. Jenkins' obvious intention to pull a fast one on the inexperienced greenhorn with his laughable offer." His index finger paused in a feather-touch at the corner of her mouth, raising goose bumps all over her body. "But, mostly, you."

"Me?" Emma frowned. "I'm funny?"

"No." He shook his head. "It was your stance when I stepped from the Bronco." His gaze swept her face, returned to her mouth. "You're such a small, delicate-looking woman… And yet, there you were, expression defiant, ready to fight the man."

Emma lifted her chin. "I live in a large city, Mr. Conyers. And I'm not a fool. I've had training in self-defense."

"Figured." He smiled. "Still, it struck me as funny. And the name's Mace."

In retrospect, now that the high tension was over, and the defensive rush of adrenaline had slowed,

Emma could see the humor in the situation, while realizing it would have been sticky if Mace hadn't appeared on the scene. But, since he had appeared, she could afford a smile and a rejoinder.

"At least one of us was amused," she conceded, taking two steps away from him and the disturbing feel of his absently stroking finger. "And I must admit, Jenkins looked pretty amusing, too, when he turned that fish-belly shade of white after seeing your U.S. marshal's credentials."

Though he raised a brow, wryly smiled, he didn't pursue her. "Retired."

"Huh?" She frowned.

"I said, I'm retired." His smile turned rife with self-satisfaction. "I just didn't think Jenkins had a need to know that bit of information."

So he was not, in fact, a lawman, Emma thought, wondering why the news made her feel better or why it should mean anything to her one way or another.

He was safer not being a lawman.

The thought came out of nowhere. Startled and unnerved by the idea that she cared either way if he was safe or not, Emma banished it to the nether regions of her mind.

"It's too quiet in here." Frowning, Mace sent a quick glance around the room. He gave an audible sniff. "And nothing's cooking. Where's Nancy?"

Uh-oh. He would notice Nancy's absence right off, Emma thought, releasing a silent sigh.

"She's visiting family in Denver this weekend," she admitted, suppressing another sigh.

Emma had been hoping to somehow keep him out of the house, come up with a way to conceal Nancy's absence from him, even to postponing his tour of the house until after the housekeeper returned, feeling it safer he not know she was alone.

So much for hopes.

"I think it's safe to go out now."

Her wandering attention snagged by the dry sound of his voice, the word "safe," Emma glanced at him in confusion. "I beg your pardon?"

"The dust has settled." He flicked a hand to indicate the yard. "It's safe for us to go out, to begin my inspection of the property."

"Oh." Feeling foolish as well as inattentive, Emma strode to the door. "Yes, of course, let's go. The sooner we get started, the sooner we'll be finished."

She could have sworn she heard him chuckle as he quietly pulled the door shut.

Chapter 4

They had been riding for over an hour, and the air was getting decidedly colder. The sky seemed to be steadily lowering, and was a suspicious whitish-gray.

Though they had covered only a very small section of the ranch, Mace felt a growing certainty inside, well pleased by what he had seen thus far.

Emma had given him the total acreage of the property—a number that had, she frankly admitted, stunned her from the day she had learned of the size and scope of her inheritance, and still continued to amaze her.

Mace had merely nodded at the stated figure, commenting, "It's small in comparison to the large cattle spreads, but I wasn't looking for a really large place.''

Emma hadn't responded, but from her expression, Mace knew she was speculating on exactly how big a really large ranch might be. Like most Easterners, she obviously couldn't imagine the size of such a place.

''It's so wide-open, so...so spacious,'' she murmured in awed tones. ''Seeing it has sharpened my perspective about how very big this country really is.''

''Yeah,'' Mace had agreed, musing on how small she was, how fragile-looking. The thought reactivated the range of emotions that had swept through him when he'd pulled the Bronco to a stop in the ranch yard earlier.

First and foremost, there was the eruption of sheer rage he'd experienced at the sight of Jenkins moving toward Emma in a threatening manner. Mace had literally seen red, and knew that if the man so much as touched her, former lawman or not, he would take Jenkins apart, break him into small pieces.

Then there was Emma herself, the sight of her small, slender body, poised for battle, had tempered Mace's fury with tender amusement.

Finally there was the shock from the depth of the sense of protectiveness Mace felt toward her. He wanted to wrap her in cotton, cradle her in his arms, close to his strength, keep her safe from everyone...but himself.

The mere thought of cradling Emma in his arms caught his imagination, took flight into the realm of erotic fantasy. Mace no longer saw the sun-dried terrain. Lost in his self-created world of hot nights, and hotter lovemaking, Mace was unaware of how cold the air had become, until the object of his sensual intent brought him to attention.

"You know," Emma mused aloud, shivering from the chill that obviously penetrated her jacket, and whatever she had on beneath it, "I have friends back in Philly who are still spending weekends at the Jersey shore, tanning in the hot sun, splashing in the surf." She huddled inside the meager warmth of the lightweight garment. "It's hard to believe that here in Colorado, autumn doesn't officially begin until the beginning of next week."

"Know what you mean," Mace said, belatedly raising his head to study the sky. "Colorado has some strange weather patterns. In the higher elevations, it's not unheard-of for snow to fall as late as the end of June, or for Denver to post sixty-degree temperatures in the dead of winter."

"Well, I can recall brief mild spells in January in Philly," Emma said. "But I can't remember ever hearing anything about snowfall in June."

"These central plains states are known for their late spring blizzards." He chuckled. "I heard a Yellowstone Park ranger on TV once say that Wyoming had two basic seasons, winter and July. I think it applies to all these states."

"I think it applies to preautumn, as well," Emma muttered, clenching her teeth against their audible chattering.

He turned to flash her a grin, but scowled instead. "You look like you're freezing," he exclaimed, cursing himself for not noticing sooner. "Why the hell didn't you tell me?"

Clearly unwilling to risk parting her teeth, Emma moved her shoulders in a stiff shrug.

"Let's go." A quick, almost imperceptible movement of his hands, a slight pressure from his knees, and the big stallion wheeled around to face the way they had come. The sudden maneuver must have startled her.

"Are you trying to give me heart failure?" she yelped. "That cutting action reminds me of those performed by cowboys on documentaries I've seen on TV about the Old West." Emma set Glory dancing sideways by her abrupt pull on the reins. "Where do you want to go now?" she asked, her voice sharp with impatience.

"Back to the house," Mace answered, reaching out to grasp Glory's bridle, bringing her to a halt. "The temp's falling rapidly—and I've seen enough for today."

Even riding in a direct line, at a brisk pace, it still took them nearly an hour to get back to the house. By then, Emma was chilled to the bone, and felt positive the temperature had dropped to below freezing.

"I'll make a deal with you," Mace said, before he had even dismounted in the yard. "I'll take care of the horses, if you'll make a pot of coffee and something hot to eat."

Convinced he was more intent on getting her out of the cold, than he was in either food or drink, Emma nevertheless wasn't about to turn down the offer.

"You're on," she accepted, swinging her leg over Glory's rump, jumping to the ground and making a beeline for the warmth of the house.

The reading on the thermometer hung on the outside frame of a kitchen window proved her guess correct: the needle hovered over the thirty-degree mark.

Incredible. Shaking her head in wonder of the vagaries of the weather, Emma shrugged out of her jacket, but decided to leave on the sweatshirt until her bones defrosted.

The coffee was dripping through the filter basket into the glass carafe, the rich French roast aroma permeating the kitchen, and Emma was stirring the chicken gumbo soup she'd dumped from two cans into a pot, when a short rap on the door was followed by Mace's entrance into the room.

"It's snowing," he announced, removing his jacket and Stetson and hanging them on the hooks on either side of her own jacket.

Certain he was teasing the greenhorn, Emma swung around to give him a skeptical look. "Of course it is," she muttered, shifting her gaze to peer out the window. The white stuff was fine, barely visible, but definitely snow. Her eyes widening with a mixture of disbelief and delight, she laughed and turned back to him. "It *is* snowing."

"That's what I said," he drawled, sauntering to her. "I knew I heard it someplace."

Emma rolled her eyes. "Cute," she retorted, turning, ostensibly to resume stirring the soup, but in fact because his very nearness was too disturbing.

His height, the breadth of his shoulders, made her feel so small by comparison—of course, at five-three, she *was* small, but, even so, she had never felt quite so...so completely vulnerable, almost overpowered by any man.

Why was it, then, that she didn't feel in any way threatened by him? Emma mused, sliding a quick, sidelong look at him. On the contrary. She felt comforted, protected—and, yes, excited and emotionally charged.

"Lunch is almost ready." Sighing in silent dismay at her own jumbled thoughts, Emma gave another vigorous swirl of the spoon in the soup. "You may set the table."

"Sure," he agreed, affably. He sniffed. "Do I smell chicken gumbo soup?"

"Yes." Emma shot an uncertain look at him. "Don't you like chicken gumbo?"

"Love it." Moving to the countertop bread-keeper, he took out a loaf and loaded the four slice toaster. "But you gotta have toast to dunk in chicken gumbo."

Emma turned off the burner under the soup pan, then slanted a wry look at him. "Gotta dunk?"

"Yes." His expression and tone were solemn, serious. "It's the law."

Unable to hold it in, she burst out laughing.

Never having dunked toast into soup in her life— crackers, yes, toast, never—Emma was pleasantly surprised to find herself dunking away, and thoroughly enjoying it.

Come to that, she thoroughly enjoyed the soup, the coffee and, most especially, Mace's company.

As if by unstated but mutual agreement, they lingered at the table, savoring second cups of coffee, generous wedges of Nancy's mouthwatering apricot crumb pie and surprisingly genial and easy conversation.

Without a qualm, Emma found herself relating the bare-bones but salient details of her completely unexpected and startling inheritance.

"Although he was always referred to by every family member as 'Uncle,' Kirk Hartman was my father's great-uncle. A loner and apparently the black sheep of the family, I had only ever met him once."

She paused, frowned, thinking back. "I believe I was around four or five at the time. And the only thing I can remember him saying to me was that I had his hair and eyes." She smiled in remembrance. "I recall being confused by his claim, puzzling over how I could have his hair and eyes, as he so obviously had his own."

Mace laughed along with her, but offered no comment.

"So," she continued, "you can imagine my surprise when, out of the blue, and after years of hearing not a word about him, I received notification from his lawyer informing me of his demise. He had named me in his will as the sole heir of his estate."

Mace's expression turned contemplative. "Yesterday, Nancy told me he had taken up horse breeding. What happened to the rest of the herd?"

Emma sighed. "According to Nancy, Kirk had been diagnosed with terminal cancer and told he had about six months to live." Her voice soft with compassion for the relative she had never really known, she went on, "Stoically accepting his fate, and determined to leave the inheritance debt free, he set about selling off the herd."

"All except Glory."

"Yes." She nodded. "Uncle Kirk must have had knowledge of my youthful passion for riding, for he specifically noted that Glory was to come to me."

"But you are free to sell her, if you decide to do so?" he was quick to clarify.

"Of course." Emma gave him a droll look.

"There were no strings or strictures on either Glory or the property."

Mace was quiet, pensive, toying with a teaspoon while she refilled their cups. "You said you hail from Philadelphia," he said as she slid into the chair opposite him.

"Mmm," she murmured, nodding around the coffee she'd tentatively sipped.

He frowned. "How come you decided to make the trip out here, try to sell the place yourself, instead of placing the property in the hands of a local Realtor?"

"Two reasons," she answered. "Although I have been to the West Coast on several occasions, all I'd ever seen of the middle of the country was from the window of a plane. But, my primary reason was that I am a real estate agent myself. A rather successful one, at that, I might add." She shrugged. "By handling the sale myself, I'll be killing two birds with one stone, so to speak."

"Not to mention saving the commission you'd have to pay another agent," he concluded in dust dry tones.

"That, too," she conceded, before expanding on her explanation. "Actually, there was one other reason."

She paused for another sip of coffee, and to carefully choose her words. "I had been working steadily and hard for some time…three years, in fact, not even taking advantage of my vacation time.

I was tired and needed a break.'' Again, she moved her shoulders in an intended light shrug that didn't quite make it. ''I considered coming here to handle the sale myself as an opportunity for a minimal working holiday, with ample periods of rest and relaxation.''

Mace's appealing male lips curved into a commiserating, knowing smile. ''In other words, you're burned-out.''

''I most certainly am not burned-out.'' Sparked by the echo of her friends similar opinion, Emma's denial came swiftly, too forcefully.

''Nothing to get riled up about,'' he murmured in soothing tones. His too knowing smile matured into a grin. ''I'm burned-out, too.''

Bristling, Emma fairly leaped from her chair, caught on the raw of a very sore emotional spot. ''I tell you, I am not burned-out, dammit.''

Lips twitching with inner laughter, he held up his palms in surrender. ''Okay, have it your way.''

''I intend to,'' she snapped, clattering dishes as she started clearing the table.

Pitching in to help, Mace cleared his throat. ''I, er, thank you kindly for lunch, it was delicious.''

On a path to the dishwasher, Emma's head snapped around, and she glared at him, suspicious of his oh-so-polite tone. Her suspicions were proved valid by the evidence of his lips losing control of the amused twitch.

"You're welcome." She winced inwardly, chagrined by the near snarl she'd produced.

He had the gall to laugh.

She practically threw the dishes into the washer.

More, he had the brass to comment.

"You *are* uptight, aren't you?"

His shot hit its mark. Drawing a deep breath, Emma counted to ten, then worked her stiff lips into a faint semblance of a smile. "What I am, is bored by this conversation," she retorted, her voice strained by the effort required to sound reasonably normal.

"Okay," he agreed, amiably. "What do you want to talk about?"

Once again, he was standing too close, making her feel small, delicate, vulnerable. Memory swirled, vivid and disturbing, of being crushed to the long, hard length of him, her mouth a quivering captive to his senses shattering kiss...and other urgent, mindless, hot, melting sensations she had no desire to analyze.

"I don't want to talk." Dumping detergent into the designated hollows, she slammed shut the door, locked it and flicked the dial to start.

"Then what do you want to do?"

Do? Heat swirled in unthinkable places. Emma's throat went dry...while lower regions grew moist. In a near desperate bid to distance herself from the powerful, magnetic tug emanating from him, she moved away to stare out the window at the novel display of flurrying white.

Inspiration struck.

"I want to walk in this crazy September snow."

"Then I suggest we get to it," Mace drawled, sauntering to the coat pegs by the door. "Because it most likely won't last long, and will melt fast after it stops."

Trailing after him, she watched him shrug into his long, sheepskin-lined jacket, frowning when, instead of her shorter, lighter garment, he lifted from a peg an old heavy wool hip-length navy pea coat.

"That's Nancy's, not mine," she said as he turned to hand it to her. "And too big for me."

"Maybe so," Mace replied, moving around her to drape the coat over her shoulders. "But it'll keep you a helluva lot warmer than that fancy showpiece of yours."

Emma didn't argue; she couldn't. She was too busy trying to control the shiver activated by the brush of his fingertips against the sensitive skin at her nape. Shoving her arms into the sleeves, she stepped away from him.

The sleeves covered her hands to the cuticle of her fingernails; the body of the coat, which on Nancy circled her hips, hung midthigh on Emma.

Feeling diminished, somewhat like a little girl playing dress-up with her mother's clothes, Emma, stiff and resentful, yanked open the door and stomped out onto the porch.

Resentment changed to reluctant gratitude with the first blast of frigid wind that slammed into her, through her, stealing her breath.

Emma quickly fastened the buttons on the panels she had left hanging open, flipped up the wide collar, then curled up her fingers inside the warmth of the long sleeves.

"Thank you," she muttered when Mace plopped onto her head the beat-up hat she had worn when riding.

"You're welcome." Casually slinging the added warmth of his arm over her shoulders, he led her from beneath the meager protection of the porch roof, into a stinging cold world of lowering slate-gray clouds and tiny delicate white, wind-driven snowflakes.

Emma was enchanted. Cold, but enchanted. Laughing, she slipped from beneath Mace's arm, and ran into the middle of the yard. Flinging back her head, she opened her mouth and stuck out her tongue to catch a flake, to feel the cold of it melt in the warmth of her mouth.

Instead of the cold of lacy snow, her mouth was captured by wind-chilled male lips, her tongue imprisoned within the heated cavern of Mace's mouth.

The arm he had so casually draped around her shoulders was joined by his other arm, both tightening as he turned her, molded her slight form to the firm, and swiftly hardening angles of his body.

Emma's feeble attempt at protest was smothered

by his tongue thrusting into her mouth. Suddenly she no longer felt the sting of the wind, the cold of the pelting snow. She was hot, so hot, so needy... so...so...

Out of her tiny mind.

The thought instilled enough strength for Emma to tear herself away from him. Instantly she felt the cold again, the biting wind, the stinging splat of snow against her face...and a clawing emptiness deep inside her.

Mace stood watching her, quiet and still. But his eyes, dark and compelling, probed into hers, willing her to admit to the need clamoring within, surrender to the inevitability of the sensual attraction shimmering between them.

Emma was sorely tempted. Lord, she had never felt such an overwhelming temptation.

And he knew it. Emma felt certain that with the laser probe of his dark eyes, he couldn't help but see the conflict tearing her apart inside.

"I want you so badly I can taste it, Emma."

His low voice, threaded with leashed passion, slashed through Emma with the searing sting of a flaming firebrand, igniting her senses, heating her blood.

Her breath constricting, her imagination expanding, she stared at him, wide-eyed, unable to think, move, caught in the web of his compelling eyes, his blunt admission of desire tapping into the need clawing inside her.

"I... We..." She halted, swallowed, stammered on, "I...don't...we barely know each other. I...for all I know, you could be married."

"I'm not." His tone rang with absolute honesty. "I was once, but that ended a long time ago," he went on, his lips curving into a faint smile of bitter remembrance. "Are you? Married or currently, er, attached?"

"No," she admitted.

"So, then, what's the big deal?"

Big deal? Big deal! Emma stared at him in blank disbelief. They were virtual strangers, and had practically been devouring each other...and he wonders what's the big deal?

"For God's sake, Mace, how can you even ask me that?" she demanded. "We've only just met."

"I know." Mace exhaled, shook his head, then drew a deep harsh-sounding breath. "Damnedest thing—nothing like this has ever happened to me before, not with my former wife, or any other woman, not even when I was an overeager teenager," he admitted with surprising candor. A wisp of a smile shaded his taut lips. "Hell, Emma, I don't know, but I felt it...this strange, instant attraction between us, from the moment you walked into the kitchen yesterday."

Emma understood, only too well, for she had felt the same immediate and startling, almost inexorable attraction at her first sight of him.

What could she say? The impulse to deny the attraction was strong, but inevitably pointless. She had betrayed herself, her weakness, with her hungry, melting response to him, both yesterday in the stables, and mere moments ago.

"I can't deal with this now...I just can't." With an abrupt about-face, she walked away from him, unmindful of the sharp wind, the cold snowflakes tangling in her lashes, wetting her cheeks.

Mace was alongside her in a moment, adjusting his stride to hers. "Do you want an apology?"

As if an apology from him would be sincere, after hearing him admit to wanting her so bad he could taste it, Emma thought, shaking her head, snapping, "No."

"Then... Do you have any idea where you're going?" Not an idle question, since she was not heading either back to the house or in the direction of the stables.

"Nowhere. Anywhere." She shrugged, not daring so much as a quick glance at him. "I told you before, I just want to walk in the snow."

"Okay, we'll walk in the snow." Pitched low, his voice had a soothing, settling tone, not unlike a shaman's croon. "But, would you mind a stroll around the house? I'd like a look at the structure in daylight."

Emma hesitated, then shrugged again. What difference did it make where she walked? she asked herself. She really wasn't paying attention to the weather, anyway. She was much too aware of Mace, pacing beside her, to notice such mundane things as the wind, the cold, the lacy white stuff.

She could still taste him, on her lips, in her mouth. The hard angles of his muscular body, and even harder ridge of his erection, seemed permanently imprinted on her flesh, her senses, her rioting hormones.

Bemused and confused, Emma tried to figure out what it was about this man, this Mason Conyers, that set him apart from all the other men she had ever known, made him, his nearness, his touch irresistible to her.

He was attractive, sure, but she had met many men as attractive, even more so, than Mace, and had found nothing at all irresistible about any one of them...including the one whose engagement ring she had briefly worn.

Of course, none of those other men were quite so blatantly masculine as Mace, nor had any of them possessed such raw and powerful sexuality. But Emma had never been impressed by mere manliness, so there had to be something else about him, some element other than sheer male sexiness that spoke to, connected with something inside her.

Quiet strength.

The sudden thought compelled deeper examination.

Yes, Emma reflected, she had been struck at once by the pervading quality emanating from him of quiet, steady, dependable strength of character.

Without a taint of vanity, Emma acknowledged owning her fair share of the same character traits.

Like to like?

But that didn't make any kind of sense to her. How could it when they were so very different? She was ambitious, a go-getter, she thrived on the rattle and clang of the city, the give and take of the business world.

And, by his own admission, Mace was burned-out, tired of it all, looking for solitude and inner peace.

Though Emma allowed that the bucolic atmosphere of the ranch was fine for a break in her hectic routine, she felt certain a steady diet of the peace and quiet would drive her nuts.

So strike like to like.

Into introspection, Emma trooped along, unconscious of having circled the house three times. That is, until Mace brought her to a halt in front of the porch.

"Walked it off yet?"

Blinking herself to attention, Emma angled her head to frown up at him. "Walked what off?" she asked, mystified. "What are you talking about?"

"We were about to begin a fourth circuit of the house," he informed her in dry tones. "And, seeing as how you look nearly frozen, I was just asking if you hadn't yet walked off the anger and excess energy driving you on."

"We've walked completely around the house

three times?'' Emma asked in amazement, choosing to ignore the bit about anger and excess energy.

''Three times,'' he concurred, lips twitching. ''And I don't know about you, but I've walked in this crazy September snow long enough.''

It was only then that she felt the cold, clear into her bones. Feeling more an idiot than a savvy businesswoman, let alone one with an edge, Emma sighed. Even she heard the tired sound of defeat in her soft exhalation.

''Time for a hot drink,'' she muttered, mounting the steps to the porch.

''Followed, maybe, by a tour of the house?'' Mace suggested, trailing her inside.

Chapter 5

Emma heaved a sigh in appreciation of the warmth of the kitchen, not realizing until that moment how very chilled she felt. She shrugged out of Nancy's coat, and hung it and her hat onto hooks before responding to Mace's less-than-subtle remark. "If you insist."

He slanted a wry look at her. "You're a real estate agent yourself, would you advise a prospective client to buy a property without a thorough inspection?"

"No, of course not." Impatient with him—more with herself—she crossed to the stove, leaving wet running shoe tracks on Nancy's clean floor.

Mace proceeded to show keener foresight by pulling off his boots before stepping away from the throw rug laid right inside the door for just such purposes. The sight of his heavy-duty socks made her uncomfortably aware of her own lightweight, damp hose.

"Your feet have got to be wet, and cold," he said, as if he had read her mind. "Why don't you go change into something dry and warm—I'll start a pot of coffee."

Emma wanted to protest his take-charge attitude, but she wanted to get out of her squishy socks more. She also wanted to distance herself from him, if only for a few minutes in which to breathe without constraint.

"Okay, thanks," she said, skirting the table, opposite him, heading for the hallway to the stairs. "I'll only be a moment."

"Take your time, I'm not going anywhere."

That, of course, was what she was afraid of, Emma ruefully acknowledged, zipping along the hallway and up the stairs. His continued presence, his nearness, the tension shimmering inside her just knowing he was there, closeby…touch close, was getting to her, undermining her no-involvement resolve.

Emma was gone for a few more than a few minutes. In fact, she had taken the time to have a quick hot shower to chase the last of the chill from her body, at least the chill caused by the cold weather. The deeper, inner chill of heightened sensual excitement instilled by the man making free with her kitchen remained to torment her.

When Emma returned to the kitchen, she was struck by the tantalizing aromas of fresh coffee and the mouthwatering scent of cinnamon rolls warming in the oven. A sweeping glance of the area gave evidence that Mace had mopped up the tracks made by her wet running shoes.

"You have been busy," she commended, indicating the floor with a hand gesture.

"Hmm," he murmured absently, spreading icing onto the pastries. "I found the package of rolls in the fridge and couldn't resist." He flashed a quick grin at her. "Hope you don't mind."

"How could I...after you were kind enough to clean up the floor for me?" she said, covering the shiver-inducing effects of his sexy grin by moving to the coffeemaker to fill the two cups he had set out.

He shrugged. "All it took was a couple of swipes with some hand towels."

Surprisingly, after all the mind- and nerve-crunching tension between them earlier, Emma found herself relaxing over the coffee and rolls, willing to join with him in an unstated but mutually accepted truce.

Stilted at first, conversation eased between them as the warmth of the kitchen enveloped them, and they laughed together when they caught sight of each other licking melting icing from their fingers.

"You appear to be at home and competent in the kitchen," Emma observed, again gesturing to the floor.

"Had to be." His smile was crooked. "I've been fending for myself for a long time."

"Your…marriage?" she dared to ask.

He sighed, but answered. "It was a mistake. We learned too late that we wanted different things, lifestyles. It was a classic example of marry in haste, repent in leisure."

"I'm sorry." What else could she say?

"I'm not." His voice was flat, emotionless. "We were both young, too young. She was pretty, vivacious and she craved attention, excitement. Understandable, I suppose, since she drew men like honey draws bears, men with a lot more to offer her than I had at the time."

He had to be referring to money, the good times it could buy, Emma decided. For she couldn't imagine many men with a lot more to offer than the steady strength, the easy manner, the fine character traits Mace had revealed to her in such a short period of time.

"I was engaged once," she offered, unquestioned. "That didn't work, either."

His dark, compelling gaze fixed squarely on her eyes, he softly said, "I won't say *I'm* sorry."

A tremor rippled through Emma. Awareness of the magnetism of him, sexual in nature, raw in intent jolted her out of her chair and into a flurry of activity clearing away the remains of their snack.

He didn't offer to help this time, but simply sat there, watching her, causing her normally efficient movements to falter and fumble due to her shaky hands.

Mace's requested tour of the house commenced when, telling herself to grow up, Emma set the dish-cloth aside and turned to confront him.

"Let's get this house inspection over with," she said, marching past him to retrace her recent steps along the hallway to the stairs.

It was late afternoon by the time Mace had finished his thorough examination of every nook and cranny of every room of the house, even the storage loft above the second floor. Having grown impatient with his distracted attention to the most minute detail, Emma had left him at it to return to the kitchen to hunt up something for dinner.

Flicking on the switch for the overhead light, Emma frowned in consternation as, startled, she took notice of the time, the deepening darkness and the chilling sound of the wind as it wailed around the corners of the house.

Thinking it was surely to early for such complete darkness, she turned on the radio before going to the fridge. The commentator's voice stopped her dead in her tracks.

"...and the roadways are already slick and dangerous," he announced.

Roadways? Where? Emma frowned. Must be around Denver, she figured, since she knew Nancy kept the radio tuned to a Denver station. Had the snow turned to an icy rain, coating the roads, making travel hazardous?

Nancy! Nancy had traveled to Denver that morning. Concern for the older woman twisting inside her, Emma stared at the radio, concentrating on the ongoing commentary.

"Yep, folks, Mother Nature pulled a fast one on us, and instead of a harmless preseason snow shower, the weather service is now reporting that we're in the grip of a full-blown blizzard, and the snow is coming down harder with each passing hour. There's already close to a foot of snow on the ground, and it's piling up fast, making driving a nightmare. Authorities are advising everyone to stay inside if possible, and to use extreme caution if you must…"

"What's all the excitement?"

Startled by the unexpected sound of his voice, Emma whirled to find Mace standing in the doorway, frowning at the continued rapid-fire report from the commentator.

"Oh…Mace, it's incredible but, apparently, Denver is in the midst of a raging blizzard," she said in tones of sheer disbelief.

"Denver? Only the city of Denver?" He arched a skeptical brow. "I don't think so."

Emma bristled at having her word doubted. "What do you mean you don't think so?" she demanded. "I was just listening to a report about it on the radio."

Shaking his head, Mace moved to the door. "I meant, I don't think it likely that the blizzard is confined to only the city of Denver," he explained, eye-

ing a row of light switches on the wall next to the
door. "I saw the trouble lights mounted to the
roof—which switch?"

"The last two," Emma said, crossing to him.

Hitting the switches, Mace pulled open the door
and stepped onto the porch. A sensation, part impatience, part anticipation stirring inside her, Emma
followed him out. Blinking at the glare of the trouble
lights, a softly exclaimed "Oh" whispered from her
lips at the sight that met her amazed gaze.

No longer fine and wispy, the now wind-driven,
heavier snowflakes swirled at a near sideways angle
before landing atop the already substantial blanket
of white covering the yard. The fall was so dense,
she could barely make out the solid forms of the
stables and other outbuildings.

"Isn't it beautiful?" she murmured, entranced by
the whirling dance of the lacy flakes.

"Yeah." Mace slanted a wry look at her. "Beautiful and deadly." Sighing, he turned to go back
inside.

Beginning to feel like a well-trained pet, she followed on his heels, frowning when he reached for
his jacket.

"You're going back outside?" Dumb question,
Emma silently chided herself. Why else would he
be putting on the garment, if not to go out again?

He nodded, and settled the Stetson on his head.
"I'll go see to Horse and Glory, then…"

"Wait," she said, heading for the fridge. "I'll
give you carrots for them."

A smile softened the grim set of his features. "You never forget, do you?"

"I'd better not." Her chuckle was muffled by the open fridge door. "Because, even after only a week, Glory now expects the treat."

Moments later, shivering, Emma watched from the open doorway as, head bent against the force of the wind, carrots in hand, Mace trudged through the deepening snow to the stables. She didn't step back inside the warm kitchen until he had pulled the wide stable door shut behind him.

Dinner. The thought spurred Emma into action. Mace would probably be cold and ready for a hot meal by the time he finished settling the horses for the night.

But what to make? Emma's cooking skills ran to scrambling eggs, warming canned soup and frozen dinners. She went to the fridge, hoping to find something substantial that even she couldn't ruin, if only a steak she could thaw and toss under the broiler.

To her heartfelt relief, she discovered several containers in the freezer, either leftovers or dishes Nancy had prepared in advance for quick meals at a later date. Emma withdrew a container labeled chicken stew, set it in the microwave and programmed it for defrost.

In the fridge, she found a tubular package of bake and serve biscuits nestled on a shelf next to a package of cinnamon rolls like the ones Mace had found earlier.

This she could handle, Emma told herself, getting to work.

Everything was just about ready by the time she heard Mace stomping snow from his boots on the porch. The table was set. A wooden bowl of tossed salad greens and two bottles of dressing were placed to one side. Transferred to a microwave dish, the aromatic stew bubbled. One minute remained on the oven timer she had set for the baking biscuits. Coffee was trickling through the basket into the glass carafe.

The oven timer rang as Mace opened the door and stepped inside. An instant later the microwave emitted three musical beeps and shut off.

"Perfect timing," Emma said, feeling rather proud of herself. "We can eat as soon as you've washed up."

Mace hesitated just inside the door, a tiny frown line scoring his brow, then he sighed. "Okay. It sure smells good," he said, tugging off his boots.

"I can't take the credit for it." Emma grinned. "Nancy made it. All I did was defrost and heat it." She turned to the stove to slide the tray of biscuits from the oven.

"Anything I can do to help?" he asked, shrugging out of his jacket and hanging it and his hat on a hook before crossing to the sink to wash his hands.

"You can bring that plate of biscuits," she said, carefully setting the dish of stew on the table.

Mace waited until Emma was seated before sitting down opposite her. "As soon as we've finished eat-

ing and clearing up, I suppose I'd better get moving.''

Emma paused in the process of buttering a steaming biscuit to stare at him. "Get moving? Where?"

"Back to town," he said, ladling a generous helping of stew onto his plate. "Driving's likely a bitch
already."

Without a thought beyond the caution advisory
issued by the authorities, Emma reached out to grasp
his arm. "But you can't drive back to town in this,"
she protested. "The reporter on the radio said that
the roads are extremely hazardous. An appeal has
been issued by the authorities for motorists to stay
off the roads unless it's absolutely necessary to
drive."

He stilled. His gaze dropped to her hand grasping
his arm. When he raised his eyes to hers, they were
dark, intent. "Are you inviting me to stay here tonight?"

The simmering inner sexual tension that had diminished somewhat with his absence from the
house, her activity getting the meal together,
slammed back into Emma, stronger, more compelling than ever.

If Mace stayed the night…would he…could
she…might they then…

Stop it, Emma chastised herself. She was an adult,
a mature, reasonably intelligent woman, not a trembling, overexcitable, imaginative teenager.

Gathering her not insignificant resources of calm,
cool control, she maintained his intense stare. "Of

course,'' she said, her tone indicating that the answer should have been obvious to him. ''Why not?''

''You know why.'' Though low, his tone rang
with clear and unmistakable meaning.

''Because you're so irresistible?'' Emma injected
a note of mockery into her voice, and arched a brow.
''And because I'm alone here, a woman defenseless?''

He actually laughed. ''Defenseless? You? I don't
think so. You forget, I saw you this morning, primed
and ready to go hand to hand in combat with that
old coot.''

Emma knew too well that taking on Jenkins was
one thing, Mace, however, would be a whole different story. Her expression admitted as much, as
she swept his formidable form with a pointed look.

A warning, provocative glow brightened his dark
eyes. His voice was a blatantly sexy purr. ''I do like
the part about being irresistible, though.''

Suppressing an inner burst of excitement, Emma
made a rude, snorting noise. ''Oh, shut up and eat
your dinner,'' she ordered. ''Before it gets cold.''

Laughter dancing in his eyes, and along her nerve
endings, Mace dug into his food.

Fighting the demoralizing effects of his magnetic,
sensual attraction, Emma remained silent throughout
most of the meal, her thoughts consumed by spec-
ulation about the long evening ahead. Possible what-
ifs ran around in circles inside her mind.

What if the storm stranded them for days?

What if the power failed and they were left without electricity? Without heat?

What if? What if? What if? One what-if after the other in relation to the blizzard, all valid, and all conjured to avoid the most important what-if of all.

What if Mace ultimately proved himself to in fact be irresistible to her? She had firsthand experience of the lure of temptation, the temptation to lose herself in the heat of his body, the heaven of his mouth...

What if she were to succumb?

"Relax, Emma," Mace finally said, jolting her from her reverie. "I'm not into ravishment."

Too bad.

The sudden thought both shocked and amused her. Emma knew what had sparked the thought, of course. Were he to ravish her, she could taste, revel in the sensual pleasure she felt certain Mace would provide, while at the same time, absolve herself of any personal responsibility.

It was almost funny. No, it *was* funny. Emma laughed. Her laughter eased the strained atmosphere in the room, the taut silence between them.

After that lessening of tension, the evening passed so smoothly, so companionably, it was anticlimactic.

Smiling, Mace reassured Emma when she voiced her concern in regards to two of her what-ifs. "We won't be stranded, at least not for long. It's too early in the season. As to a power failure, that wouldn't last long, either," he went on with an unconcerned shrug. "There are candles in the top end cabinet drawer—I saw them yesterday when I was hunting for utensils to set the table." He gestured to the breakfront along the opposite wall. "And that old-fashioned oil lamp on the bottom shelf is not just for decoration—it's over half full of oil and the wick is trimmed. So we'll have light.

"There's a generator out back—I noticed it during our triple traipses around the house."

She tossed a wry look at him.

He laughed. "The generator is big enough to keep the electrical appliances running, and the heater at short intervals for a while. For supplemental heat, there's the fireplace in the living room, and plenty of firewood in that enclosed area at the end of the porch."

Emma felt like an idiot. Not only had she considered the lamp nothing more than a homey touch, but she had also never even thought to look what might be inside the boxlike enclosure at the far end of the porch. But she also felt relieved, and didn't hesitate to tell him so.

"I guess I came across as the greenest of greenhorns," she concluded, her smile rueful.

"Personally," he murmured, flashing a bone-liquifying smile, "I'm kinda partial to green."

As it turned out, none of Emma's concerns were realized. There was no interruption in electrical power. The candles remained close to hand on top of the counter where Mace had set them. The oil lamp stayed in place on the shelf. However, Mace did collect some of the wood to build a cheery fire in the living room.

Hours later, sleepy and out of conversation, curled into the corner of the sofa set at an angle to the fireplace, Emma sighed with contentment and stared into the dwindling but still mesmerizing flicker and dance of the flames.

Unseen by Emma, Mace lounged in a lazy sprawl in a deep, cushy chair opposite, and stared in contentment at her.

"There's something soothing and comforting about a crackling fire on a cold, snowy night," she murmured, raising a languid hand to smother a yawn.

"Hmm...cozy," he agreed, his own eyelids drooping. "But neither one of us will feel soothed, comforted nor cosy if we fall asleep where we are, and wake up in the morning cold and stiff in front of a dead fire."

"You're right, it is getting late," she agreed, too sleepy to feel more than the tiniest twinge of alarm about sleeping in the room next to the one she had allotted to Mace. Uncurling her legs, she stood up, yawning again.

"You go on up, I'll bank the fire and turn off the lights." Standing, Mace raised his arms over his head and arched his spine in a long stretch.

For a moment, Emma stood, transfixed by the sight of him, his broad chest and tapered waist, his flat, almost concave belly, narrow hips and long legs.

She swallowed, and swallowed again against the sudden dryness in her mouth and throat. And she was warm, too warm, in all the wrong places. Her breasts tingled and ached, as did sections lower on her anatomy.

He raked a hand through his mink-dark gray-sprinkled hair, making her fingers itch to slide into the thick, wavy silky-looking locks.

Mace glanced at her as he lowered his arms, his eyes reflecting the dying flames in the hearth. He smiled. Her breath lodged in her throat.

"You'd best get moving, before you fall asleep on your feet." His voice was low, a seduction of and by itself. "Good night, Emma."

Coming to her senses, the warmth in her cheeks owing nothing to the fire, Emma turned away from the allurement he exuded, and with a mumbled, "Good night," she fled, certain she'd find little rest with him right next door.

Her bedroom was cold. Shivering, Emma quickly stripped off her clothes and pulled on her short cotton nightshirt. Howling like a departed soul in torment, the wind slammed against the windows, as if demanding entrance.

And yet, Emma felt safe, secure, protected.

Mace was right next door.

Naive, perhaps, she mused, tugging the covers loose. But there it was. She trusted him.

She was out for the count within minutes of slipping between the chilled sheets.

Chapter 6

Emma woke to watery sunlight and the quiet still-
ness unique to snow-muffled mornings. The overnight chill permeated the room, and for a moment,
she burrowed deeper into the warmth of the covers.
But the tantalizing scent of coffee and frying bacon
soon lured her from the cocoon of blankets.

Minutes later, after a dash to the bathroom to
wash her face, brush her teeth, drag a brush through
her sleep-ruffled hair and belt herself into a robe,
Emma strolled into the kitchen.

"Morning," Mace greeted her from where he
stood next to the stove, breaking eggs into a bowl.
"Scrambled eggs all right with you?"

"Fine," Emma answered, crossing to a window.
"Anything I can do to—" She broke off with a soft

"Oh" on sight of the winter-white landscape that met her eyes. It had stopped snowing. The wind had died. The sky was an incredible benign blue. Strengthening sunlight flashed blinding light off the mantle of white. "It's...it's so beautiful," she murmured, inexplicably sorry the storm had ended. "Like a country scene on a Christmas card."

"Yeah, Christmas. Wonderful," Mace drawled, his tone edged with derision. "The temperature's rising, and the snow will be gone, and with it your Christmas card scene."

Emma turned to frown at him. "You don't like Christmas?"

"Just another day," he said, pouring the egg mixture into a large frying pan.

"But..."

The bread popped up in the toaster. "You want to get the toast and bring the bacon?" he interrupted, nodding at a plate on the counter. "The eggs are about ready."

They were halfway through the meal before Emma gave in to curiosity. "Why don't you like Christmas, Mace?"

"I don't actively dislike it," he countered.

"But you just said—" she began in protest.

"I know what I said," he cut in on her. "I said it's just another day, and to me, that's all it ever has been."

"You've never celebrated the holiday?" Emma stared at him in amazement. "Surely as a child..."

A quick shake of his head silenced her. "Look, I

grew up dirt-poor, and under those conditions, there never was anything to celebrate. I was twelve when my folks gave up the struggle, dying within less than a year of each other.''

"Oh, Mace," she murmured, recalling the wonderful childhood and delightful holidays she had enjoyed with her family. "I'm so sorry."

"Don't be." His voice was rough with rejection of her sympathy. "I was placed into foster care with a horse breeder." A cynical smile curled his lip. "Actually what he was looking for was a legal slave...and he found it with me. There wasn't much celebrating going on there, either." He shrugged. "But that was okay, I never knew what I was missing."

Emma was appalled. "But you must have gone to school...had friends with more normal home lives?"

He shook his head again. "I was home taught, first by my father, who didn't know much about anything, then by my foster father, who knew a lot...about horse breeding and, strangely, the law. He had a small library in his study, and I studied every book, some of them twice."

"So after you came of age, you went into law enforcement," she concluded.

"Right." He got up to pour more coffee for them both. "But my goal had always been to save enough for a place of my own to breed and raise horses. I didn't have the time or inclinations for holiday celebrations."

Emma hesitated, knowing it was really none of her business, but again curiosity won. "You must have made some friends, and you said you were married," she reminded him. "You must have shared holidays with your wife and friends."

He laughed; it was not a happy sound. "I was married all of seven months, from March until October. That's all the time it took for my wife to realize that I wasn't about to lavish every damn dime I earned and had saved on financing the life-style she craved. She took off with a gambler heading for Vegas—that's where the divorce papers eventually came from."

Rising, Emma began clearing the table. "And your friends?" she asked.

"Had families of their own," he answered, working along side her. "I didn't want to intrude."

No, he wouldn't, Emma reflected, absently loading the dishwasher. He wouldn't want the sympathy, if only implied, she knew, having had her own refused. Nevertheless, she sympathized with him, whether he wanted it or not.

But sympathy wasn't the only emotion she felt, nor the strongest, Emma acknowledged, feeling an electric jolt zing through her when his hard body came in contact with hers at the sink. She glanced up to find him staring at her, his dark eyes shimmering with desire.

"Comfort and joy," he murmured, moving even closer to her. "The refrain never had much meaning to me before now." Raising a hand, he trailed his fingertips down her cheek to the corner of her mouth.

Beneath the heat of his gaze, his touch, Emma was melting faster than the snow beneath the warming rays of the sun. Her breathing erratic, she whispered, "And…now?"

He smiled, the curve of his lips pure enticement. "Now comfort means having this property, this house." He slowly lowered his head; his breath bathed her mouth. "And joy means having you, in my bed."

Yes. Yes, her senses urged, clamoring for the promise of sensual pleasure he offered.

No. No, be reasonable, her intellect cautioned.

"I…I… The horses," she blurted out. "We have to see to Glory and Horse."

"I did that," he said, his mouth drawing ever nearer to her own. "I've been up since dawn, mucked out the stalls and took care of the horses." His lips skimmed over hers, blurring intellect. "Then I had a shower…in your bathroom…all the time wishing you were in there with me."

"Mace…I…"

His mouth took command of hers in a searing, mind-bending kiss. His tongue speared into her mouth. She felt the effects in every atom of her body.

Emma's senses pummeled intellect into the dust of physical desire. Surrender was not only easy, but it was necessary. Her body raging for the touch, the possession of his, she curled her arms around his neck and melted into his kiss.

The world tilted when, his mouth still fastened to hers, Mace swung Emma up and into his arms. His strides long, purposeful, he carried her down the hallway and up the stairs to her bedroom.

Drowning in his kiss, frantic with a need to touch his skin, feel it next to her own, she began working on his shirt buttons before he had set her on her feet next to the bed.

Within moments, the carpet was strewn with their discarded clothing and Mace was bearing her down to the mattress.

The bed was still warm; it swiftly became warmer.

Murmuring enticing, exciting words of the pleasures they would share, Mace inflamed Emma's imagination with verbal images, while he ignited an inferno in her body with his hands and mouth and tongue.

Never, never before had Emma felt the exquisite sensations Mace aroused in her. Her hands caressed and gripped him in turn. She was on fire, a flame burning out of control, craving the quenching release only he could provide.

She cried out when, at last he entered her, arching into him to encourage his driving force.

She cried out again when she crested the pinnacle of pleasure, and heard his low, harsh cry as he followed her into shattering ecstasy.

Other than necessary trips to the bathroom, occasional forays into the kitchen for sustenance, and one hurried dash to the stable to see to the needs of Glory and Horse, Emma and Mace spent the remainder of the day, and the entire night, in bed, seeing to the more physical and earthy, and seemingly insatiable needs of each other.

The scenario was repeated throughout the following days, Emma and Mace melting into each other, as the early autumnal snow melted into the ground.

Although she tried to ignore it, Emma knew that at some point, reality would have to intrude. Because, no matter how absorbing, how thrilling, how enchanting the distraction of self-indulgence, one could not spend one's life in bed. And she did have a life outside the bedroom.

Reality intruded with a double whammy around midmorning the next day. The first blow made itself felt with the unexpectedly early return of Nancy from Denver.

It was a perfect autumn day, the sky a clear blue, the sunshine bright. The temperature in the mid-sixties. Except for shallow patches in the shady side of buildings and trees, the snow had melted into the ground, making the yard a mud-puddled mess. Fortunately, since Emma and Mace were still in the stable after having exercised Glory and Horse, they were both fully dressed. Emma knew it might have been a different story had Nancy arrived a half hour later.

"Hey, there," she hailed them as they walked from the stable to investigate the identity of the new arrival. "You guys want to help me here? I've got the trunk loaded with groceries I picked up in town."

"You must've left Denver pretty early, stopping for groceries and still getting here so soon," Mace said, hefting four plastic store bags from the trunk.

"I did." Nancy nodded. "I was worried about Emma, being alone here through that storm and all."

"But I told you when I phoned you the other day that I was fine," Emma said, suddenly overwarm in her suede jacket. Grabbing the last bag, and Nancy's suitcase, she turned and started for the house.

"I know, but…" Nancy broke off with a shrug. "I didn't know how bad the storm was here." She glanced around the yard, noting the mud instead of snow. "Denver got blasted—driving's still a challenge there." Trailing behind Emma, Nancy cast a look back at Mace. "Does your being here mean that Emma's decided to sell the place to you?" she asked in her usual blunt fashion.

"We're negotiating," Mace answered in dust-dry tones, setting the bags on the porch to tug off his boots.

Oh, was that what they'd been doing in the bedroom? Could have fooled me, Emma thought, kicking out of her own ankle boots before entering the house.

Reality's second blow came with the ringing of the phone while they were stashing the foodstuffs.

"I'll get it," Nancy said, going to the wall phone. Then, "Yes, she's here," she said into the receiver, turning to hold it out to Emma. "It's for you. A Mr. Gardner."

Her boss? Emma frowned as she took the receiver. "Hello, Mark, what's up?" she asked.

"You'd better be," he said, skipping the niceties. "In the air, I mean, on a plane, heading back here on the first available flight east."

"But..." she protested. "I can't leave right now, I'm in the middle of *negotiations* with a prospective buyer." She slanted a quick look at Mace to see if he'd caught the slight emphasis she placed on the word he had used in describing their association to Nancy.

Mace sliced her a wicked grin. She didn't have time to savor her tingling reaction to his grin, the glint in his dark eyes. Mark's voice exploded in her ear.

"You can handle that from here...or turn it over to a local Realtor there, but you've got to get back."

Certain the others couldn't help but overhear his sharp voice, she said, "Hang on a minute, Mark." Placing her palm over the mouthpiece, she turned a beseeching look on Nancy and Mace. "If you wouldn't mind?"

"'Course not. I need to unpack anyway," Nancy said, picking up her case and heading for the hallway.

Going to the fridge, Mace took out two carrots. "I'll be in the stable," he murmured as he passed her on his way to the door.

Sighing, Emma lifted her hand from the mouthpiece. "Okay, Mark, why must I come back?"

"You recall that big commercial property deal you were working your tush off on a couple of months back?" he barked. "The one that would have made the agency, and you, a lot of money? The one you thought fell through?"

"Yes, of course I remember, but..."

"But, hell," Mark said. "It's on again, and this time that group is serious, and they insist they'll only deal with you. I made an appointment for you to meet with them on Friday morning, nine sharp. So get packing and cracking," he ordered, and hung up on her.

Emma stared at the phone for several moments after cradling the receiver for the second time. Before she could give in to temptation to call Mark back and tell him to soldier on by himself, she had called the airline— She was booked on a late flight out of Denver to Philadelphia.

It was over. Whatever it had been between her and Mace, a fling, a brief affair, it was now over. She blinked against the sting of tears.

Of course, she had known it wouldn't last, couldn't last. She and Mace were from two altogether different worlds. He longed for the peace and quiet of the country; she preferred the fast-paced action of the city.

Opposites attracting, then separating, like two ships, connecting for a moment, then passing in the night.

Groaning in despair of her descent once again into the clichéd, Emma impatiently brushed the moisture from her cheeks and headed for the stable to say goodbye to Glory…and to Mace.

It was cold in Pennsylvania, even for December. The hem of her ankle-length wool coat flapping in the wind, Emma hurried to her car parked on the vehicle packed lot surrounding the malls at King of Prussia.

Less than two weeks remained until Christmas. Shopping had been a challenge, what with the throngs of people jamming the walkways and the stores, the repetitive holiday music blaring from numerous speakers, the lines at the cash registers.

Emma felt exhausted. She had finished, crossed off the last name on her list of friends and co-workers. The mere thought of wrapping the gifts was daunting.

It was a new experience for Emma. Always before, she had enjoyed dashing around, selecting special gifts for family, friends and co-workers. Apart from the gift she had bought and mailed to Nancy who, at Mace's request, had happily agreed to stay on at the ranch as housekeeper, this season, she couldn't get into the swing of shopping, couldn't work up any enthusiasm for the whole process.

Emma's lack of holiday spirit had little to do with the fact that, in October, out of the blue and with obvious hesitation, her parents had informed her of their desire to accept an invitation from friends in

England to join them in their country home for an old-fashioned Christmas celebration.

"Of course, you're also included in the invitation," her mother had been quick to clarify.

"I can't take the time." Emma had been just as quick to decline. "But it does sound like fun, and I think you two should go," she'd insisted. "I've received several invitation from friends, and besides, with my schedule, I probably won't even notice. One Christmas on my own won't hurt me," she'd assured them, aching inside for the man who had told her he spent every Christmas on his own.

Though her mother and father had voiced token protests, Emma had seen them off at the airport two days before. The thing that surprised her was that she really hadn't minded.

She also hadn't minded turning down the invitations she had received from friends, telling herself she simply wasn't in the mood for the usual holiday frivolity.

And yet Emma should have been feeling on top of the world. Not only had she completed the sale on the large commercial property, but she had also negotiated several other lucrative sales, commercial and residential, in addition to recently making final settlement with Mace on her own ranch property, as well as the separate sale of Glory to him.

But none of those accomplishments, the healthy commissions she'd earned, the profits garnered from the sale of the ranch and Glory, had lifted her declining spirits. Though she tried to tell herself she was merely tired, Emma knew she was lying to herself.

What Emma was was haunted, and not by any Christmas ghosts. She was haunted by memories, one in particular. The memory echo of Mace's voice, the last words he'd spoken that last day, haunted her day and night.

Don't go back, Emma. Stay with me, live with me, sleep with me…love me.

That day Emma had been tempted—sorely tempted—to toss it all…her career, her town house, the energy she had always drawn from city life, turn her back on it all for the safe haven of Mace's arms, the heaven of his kiss.

Uncertain and frightened by the way Mace had made her feel, emotions he had aroused in her, deeper and more intense than any feelings she had ever experienced before, Emma had fought temptation and bolted for home telling Mace he could buy the ranch.

Now, almost three months later, she felt empty and lost. The energy of the city no longer charged her, her town house felt alien, her career gave little satisfaction.

Love. Was it possible to fall in love so quickly? The question was another of the specters haunting Emma. Could she, could he, have fallen in love in so short a time?

Emma pondered the question as she finished wrapping the last of the gifts she had purchased that afternoon. The echoing specter whispered through her mind.

Love me.

Could she? Did she? she asked herself, a vision of him, vivid, heart-stopping, forming to tease her.

"Yes." Emma cried aloud, surrendering to the realization of the inevitable. "Yes, dammit, I love him."

Revitalized, she jumped up and ran to the phone, hoping, praying for a timely flight cancellation miracle.

Emma flew into Denver on December 21. She didn't rent a car. She bought one. While waiting for the requisite paperwork to be completed before taking possession of the car, she went on a shopping spree.

She hummed along with the canned Christmas music in the stores, smiled at the jostling crowds, wished each and every harried salesclerk a happy holiday.

She drove out of Denver on the twenty-fourth, the trunk and back seat of her new vehicle loaded down with the bounty of her shopping spree.

It was snowing. The day before Christmas, and it was snowing! The promise of a white Christmas sent Emma's high spirits soaring.

By the time Emma reached the turnoff to the private ranch road, driving was becoming a little chancy. She exhaled a deep sigh of relief when she brought the car to a stop in the yard near the house.

"Emma!" Nancy's cry of surprised delight from the kitchen doorway was music to Emma's ears as she stepped from the car. The older woman crossed the porch and started down the steps.

"Hi!" Emma called back, leaving the car door standing open as she rushed forward.

Laughing, crying, they flew into each others' arms like long-lost friends, reunited after a separation of many years instead a mere three months. Standing in the yard, oblivious to the cold and falling snow, they chattered away, their words clashing, overriding each other.

"I missed you so..."

"Oh, I've missed you, too. I..."

"...and I kept hoping you'd come back, and I know Mace felt the same...even though he never said so."

Mace. Emma blinked against a fresh rush of tears. But the mention of his name reminded her of her mission. A frown scoring her brow, she glanced at the house, then at the stable. "Where is Mace?"

"He left soon after lunch," Nancy answered, also frowning. "Didn't say where he was going, just that he had something to do, and didn't know when he'd be back."

"Perfect." Emma laughed at Nancy's startled look. "Go get your coat on," she ordered, turning to walk back to the car. "I've got a pile of stuff to unload."

"But..."

"Hurry, Nancy, please," she said, slamming shut

the car door and moving to the trunk. "We've got a lot to do before Mace gets back."

When all the boxes and packages were brought into the house, and Emma had outlined her plan, Nancy joined in with gleeful anticipation.

First, they stashed the lavish selection of delicious-looking foods carefully packed in fancy boxes. Nancy's expression went from curious to delightfully astounded at the variety of goodies, ranging from smoked turkey and salmon, to delicate cookies, small cakes, decadent candies and even a Christmas pudding, all of which Emma had splurged on in an expensive gourmet shop.

Then they tackled the serious work.

Chatting, laughing, they worked throughout the afternoon, Nancy exclaiming in ever-increasing amazement over the array of decorations revealed inside the packages.

The tree, a live six-foot blue spruce, proved the biggest obstacle. But, after rearranging furniture to make room near the large front window, they finally managed to manhandle the tree into the stand, anchoring it with twine strung from the trunk and fastened to either side of the window frame. The remainder of the afternoon was spent trimming the tree and draping real-looking but plastic long holly garlands with deep red berries intertwined with tiny twinkle lights on the mantel above the fireplace and around each window and doorway. It was long past dinnertime when they finished.

"Oh, Emma, it's beautiful," Nancy murmured in awed tones. "So beautiful."

"Yes," Emma agreed. "And after all that work, I'm so hungry." She frowned, beginning to worry, for although it had stopped snowing, several inches had accumulated on the ground. "I wonder what could be keeping Mace. The roads must be treacherous by now."

"Now, don't fret," Nancy said, turning to go to the kitchen. "Mace can take care of himself. Meanwhile, I think we'd better go ahead and eat."

Dinner was long since over, and still there was no sign of, and no word from Mace. With each passing hour, Emma became more tense and worried. Nancy was clearly concerned as well.

Wanting to spring her surprise for Mace with a burst of light, Emma and Nancy sat in the living room, their only source of illumination the leaping flames of the fire they had built and the flickering light from the TV neither one of them paid any attention to, except for news breaks.

At frequent intervals, Emma paced from the living room to the kitchen window, hoping to see the headlights of Mace's Bronco coming up the road.

"I'm going to call the authorities," Emma said near midnight, feeling sick in the stomach with dread.

"Yes, I think you—" Nancy broke off, springing out of her chair. "Wait, I think I hear—" Breaking off again, she hurried to the kitchen. "It's him,

Emma,'' she called back, relief plain in her voice. "He's home."

Saying a silent prayer of thanks, Emma flicked off the TV and sat unmoving, waiting. She heard the sound of his boots thumping to the porch floor, the door being flung open and then Nancy's scolding voice.

"I've been worried about you, Mace. Where in tarnation have you been all this time?"

"In Denver." Mace's voice had a tired, defeated sound, but it still sounded wonderful to Emma.

"Denver... What were you doing in Denver?"

"I was at the airport, trying to buy or beg a seat on a plane east to Philadelphia." He sighed. "I was waiting on standby, my name near the bottom of a long list, but still hoping, when the weather settled the matter. The snow's still falling there, and the runways are icing up." He heaved another sigh. "They canceled all flights."

East? Philadelphia! While she had been waiting here for him, Mace had been trying to fly east to her! The realization brought a film of fresh tears to Emma's eyes, and a surge of hopeful anticipation to her heart.

"You must be starved," Nancy said, her brisk tone failing to conceal her concern. "I'll just warm up—"

"No, thanks," Mace interrupted in a gentle, yet dejected tone. "I ate at the airport...since there was nothing better to do. But I could use a cup of decent coffee, if you wouldn't mind...?"

"'Course not," Nancy assured him before raising her voice to give Emma a heads up, she continued, "You look beat, Mace. Why don't you go into the living room, get comfortable in front of the fire? I'll call when the coffee's ready."

"Okay. Thanks. I am kinda tired." The disheartened sound of his voice caused a pang in Emma's chest.

The pang gave way to a tingle of excitement as she heard him start along the hallway, his stocking-footed steps unusually heavy with weariness.

Slipping off her chair, Emma crept to the electrical wall socket close to the tree. Picking up the plug to the cord to the main outlet power strip to which all the decorative houselights were connected, she held it at the ready.

"Why is it so dark in here?" Mace grumbled.

Turning her head, Emma waited, breath bated, until she saw him step into the doorway. She pushed the prongs into the socket. Instantly, the house lit up like a…well, like a Christmas tree. Emma quickly turned her head to catch his reaction.

His expression, part disbelief, part wonder, was priceless, well worth every dollar she had spent, every hour of her labor, every quiver of trepid anticipation she had endured. Barely breathing, she slowly stood to face him.

"Emma?" His voice was a fearful whisper of hope that swiftly expanded to a near shout. "Emma!"

"I…I wanted to bring Christmas to you," she

said, her own voice soft, cracking with emotion, riffling with excitement as he strode to her.

"It's wonderful," Mace said, skimming a glance around the bright, gaily decorated room. "All of it," he murmured, pulling her into his arms and crushing her to him, as if to never let her go. "But even without the decorations it would still be wonderful because you're here." He raised a hand to lift her head to face him, a glow backlighting his dark eyes. "You are Christmas to me—Christmas, and every other day of every week."

"Oh, Mace, I..." she began, tears streaming down her face. "I..." He silenced her with his mouth.

His kiss was hard, deep and contained an element of desperation. Emma responded in kind, starved for the taste of him, the feel of him, the essence of him. When it ended she could barely breathe, and didn't care.

"I love you, Emma," Mace murmured against her tingling lips. "Stay with me, bring Christmas to all of my days."

"I love you back," she said, crying tears of happiness. "And, yes, I'll stay." She sniffed, then laughed. "Stay? I'll probably cling."

"Interesting." His smile sexy as all get out, he lowered her to the carpet in front of the glittering tree. "Wanna give me a clinging demonstration?"

"Mace, we can't," Emma moaned, suddenly remembering they were not alone. "Nancy will..."

"I'm off to bed, folks," that wise woman called

from the staircase. "Coffee's ready whenever you are. See you in the morning," she went on, her voice growing fainter as she mounted the stairs. "Merry Christmas."

"Now, about that clinging," Mace whispered, his fingers tugging at the hem of her sweater.

Within minutes, with both of them divested of their confining clothing, Emma clung to Mace for all she was worth, all the way to heaven and back.

His chest heaving from his exertions, Mace lifted his head from the curve of Emma's neck to stare at her, thrilling her with his love for her blazing from his eyes.

"Now that's what I call comfort and joy."

They never did get to Nancy's fresh coffee.

* * * * *

*Look for Joan Hohl's next story for
Silhouette Books—part of a special
two-in-one collection available in April
from Silhouette Romance.*

Dear Reader,

Season's Greetings!

No matter how frazzled I become during the countdown weeks prior to the holidays—shopping, wrapping, decorating, cooking and (shudder) cleaning—that salutation of goodwill, whether emblazoned on a card, or offered verbally with a smile, never fails to lift my spirits and make it all worthwhile.

And so, I am pleased and gratified once again for the opportunity afforded to me by the good folks at Silhouette to send my greetings to you, both in this letter, and with my holiday story, "The Gift of Joy."

To my mind, all gifts given from the heart, be they of great financial value or an inexpensive but thoughtfully chosen token, are gifts of joy. They are to be cherished and treasured throughout our lives.

Some of the gifts that live in my memory are the wonderful Christmas stories that I have read over the years. Stories that made me laugh. Stories that made me cry.

I hope my story, "The Gift of Joy," about a lonely man who has never really experienced Christmas, and a woman who discovers the true meaning of giving, brings a smile to your lips and, perhaps, a bit of joy to your holidays.

With love,

A CHRISTMAS TO TREASURE

Sandra Steffen

For my mom and dad. Again. Always.
Merry Christmas!

Prologue

Max Fitzpatrick swiped the sleeve of his sweatshirt across the foggy glass and peered through the attic window. He sure loved this old house, but he liked this room the best because when the sky was clear, he could see all the way to the harbor from here. He couldn't see much past the house next door today, so he watched the big, fat snowflakes drifting from the sky like feathers, turning the air and ground white and everything else hazy.

His mother was pounding an Apartment For Rent sign into the front yard below, and he was supposed to be lugging the suitcases out of the closet so she could start packing as soon as she came in. They were going up the coast to Aunt Maggie and Uncle Henry's like they did this time every year. Tomor-

row, they would all go to the Thanksgiving Day
Parade, and then they would go back to Maggie's
kitchen where they would stuff themselves on turkey
and mashed potatoes and gravy and three kinds of
pie. On Friday they would go shopping. And Max
and Shiloh would get their pictures taken with Santa.
It was part of the tradition.

He was supposed to be thinking about what he
wanted for Christmas. That was easy. He wanted the
same thing he'd wanted last year. And the year before that. He wanted a dad. A real one. Not just
somebody who sent a postcard once or twice a year
or who called and left a message on the answering
machine when he knew darn well that Max and Shiloh were in school.

Max had found out about Santa last year. Once
he'd gotten used to the idea, he hadn't been all that
surprised. He sorta understood why he hadn't gotten
what he wanted yet. He didn't think a dad was
something Santa could have managed all by himself,
even if he had been real.

Max needed his mom for that.

And his mother wasn't planning to get married
again. He'd heard her say it to her best friend lots
of times. She said Uncle Henry was one of the few
men left on the planet who had staying power. She
always looked relieved when Max and Uncle Henry
wrestled around and did guy stuff like making cool
noises with their hands in their armpits.

Mom called weekends at Uncle Henry's quality
time. Max liked Uncle Henry a lot, but he wanted

more than a few hours of quality time. He wished Mom would get married again. Not to Uncle Henry—he was already married—and not to somebody like Lumpy Graham's dad, who sat around watching TV while he yelled for Lumpy to bring him a beer.

Max paid close attention to the men he saw. Some were tall, some had beards, some wore ties and others tool belts. A lot of them were kind of grouchy, although Mom said not all men were. Max didn't care if the man who became his new dad was a little grouchy on the outside, just so long as he was nice on the inside and was good to Mom and Shiloh and him.

A movement down below drew his attention. Nadine Boak, their next-door neighbor, strolled over and started talking to his mom. He liked Nadine, the way she talked and the color of her hair, and the way she cried black tears when she watched a sad video. Unlike his mother, Nadine was always looking for a man.

Max was in the middle of a heartfelt sigh when the door creaked open and his little sister crept in. "Hey, Maxie."

Shiloh was the only person in the world who could get away with calling him that.

"I got something to go with what you're making Mama for Christmas. Wanna see?"

Max eyed his five-year-old sister. She was whispering, which meant she either had a secret, or she'd done something she could get in trouble for. Waiting to see which it was, he followed her down the back stairway.

He and Shiloh both knew where all the creaky boards in the stairs were. The fact that Shiloh painstakingly avoided them made Max even more suspicious.

"What have you done?" he whispered the instant they entered her cluttered room.

Shiloh was skinny, and no matter how much she ate, she stayed that way. Still, she was tough for a girl, and she liked to do things for herself, which made her both fun and kind of exasperating. "Haven't done anything, leastways nothing wrong. Look."

She took a dusty, velvet bag out from underneath her pillow and dumped the contents into the middle of her bedspread. "Isn't this the prettiest ocean glass you ever saw?"

Max took a closer look. It was pretty, all right, sparkling like crazy underneath Shiloh's bedside lamp. "Where'd you get it?"

Dropping them back into the velvet bag one by one, she said, "I didn't take 'em, honest. I found them. Under a floorboard in the hall up in the attic. Do you think some other little girl put them there a long time ago and then forgot them?"

Max considered the possibility. He, Shiloh and their mother had lived in this house for five years now. The inn had belonged to his grandma before that. Shiloh was probably right. Some boarder probably found the ocean glass and tucked it away and then forgot all about it. "Finders keepers, losers weepers," he said.

Shiloh beamed. "A lady on the home and garden channel Mama was watching the other day glued a whole buncha buttons and stuff onto a flowerpot. This ocean glass is way prettier than buttons." Sliding the bag out of sight, she pushed a straggly strand of hair out of her face and said, "You can have 'em for the flowerpot you're makin' Mama. On one condition."

Max grinned at Shiloh. He couldn't help it. She was four years younger than he was, and half his size. She was hardly in any position to name conditions. It never fazed her. He liked that about her. Since a guy could get beat up for admitting that he liked his sister, he kept it to himself.

"What condition?" he asked.

"You can have it as long as you let me help."

"Okay," he said. "You can help as soon as we get back from Uncle Henry and Aunt Maggie's."

Shiloh was still beaming when their mother's voice carried up the stairs. "Max? Are you getting those suitcases?"

He made a beeline for the door. "Me 'n' Shiloh were talking. I'll get them right now."

"Good. The snow's really coming down out there. I want to get an early start up the coast. I'm almost done with everything down here. Oh, by the way. Nadine said not to worry. She'll feed your goldfish while we're gone."

Max sighed. Goldfish were okay, but everybody

knew he would rather have a dog. With his chin practically touching his chest, he thought about the one thing he hadn't told anybody—except that man dressed up like Santa last year—not Mom or Nadine or Shiloh or Uncle Henry, or even Lumpy. What he wanted more than a dog, more than anything, was a dad.

He didn't know where he was ever going to find one. He only knew that he would recognize him the minute he saw him. He didn't know when it would be, either. But he was going to keep his eyes open, just in case.

He hoped with all his might it would be soon.

Chapter 1

Crea-ea-eak.

Colter Monroe stirred. Reluctant to return from the oblivion of sleep, he buried his head underneath his pillow.

Creak. Snap. Creak. Thud.

He opened his eyes. What the hell was he doing awake?

Crea-ea-eak.

Oh, no. Groaning, he flopped onto his back. He knew that sound, dammit. Someone was coming up the stairs. Again. Not another intrusion by the bleached blond bombshell. If he was lucky, she would go away. He held his breath until more floorboards creaked out in the hall.

The knock on his door brought a renewed curse

to his lips, and his feet to the floor. It also reminded him that he'd used up the last of his luck nearly a year ago.

Running a hand over his sleep-gritty eyes, he rose stiffly. All he wanted was to be left alone for the next, say, twenty or thirty years. Was that too much to ask?

He'd made his wishes perfectly clear when he'd checked out the attic apartment two days ago. No meals. No conversation. No contact. The blonde couldn't have been stupid enough not to have understood. Nobody was that dumb.

He'd ignored her blatant come-on when he'd given her the deposit and hauled his meager belongings up two flights of stairs. By the time he'd mumbled a gruff "No thanks" when she'd knocked on his door an hour later to give him an extra key, and whatever else he wanted, he'd realized she was desperate, not dumb. That may not have been worse, but it was definitely scarier.

He'd refused her invitation to join her for a drink yesterday. He hadn't bothered to explain that he didn't drink, at least not anymore. He didn't soften his rejection with a compliment, or harden it with an insult.

She might have looked like one of those women who'd been played with hard and put away wet, but she wasn't ugly, not by a long shot. He just wasn't interested. In anyone. Or anything.

He'd seen a minivan parked in the driveway when he'd returned with a few groceries earlier, so he'd figured she must have company. He'd assumed she'd finally gotten the message.

The knock on the door came again.

Dammit to hell, he'd assumed wrong.

He was across the narrow room and was sputtering up a blue streak before he yanked the door all the way open. "Look, lady, I don't want any, so go curl up and purr in someone else's lap, all right?"

His eyes focused about the same time he got a whiff of soap and clean, winter air. If he hadn't been so groggy with sleep, he would have noticed that he hadn't gagged on strong perfume the instant he'd opened the door. He might have even been thankful. If he hadn't been so groggy with sleep, he might have known what to say to the dark-haired woman looking at him with guarded, green eyes.

Well, what do ya know? It wasn't the blond bombshell after all. "What do you want?" he ground out between clenched teeth.

Moss-green eyes went wide a moment before narrowing. Since he figured it was slightly possible that he had it coming, he prepared himself for some scathing retort.

She didn't so much as utter a single noxious comment. She didn't even appear to bite back a curse. In fact, the only change that came over her entire expression was a slight lift of her eyebrows as she said, "I'm Rosanna Fitzpatrick. No doubt you've met my former best friend."

Former? The sarcasm was evident in the tone of her voice. So was the dry humor. He hadn't laughed in a long time, and he told himself he didn't give a rip whether the woman had a sense of humor or not. He didn't even care that she was pretty, and had a damn nice smile. All he wanted was to be left alone. He'd made it clear to the blonde. It was time he made it clear to the raven-haired former best friend.

"If you'll excuse me." He started to close the door.

"Wait."

Rosanna studied the man Nadine had allowed to rent the attic apartment. Colter Remington Monroe had seemed like a lot of name when she'd first heard it. Nadine had insisted that he was a lot of man. Rosanna had to agree. The room was pitch-dark behind him. The only light in the hallway came from the antique wall fixture around the corner. It washed the walls with a warm, golden glow, but the light only fell across the lower half of the man's face, leaving the rest in shadow. His hair was dark, and a little too long to be considered civilized; his whisker stubble was more than a day old. If he had bedroom eyes, she was going to wring Nadine's neck.

"I'm sorry to bother you," she said.

He held up his hand in a halting gesture. "I don't know what's going on between you and your best friend, and frankly, I don't care. I made it clear to the woman who rented me this room that I don't want to be disturbed."

"I'm afraid there's been a little mix-up."

"Oh, hell, why am I surprised? What kind of mix-up?"

She withdrew an object from her pocket and slowly opened her hand. "I believe this is yours."

He sprang forward with the grace and stealth of an alley brawler, snatching the badge from her with a touch so light she barely felt the brush of his long, blunt-tipped fingers. She might have jumped backward, if she hadn't finally gotten a glimpse of his entire face.

His cheeks were slightly hollow, and Lord, they were pale. His eyes were dull and lifeless, the kind of eyes that knew searing pain. He wasn't looking at her, but at the badge in his hand, causing her to wonder if it was somehow connected to the bleakness on his face.

"Where did you get this?" His voice was deep, emotion-filled and little more than a rasp in the early-evening quiet.

"My daughter found it." She grimaced at the white lie. She didn't bother adding that Shiloh had *found* it in the man's dresser drawer while he'd been fast asleep.

Now, she thought, sliding her hand back inside her pocket, for the next portion of this uncomfortable little episode. She was in the process of drawing the money from her pocket when she finally met his gaze. Something inside her went perfectly still. Colter Monroe didn't have bedroom eyes. It would have been easier to deal with him if he had, much easier in fact than dealing with a man who appeared wounded all the way to his soul.

She'd thought it was odd when Nadine had told her he'd paid his rent, all of it, including the first and last and current month, with cash. Cash that would buy food and heat and electricity for her and her children. She squeezed the money in her hand. A woman alone had to follow her instincts, as well as her own careful, calculated, well-thought-out rules to keep her and her family safe and secure.

The Midnight Inn, one of hundreds of bed-and-breakfast inns up and down the coast of Maine, did very well during tourist season. In the off-season, she supplemented her income by renting out the tiny attic apartment. In the past, she'd rented the room to grandmothers or college girls. She had Max's and Shiloh's, as well as her own well-being to consider. The only man she'd ever allowed to live here through the long eastern winter had been eighty-six. Colter Monroe didn't look much over thirty. He could have been an ax-murderer for all Nadine knew. Rosanna had to give the money back, and ask him to leave. It was that simple. Unfortunately that didn't mean it was going to be easy.

"I'm afraid there's been a mistake, Mr. Monroe."

His eyes narrowed. When he turned them on her, she had to swallow the nerves that rose to her throat. "We've just come from our friends' house up the coast."

"We?"

She tipped her head backward slightly, glancing

over her shoulder. ''My children, Max and Shiloh and I.''

Colter's gaze shifted to the two young kids who were watching from around the corner. There was a time when his instincts would have alerted him to the fact that he was being watched. He would have been aware of every subtle aspect of his surroundings. He squeezed the badge in his hand so tightly the edges cut into his flesh. The pain brought him back to the present, and reminded him that that was then. This was now. And now, all he wanted was sleep.

''You see,'' the dark-haired woman continued, ''I own the Midnight Inn. Nadine was supposed to keep an eye on things over the weekend. She promised to feed Max's goldfish, and get the mail. That sort of thing.''

Colter heaved a sigh. There was nothing like a woman to make a long story longer. He let his gaze trail to the children. The girl looked as if she could use feeding. The mother did, too, for that matter. The boy, Max, she'd called him, was the sturdiest of the bunch. Probably nine or ten, Colter gauged, the kid was gangly, but he wasn't reed thin like his mother and sister. Colter couldn't see the color of the boy's eyes from here, but he could feel the intensity in that young gaze. His was a different kind of hunger.

The thought came out of nowhere, and made Colter's nerves stand on end. Luckily the woman was still talking, and didn't appear to notice his discomfiture. "Nadine wasn't supposed to take it upon herself to rent out this apartment. I gave her strict instructions—"

"Look," he said, interrupting. "I told your friend—Nadine is it?—in no uncertain terms that I came here to sleep. Alone."

"That's what I'm trying to tell you," Rosanna said in a rush. "Nadine has selective listening skills. I gave her strict instructions not to rent the attic apartment to any man under the age of eighty."

His head came up sharply. "You don't like men?"

She seemed to have to dig deep to dredge up a small smile. "Men are fine." She reached into her pocket again. When her hand opened this time, it was filled with a wad of bills that looked suspiciously like the one he'd handed over to the *former* best friend.

"What are you doing?" he asked.

"I'm returning your deposit, as well as your rent money."

She hadn't gotten the last word out before the boy shot forward. "Mom, no. You've gotta let him stay. Please. You've gotta."

"Max, it's going to be all right," she said.

The boy was shaking his head and tugging on the hand that held the money. "Not if you send him away. You've gotta keep him."

"I'm not a stray dog," Colter said, louder than he'd intended.

"I'm sure he didn't mean..." Rosanna stammered.

"I know you're not a dog," Max stated, matter-of-fact. "You're what I asked for for Christmas."

No one moved, nor spoke, nor made a single sound. Only the howling of the wind and the rattle of a loose shutter filled the ensuing silence.

As if determined to straighten out the matter and restore a degree of normalcy, Rosanna squared her shoulders and found her voice. "You asked for a male boarder for Christmas?" she asked her son.

"Well. Not exactly." Slowly the boy met Colter's gaze. He didn't glance away like a lot of kids would have. He was brave. Colter would give him that. The quaver in his voice, and the audible swallow he took before continuing gave his nervousness away, although it didn't keep him from saying, "Not a boarder."

"What then?" Rosanna asked.

The boy took a sudden interest in the toes of his worn shoes, mumbling something into his chest.

"What did you say, Max?" his mother asked.

For the first time, Colter noticed that the girl had joined the mother and brother. Eyes wide, hair a mess, she tugged on Rosanna's sweater, and gestured with one finger for her mother to bend closer.

Rosanna leaned down, placing her ear near her daughter's mouth. The child made *pst-pst* sounds that must have come as quite a shock, because suddenly Rosanna looked blank, amazed and shaken.

She stared at the girl, and then at the boy, and finally at Colter. For several seconds, she didn't move.

"What is it?" Colter asked.

She shook her head. Obviously flustered, she finally said, "If you'll excuse us."

She backed slowly away, drawing her children with her. At the top of the stairway, the boy glanced back at Colter.

"What did you ask for?" Colter said, quieter than before.

Rosanna looked stricken all over again. The little girl moved as if to speak, but the boy silenced her with a gentle hand on her shoulder. Raising his chin slightly, he spoke for himself. "I asked for a dad."

Without another word, he started down the stairs, his mother and sister close behind. Listening to the symphony of creaking floorboards, Colter took a backward step, and promptly closed his door.

"Are ya gonna let the man stay, Mama, are you?"

Rosanna made a *shushing* sound before whispering, "You aren't supposed to ask me questions when you're saying your prayers."

On her knees, Shiloh squeezed her eyes shut, and got back to the business at hand. "God bless Mama and Max and Uncle Henry and Aunt Maggie and Nadine and Miss Willingham and Amy Sue Walters and Gold E. Fish. Amen."

With a hop, skip and a jump, she was on her bed and under the covers. Suddenly she closed her eyes again and said, "Oh, and the man upstairs." Opening her eyes once again, she said, "Are ya, Mama?"

If the situation hadn't been so serious, Rosanna would have smiled. Shiloh was a cyclone on two feet. And one of the two greatest joys in Rosanna's life. Her mother used to say that all good things came with equal parts pleasure and responsibility. Staring past the tufts of flyaway hair that refused to be tamed, and into impish blue eyes, Rosanna thought her mother had been a very wise woman.

"Are ya gonna let Maxie keep the new boarder?"

Rosanna's mother also used to say that when life got hard, sometimes the only thing a person could do was curse and endure with equal parts enthusiasm. As far as Rosanna could tell, this had all the makings of one of those times.

Smoothing a baby-fine strand of hair off Shiloh's forehead, she said, "Mr. Monroe is a person, and people can't *keep* other people."

Shiloh looked up at Rosanna through the guileless eyes of youth. "You told us we can ask for anything for Christmas just so long as it's homemade, and people are homemade and daddies are people, so Max can so ask for a daddy."

Rosanna didn't know what to say to that. Other than her love of anything that sparkled and her tendency to "borrow" things from people, Shiloh wasn't a difficult child. As spry and whimsical as a sea sprite, she lived in the land of make-believe much of the time, but she had a sharp mind, and she could be logical when it suited her. She laughed easily and often. Max was different. He was quiet and studious and old beyond his years. Secretly Rosanna had always been relieved that he hadn't inherited his father's tendency to have his head in the clouds. And she thanked God that her son seemed to possess no wanderlust. She'd had no idea that he yearned for a father, or believed in the magical possibility that wishes could come true.

Max was barely nine years old. She didn't want to squash his dreams. But she couldn't let him or Shiloh believe that the man upstairs was here in answer to their secret wishes or prayers. She didn't know how to make them realize that fathers didn't grow on trees or appear out of the blue, without robbing them of the innocence of blind faith and a child's dream.

"Shiloh," she said, her voice quiet, her hand soft where it touched her daughter's narrow shoulder. "You and Max have a father."

"He's a deadbeat."

At Rosanna's gasp, the girl said, "What's a deadbeat?"

"It's not a nice thing to call your father, or anyone else, for that matter."

"It's not?"

Rosanna shook her head.

And Shiloh said, "Maybe you should tell Nadine, cuz she's the one who said it."

Rosanna dropped her forehead into her hands. Actually Nadine was right. Darrell Fitzpatrick was a part-time musician and a full-time wanderer.

She'd been nineteen when she met him, and so full of her own dreams she hadn't noticed that he never seemed to have two nickels to rub together. Completely in love with him, she hadn't cared. It was only after Max was born that she began to notice Darrell's slight imperfections. Oh, he had talent, but he never quite got around to finishing the songs he wrote. He was likable, lovable, really, but he never quite got around to keeping a paying job, either, or remembering to come home at a decent hour, or to pick Max up from the sitter's when he said he would.

He'd wandered off one day when Max was two. When it finally occurred to him a week later that she might be sick with worry, he called. When it happened a third, fourth and fifth time over the next several months, she faced reality and left him. A year later she fell for his smile, for his smooth voice and his sincere promise that he'd changed. He had a job, an apartment, a car that ran. The trial reconciliation lasted longer than either his current job or the car's transmission. She left him for good the day she and Max were served eviction papers—Darrell was nowhere to be found. A month later Rosanna found herself staring at a little blue line on a home pregnancy test. Since it was a pretty sure bet that she wasn't going to make it to New York to dance in *Chorus Line,* she came back to Midnight, Maine, where she could raise her babies and help her mother turn this old relic of a house into a quaint bed-and-breakfast inn.

Her mother had welcomed her home, and although she might have said "I told you so" a hundred thousand times, life had been good for all of them. Surely, Rosanna told herself, the little bomb Max had dropped tonight wasn't the most embarrassing thing she'd lived through. It certainly wasn't the hardest. Finding herself a single mother of two at the tender age of twenty-three, or losing her mother to an unforeseen and deadly stroke three years ago had this situation beat hands down.

Tucking the covers under Shiloh's chin, she leaned to kiss that smooth little cheek. "Night, pumpkin. Remember, no more borrowing other people's shiny things."

Shiloh sighed. "I always give them back."

This time it was Rosanna who sighed. Shiloh's penchant for "borrowing" things was a constant source of concern, but after poking her head inside Max's room a few minutes later, it was Max who worried her the most.

"Night, Max."

He didn't reply. She knew he wasn't sleeping, which meant that he was sulking. And Maxwell Nathaniel Fitzpatrick rarely sulked.

Leaning in the doorway, Rosanna said, "Grandma always said if you sleep on bad feelings, they'll multiply and give you indigestion by morning."

She heard his sigh all the way across the room. She strolled closer, stopping near the foot of his bed.

She could tell he was looking at her, and could practically hear the gears turning in his brain.

"No fair breaking the rule."

She eased around to the side of his bed. "What rule have I broken?"

She could tell he was reluctant to talk to her, and imagined that he was rolling his eyes. "The rule you made about Christmas presents. You said we can only give presents that are homemade. Nothing store-bought, you always say. A father isn't store-bought."

"It'll be Christmas soon. And your father always calls near the holidays."

"He's a deadbeat." After a spell of silence, he added, "I heard Nadine, too. And I know what it means."

"He's not a deadbeat, Max."

"He changed his name to Deke. As if that'll get his songs recorded."

Rosanna folded her arms, thinking it wasn't easy to argue with that kind of logic. "I love you, Max. And we're doing okay. Better than okay, if you ask me. We have a warm house and food in the fridge and friends and each other. I'll do everything in my power to make sure that you grow up happy and secure and safe."

His sigh filled the quiet. "Just don't send him away. Not yet. Please?"

"Max—"

"Please?"

She felt guilty, and she didn't even know why.

She knew exactly where the feelings of inadequacy were coming from. Closing her eyes, she said, "I'll think about it."

Max flopped onto his side, effectively turning his back on her as he sputtered to himself that that's what grown-ups always said when the answer was no.

The resignation in her son's voice squeezed at her heart. Childhood was supposed to be the best time in a boy's or girl's life. Did she say no too often? Too easily? How could that be, when nothing felt easy?

She didn't know the answers. She didn't even know all the questions. But she knew that Max's wish for a father came from a place deep inside of him, a place he rarely let her see. And Rosanna couldn't dismiss it without doing a lot of thinking, and a lot of soul-searching.

She would walk through fire for her child. But search for a new father for him?

Years ago she'd discovered that parenthood was a balancing act. Parents had to carefully weigh and measure their children's needs and wants against what was best for them. It was always difficult, but she believed it was even harder for single parents. That didn't mean she believed that all children were better off with two parents. Sometimes security and stability were more important than living in a two-parent home. She knew Max missed a male influence. She remembered how devastated she'd been when her own father died. She'd been nine. Max's age.

She spent the better part of the next hour pacing. Thinking so hard her head ached from the sheer force of it, she strode to the back entryway off the kitchen. A firm believer in getting things over with, she opened the door, and started up the narrow back stairs that ultimately led to the third floor.

Chapter 2

Rosanna paused at the top of the second flight of stairs. Most days, she ran up and down these steps countless times, so it wasn't the workout that had made her breathless. It was a bad case of nerves.

Sidestepping the noisiest floorboards, she made her way toward the apartment at the end of the hall. By the time she reached her destination, her breathing was nearly back to normal and her speech was well rehearsed.

She raised her hand to knock, but had barely brushed her knuckles on the surface before the door swung open a few inches.

"Come on in."

The words sounded muffled, as if they'd come from some distance away. It occurred to her that he'd been expecting her, and had left the door un-latched. She pushed the door open far enough to look inside.

Colter Monroe was standing at the multipane win-dow on the other side of the room, his back to her. She'd planned to have this conversation from the hall. Since it looked as if she was going to have to wing it, she placed the cordless phone on the floor in the hall and entered the room, pausing just inside the doorway.

The room was long and narrow. There was a dou-ble bed tucked under the eaves on one end of the room, a kitchenette on the other. The rag rugs she'd scattered across the painted floor were exactly where she'd placed them when she'd cleaned last week. There was a faded quilt on the bed; the fringed lamp she'd found at a secondhand store was perched on an old chest of drawers. A pine table and two mis-matched chairs graced the center of the room, the conch shells Max and Shiloh had brought home last summer displayed in its center. Other than the badge on the painted bedside table, and a scruffy leather jacket and some discarded wrappers, there was very little of Colter Monroe's personal touches in the room.

He dominated the small space all by himself.

He'd turned on the fringed lamp, and she could see the edges of his reflection in the darkened win-dow. Fleetingly she wondered what he was looking at this time of the evening.

"It's the same ocean," he said in that rusty-sounding baritone. "But it looks completely different from Miami."

So, she thought, he was from Miami. Curious, she asked, "Is this your first trip to Maine?"

"I made it as far north as Philadelphia once."

Folding her arms, she eased slightly closer. "What do you do in Miami?"

He didn't answer for a long time. When he finally spoke, his voice was flat and devoid of all emotion. "I was a police officer."

"Was?" She wished he would turn around so she could see his face and read his expression.

With a lift of one shoulder, he said, "Technically I'm on a leave of absence. But only because my sergeant wouldn't accept my resignation. It doesn't matter. I don't plan to go back to it."

To police work? Rosanna wondered, or to Miami? Really, if he would just turn around.

The next thing she knew he was facing her. Staring into those dark, insolent brown eyes, she remembered one of her mother's favorite old sayings. "Be careful what you wish for." She had assumed it would be easier to talk to him face-to-face. There was nothing easy about facing off opposite the man on the other side of the room.

His jeans were faded, low slung and slightly baggy. Something had happened to him in Miami, something tragic enough to melt some weight off his large-boned frame and put a haunted look in his eyes and dark hollows in his cheeks.

"What *do* you plan to do, Mr. Malone?"

Colter rotated a kink from between his shoulder blades, and rubbed at another knot in the back of his neck. He didn't have many plans beyond sleeping. If Rosanna let him stay, that is.

He groped his chest pocket for a cigarette, and came up empty-handed. He'd given up smoking and drinking a while back—fifty-two days to be exact. He hadn't done it out of a fear of dying. It was more a fear of going on the way he'd been...living, but not feeling. He'd spent too many months drinking too much and working too hard.

He'd clawed his way out of that black hole. He'd quit his vices first, and eventually his job. Rosanna had asked him what he planned to do now. Glancing at the bed on the far side of the room, he said, "That depends on you."

On her? Rosanna thought on the interminable stretch of silence that followed. Their gazes met, held. Her heart pounded an erratic rhythm. She cleared her throat, pretending not to be affected. He, on the other hand, made no attempt to hide the fact that he was watching her. Above the hollows in his cheeks, his eyes were steady. She glimpsed integrity in their depths. It moved her and made her uncomfortable at the same time.

"On me?" she asked.

He took a step in her direction. "Have you decided what to do about me?"

Rosanna thought it was a loaded question. Once upon a time, she'd been a fanciful, romantic woman. Not anymore. She knew her strengths and her weak-

nesses. She was a modern day woman with a fair
mind and an honest soul. And she honestly didn't
know what to do about Colter Remington Monroe.
Lord, what a name.

"Do your friends call you Colt, Mr. Monroe?"

"I don't have many friends."

"Really. A man with your warm, outgoing personality."

The twitch on his lips couldn't be classified as a
smile. Heaven forbid. A grin might crack his face.
Still, the quirk of that mouth leaned the tiniest bit
toward humor.

It never occurred to her to hold back her smile.
She slanted it at him, and quietly said, "You can
stay. If you still want to, that is."

Colter's eyes dropped shut and the wind dropped
out of his lungs in a heavy whoosh. He hated the
suffocating sensation that threatened to choke him.
He hated the relief that was weakening his knees
even more. He told himself it was only because he
was so god-awful tired. That was the reason he'd
dreaded the thought of stuffing his meager belongings into his bags and heading back out to the highway in search of another place to rest.

"Don't worry," she said, straightening a faded,
framed print of an old whaling vessel hanging on
the wall. "I've explained to Max and Shiloh that a
father is not something they can ask for for Christmas."

She moved on to adjust a dried flower arrangement in an old milk bottle, explaining all the while

about the homemade gifts she and her children exchanged each Christmas. He noticed she didn't stray too far from the door. She was careful, smart. And she wasn't turning him out into the night. Her voice was as smooth and mellow as a promise, friendly and chatty and warm. And completely female.

Her hair was the deep, dark brown of fresh ground coffee. It waved to her shoulders, thick and pleasingly mussed. She was wearing the same moss-green sweater set and long knit skirt she'd had on earlier. Then, he'd thought she looked a little on the scrawny side. Upon closer inspection, he saw that he'd been wrong. Rosanna was slender, but the heavy knit fabric of her skirt wasn't curving over his imagination, although he had to admit his imagination was enjoying the ride.

Maybe five-five or five-six, she was fine-boned, and she held her head high, as regal as a queen. His gaze dipped lower, over the little hollow at the base of her neck, lower, where her sweater conformed to the gentle slope, the plump curve of her breasts.

The jolt that went through him was vaguely familiar and not altogether unpleasant. Not unpleasant at all. He allowed his gaze to roam in reverse, stopping at eyes that were nearly the same shade of green as her sweater.

She'd been watching him watching her. She didn't look away. And neither did he. The throbbing rhythm and crooning melody that had settled in his chest left little doubt that he was in danger of doing or saying something that might get him thrown out of the room she'd just agreed to let him rent.

A telephone rang. The sudden, shrill sound brought his head up like a whip, and made his nerves stand on end. It rang again. From where? He didn't have a phone.

She strolled into the hall, leaned down and picked up a portable phone. Her end of the conversation consisted of uh-uh's and a series of hmms. She was back within seconds, talking as if nothing had passed between them a few seconds ago.

Maybe nothing had.

"So don't worry," she said. "I've explained to Max and Shiloh, and I will keep explaining it until they understand."

He was pretty sure he'd heard every word. Why then, was she handing him the wad of bills he'd paid in rent?

"I apologize for any inconvenience Nadine might have caused you."

"But you just said I could stay."

She smiled the way she might have at one of her children. "You can. But under the circumstances, I would prefer that you rent this room one week at a time."

He let the request soak in. And then he said, "Who was on the phone?"

She reached for his hand, pushed the bills into it and closed his fingers around his money. "Nadine. A woman alone can't be too careful. You're settled in for tonight. We can decide what to do about the rest of the month later.''

The smile she slanted at him was probably more than he deserved, what with the direction his thoughts had taken. He watched her saunter to the door. In a minute, she would be gone. And he would be alone. He wanted to say something to her. He had no idea what.

''Cole.'' The word rang out of his mouth, completely out of the blue.

She glanced over her shoulder. ''Pardon me?''

He swallowed, forced himself to relax. ''Anybody who puts up with me long enough to risk becoming my friend calls me Cole. And in answer to your earlier question, I told your friend that I wanted to become a hermit.''

''Yes. Nadine mentioned that.'' She smiled as if she'd let him in on a tender secret. The glint in her eyes was as deep as midnight, the expression on her face friendly and earnest.

He was trying to read between the lines. He knew how he looked. Hell, he wasn't sure *he* would have rented this room to the likes of him. She hadn't trusted him when she'd come up here. The phone call had undoubtedly been a check-up call from her friend. It was probably going to ring again any second. She didn't trust him, she wasn't looking to give her kids another father, and yet she'd decided to let him stay.

''Why, Rosanna?''

Rosanna paused in the doorway. It had been a

long time since a man had said her name in exactly that way—slow and husky and deep. It reminded her of yearnings for closeness and togetherness and other things she'd learned to live without. Keeping her back to him, she shook her head to clear it. "Pardon me?"

She could hear the deep breath he took. "What changed your mind about letting me stay?"

The question drew her around. She watched as he ran a hand through his hair. Following his gaze to the rumpled bed, she said, "Don't worry. Unlike Nadine, I'm not looking to have blinding sex with a relative stranger."

Did she say sex? For a split second, Cole couldn't put two thoughts together. He knew he needed to be objective here, but silently he agreed that any sex they had would be blinding. Pushing the thought away for now, he said, "Why are you letting me stay?"

Something passed between their gazes. It was almost as if a connection had formed from her soft green eyes to his dead brown ones. Awareness sizzled and arced on an electrical current, zapping him like a cardiologist's paddle.

She tipped her head a fraction of an inch to one side and quietly said, "I couldn't send a man like you out into the cold. Good night, Cole."

She slipped out the door, and quietly closed it behind her.

She'd called him Cole, his first thought when he found himself alone in the silent, drafty room.

Had there really been a connection between them? More than likely, he'd finally gone crazy.

There was nothing between them, and that was how it would stay. There was no connection. There sure as hell wasn't an attraction. She was just being nice. He should be thankful. He knew he could crawl back into bed without interruption now.

He glanced around the sparsely furnished room. No amount of willing his sudden resurgence of desire away did the trick. He had a quiet room rented for at least a week, a room in which he'd planned to do nothing but sleep. Just his luck, what he felt like doing in that bed didn't have anything to do with sleeping. He wasn't dead everywhere after all. Cole didn't know whether to be relieved or angry at the intrusion into his numb life.

He switched off the lamp, and swiped his hand across the condensation on the window. Water ran in droplets down the wavy glass. Porch lights glowed up and down the street below. Streetlights glinted yellow at every corner. It was a clear night. Stars twinkled in the sky, disappearing into blackness that must have been the ocean.

He wasn't ready to say his luck was changing, but he admitted that maybe, just maybe, it was leveling off instead of getting steadily worse. He didn't have many blessings to count. But he had a roof over his head, a bed complete with a quilt that smelled of long-forgotten summer breezes. He had enough money in his account to remain a hermit indefinitely.

He had running water, a tiny shower, a tin of coffee and enough groceries to last him several days. He would sleep, and eat, and sleep some more. He had no one to impress, no one to let down. He was an island. A hermit. Alone in the world. And Rosanna wasn't going to turn a man like him out into the cold.

He started for the bed. Halfway there, he stopped in his tracks.

What did she mean by a man like him?

"I'm not a charity case, dammit."

The peeler in Rosanna's right hand paused midway across the carrot in her left hand. As far as greetings went, Cole's could have used a little work. Picking up where she'd left off in her task, she said, "Sleep well?"

Cole was at a complete loss. He simply was not accustomed to answering that kind of innocuous question. People simply didn't give a damn whether he slept well or not.

People simply didn't give a damn, period.

He'd slept sixteen hours straight. Sixteen hours without moving, without dreaming, without thinking. All in all, he'd figured he was well on his way to becoming a recluse, a bona fide hermit. And then he woke up. After spending two hours with nothing to do except pace and stare out the window, he'd decided becoming a hermit had a small flaw.

It was boring as hell.

He was itchy, antsy. He'd eaten handfuls of cold

cereal straight out of the box. He'd fiddled with a leaky faucet, checked out the squeaky hinges on the door. He'd told himself he owed her for allowing him to stay. But he kept remembering the way she'd said, "…a man like you."

And it rankled.

He figured hermits were allowed to take walks, just so long as they did it alone. First, he would set her straight where he was concerned.

He'd stomped down two flights of stairs, making enough racket to wake the dead. The door leading to the back stairway was open, so he knew damn well she'd heard him.

He'd stood on the back rug, waiting for her to acknowledge his presence. To comment. To reprimand.

And nothing.

She didn't turn around. She didn't say a word. She didn't so much as glance over her shoulder. She ignored him, and he didn't like to be ignored.

The sight of her feminine shape had sidetracked him for a moment or two. She was wearing loose-fitting slacks today, the kind that rode low at the waist and bagged a little in the seat. As far as he could tell, she hadn't missed a beat in her task, which caused her to sway slightly to and fro, which in turn drew his eyes repeatedly to the delicate curve of her rear end.

"Did you mean it?"

He did a double take. Did he mean what? Casting her a withering glance she didn't have the decency to turn around to see, he practically growled. "If I said it I meant it."

"Good." Carrot peels sprayed onto the counter. Keeping up a steady rhythm, Rosanna thought, Lord, he was even sulkier than Max. "The shovel is in the shed."

She counted eleven passes on the carrot before his voice sounded behind her. "Shovel?"

She hummed something that passed for yes. "Since you're not a charity case, I thought you could shovel the sidewalk in return for the coffee and pumpkin bread I'm going to offer you when you're through. Max and I usually do it, but the snow is heavy, and a man could do it in half the time. And even hermits have to get a little fresh air and exercise."

She finally turned.

"Unless you would like the coffee and pumpkin bread now."

Cole had been shoveling for twenty minutes when he spotted Rosanna's kids walking toward him from the next block. He felt, what?

Better. His mind was clearer, his senses more alert. A year ago he would have assumed it was the result of the subtle stir of desire that was bringing him back to life. Now he knew it took more than a sex drive to make a man feel human, let alone alive. Maybe it was the long night's sleep. Or the exercise. Maybe it was the change of scenery: cold, dry air instead of humidity, snow beneath his feet instead of concrete or sand. He wouldn't say he was back to normal. He wasn't sure he would ever be. But at least this was a start.

He'd heard the kids talking as they approached. Once they got close enough for him to hear the actual words they said, they clammed up. He stepped to one side, nodding a greeting of sorts. Both kids eyed him in silence, then averted their faces. It seemed they didn't know what to say to him now that they knew he wasn't an answer to their prayers.

He could tell by the shuffle of their boots that they'd started to run as soon as they'd cleared him and his shovel. They stomped their boots on the back stoop. What followed was a normal litany of voices raised in greeting.

"Mom, we're home."

"How was school?"

"I'm starving!"

"Shiloh, where's your other mitten?"

The door closed, and Cole imagined boots and coats being discarded, snacks eaten, the day's events shared. Those kids probably didn't even know how normal their lives were. Cole sure hadn't when he and Gary were kids.

Pressure built up in his chest like smoke in a jar. If it hadn't happened before, he would have worried that he was having a heart attack, even though he was only thirty-two. A couple of seconds into the relaxation and breathing technique the doctor he'd seen down in Miami had taught him, the pressure subsided.

Cole went back to his task.

The boy appeared a few minutes later, the shovel in his hands almost as big as he was. "Mom says you and her worked out a deal."

Never as clearheaded so soon after the threat of what Doc Henderson had dubbed "an episode," Cole had to ask, "Deal?"

Max didn't seem to think anything of the fact that Cole's mind had obviously gone blank. "Yeah," he said, leaning into his first scoop of snow. "She says she's gonna feed you and you're gonna help out around the inn."

He and the kid worked side by side in silence for several minutes. Aiming for a level of nonchalance he used to take for granted, Cole said, "Your mother mentioned that she talked to you about your Christmas wish."

Max nodded.

"Then you know that I'm not…"

"Yeah, I know."

They each scooped up several more shovelfuls of heavy snow. If Cole felt the exertion in muscles he hadn't used in a while, he could only imagine how much work it was for a nine-year-old kid.

"I wouldn't make much of a father," Cole said, throwing snow between the street and the sidewalk. "But if you're interested in being my friend…"

Max's shovel thudded to the ground. "You mean it?"

"I said it, didn't I?"

The boy said, "You and I could, like, hang out sometimes?"

The metal edge of Cole's shovel scraped on the sidewalk as he said, "I guess we could. While I'm here, at least."

He felt Max's eyes on him. Taking a breather, Cole stuck the shovel into a snowbank, and rested his hands on his hips. The boy's cheeks and nose were red, his stocking cap slightly askew, tufts of light brown hair sticking out around his forehead. When he'd first laid eyes on the boy, Cole had thought Max seemed old beyond his years. There was a youthful glint in his eyes now, and a wistfulness that was difficult to look at.

"What would we do?" he asked.

Cole made a show of peering into the distance. "I've always been fascinated by ships."

"There are ships at the harbor."

"Yeah, I figured," Cole answered.

"You wanna go to the harbor?"

There was no disguising the excitement in that young voice.

"Yeah. I guess I do."

"When?"

"Whenever you want to. We'll have to clear it with your mom first."

Max returned to his shoveling, but not before Cole heard him say, "The harbor is like the coolest place in the world."

* * *

"Cole says he never saw real snow, except on television, until he was all grown up. Can you believe that?"

"Not even on Christmas?" Shiloh asked.

Smiling at the sheer amazement in her daughter's voice, Rosanna chose to ignore the amount of pumpkin bread Max had crammed into his mouth. There would be time to work on manners later. For now, she didn't want to mar something as simple and pure as a young boy's excitement at the prospect of taking a trip to his favorite place.

Cole and the kids were sitting around the kitchen table. Rosanna was leaning against the counter nearby. Stew bubbled on the stove, steam wafting toward the ceiling. Outside, snow was starting to fall again.

"How did Santa Claus come to your house then?" Shiloh asked, wiping her milk mustache on the back of her hand.

This is nice, Rosanna thought, sipping her coffee. It was cold outside, warm inside. The kids were happy. There was even a little color in Cole's cheeks. She wouldn't go so far as to say the man was outgoing, but he was keeping up his end of the conversation. She had no way of knowing whether he'd always had a streak of reticence in him. And really, it didn't matter, because reticent or not, he treated the kids with kindness and care.

She'd blanched when she'd overheard him talking to Shiloh about the danger of snooping in other people's drawers. He'd explained that sometimes people left harmful things lying around, things like guns

and knives and poison. He'd assured a pale-faced
Rosanna that his gun was locked up tight in his
strongbox. After that he'd moved easily from talking
about danger to talking about Santa Claus and snow.

"He prob'ly came by helicopter," Max said before slurping his milk. "Right, Cole?"

Cole's nod was completely unnecessary.

"Awesome," Shiloh exclaimed. "Did you ever
see Santa's helicopter?"

"You can't see it," Max said, his mouth partially
full. "It's see-through, like Plexiglas. You can't hear
it, either."

"Wow."

Rosanna glanced at Cole, and found him looking
at Shiloh. He turned his head, and met Rosanna's
gaze, slanting her a smile she was certain was the
first his face had seen in a long, long time. She felt
warm, flushed with a heat that had nothing to do
with the coziness of her own kitchen, and everything
to do with the expression deep in this man's eyes.

It was selfish, but suddenly Rosanna was relieved
that he didn't smile often. Because his smile was
dangerous. It made her go all soft in the head, and
warm everywhere else. It made her feel understood,
wanted. And those were dangerous feelings, indeed.

"I'm glad Santa comes to our house in a sleigh."

Shiloh's declaration broke the connection that had
a way of zinging between Rosanna and Cole. Rosanna breathed a carefully veiled sigh of relief.

"You're lucky," Cole said. "I used to wish for
snow every Christmas."

Rosanna busied herself with used plates and glasses. It gave her hands something to do, and her eyes someplace to look. "You say that now," she said, starting the water in the sink. "But people who live here year-round are sick to death of snow by the middle of January. And by the time it melts in March, we swear we never want to shovel it, smell it, touch it, or look at it again as long as we live. And then, the following November, the air turns brisk, and a scent carries on the wind, and the excitement begins all over again."

Cole's eyes closed. There was magic in Rosanna's voice, the same kind of magic that allowed a little girl to believe in invisible helicopters and reindeers that could fly. It was the kind of magic that made a man yearn to believe, too. He could have listened to that magical voice forever.

He came to with a start. It was a good thing nobody was looking at him because he couldn't have smiled if his life depended upon it. That wasn't exactly a news flash. It wasn't in his nature to smile. Just as forever wasn't in his vocabulary.

"Are ya ready, Cole?" Max asked.

The boy was standing next to Cole's chair, in a hurry to be on their way to the harbor.

"Did you ask your mother?"

He nodded, already reaching for his hat. "She says we gotta be home by supper."

"Then we'd better get started." Donning his leather bomber jacket and a pair of worn gloves, Cole followed the boy out of the warm kitchen, and into the cold.

Chapter 3

Cole pried on the wrench. The fitting wouldn't budge. Fast losing his patience, he tried again. This time he put his weight into it. The wrench slipped off the fitting, and he thwacked his knuckle a good one. Profanity spewed out of his mouth, making him glad the kids were in school and Rosanna was out of the house.

He wasn't sure how it had happened, but he'd ended up eating supper with Rosanna and the kids last night. One minute he'd been standing in the doorway, shuffling his feet while Max went on and on about the fishing boat he'd watched dock at the harbor, and the next thing they were all sitting down to piping hot stew and thick slices of homemade bread.

Wanting to repay her for the meal, he'd decided to take a look at the leaky kitchen faucet last night. Three times Rosanna had had to chase Max out of the room and sternly insist that the boy had math work sheets to do.

When he'd finished his homework, Max had called some friend named Lumpy, of all things. Cole had overheard Max recount every detail about his trip to the harbor, which had led to talk of trips the boys had evidently taken last summer. Crabbers, fishing boats, rusty cages, lobster pots, sailboats, ship building. The kid thrived on it all. Cole had already heard an entire documentary during their outing when Max had explained how local folks set lobster pots out in the summer, and how it had to warm up or else the lobsters didn't move around enough to get stuck in the cages and lobster season was crummy and nobody made any money.

After Max had gotten off the phone, Rosanna had shaken her head, saying, "He's having trouble with his multiplication tables, but ask him anything about ships or boats or fishing, and he turns into a walking encyclopedia."

Cole couldn't blame the kid. He hadn't had much use for multiplication tables when he was young, either. Back then, he and his best friend had talked of nothing but cops and robbers. But he hadn't said as much to Rosanna. Tinkering with the pipes had given him something to do to occupy his hands, someplace to look. Keeping busy hadn't kept him from thinking about the things and people he missed.

He supposed it was the coziness of another family's house that had reminded Cole of all the evenings he used to spend at Gary and Evie's place, before Gary had died. The similarity had left him feeling sore on the inside, raw on the outside. Since he couldn't fix the faucet without a washer, which would have required a trip into nearby Rockland, Cole had bid everyone an early good-night. Exhausted, he'd climbed the stairs and crawled into bed, dropping immediately into a deep, dreamless sleep that had lasted another twelve hours.

He knew he was getting better, because memories of Gary hadn't brought on another episode. He woke up feeling refreshed. He'd stared at his reflection in the wavy mirror in the tiny bathroom. Something was different. After several minutes, he'd figured out what it was. His eyes weren't bloodshot or glazed. Hell, they almost looked clear. They sure looked out of place above the three-day-old beard and too-long hair.

He'd taken the trap apart and had replaced the corroded pipe when he heard Rosanna's car in the driveway, so he should have been prepared to see her standing on the rug a few minutes later, a bag of groceries in each arm. He was on his knees, which put him at eye level with an incredible pair of legs. Her black boots covered her ankles. Thick black tights disappeared beneath some sort of a black knit skirt that kept getting tangled up around her knees as she dumped the groceries on the counter and shrugged out of an oatmeal-colored fleece coat. It required a conscious effort to avert his gaze.

Rosanna released a faint, slightly out of tune whistle. When she spoke, there was laughter in her voice. "Gee, Cole, you don't clean up too bad."

She was referring to his earlier shower and shave, and the haircut he'd gotten while he'd been out. It made him feel as shy as a pimply-faced kid at the prom. Shrugging, he answered without looking up. "Once in the winter, once in the summer."

He imagined she was smiling, but he didn't allow himself to make sure.

"What are you doing with the torch?" she asked. "I thought you were changing a washer in the faucet."

He answered while he gathered up the wrenches. "I was. I did. I swear the pipe didn't start to leak until after I fixed the faucet."

She put the milk in the refrigerator and the hamburger in the freezer. Opening a tall cupboard door, she said, "That happens a lot in this old house. One thing tends to lead to another. Where did you learn to fix leaky plumbing?"

He rose to his feet, brushed at the knees of his jeans. "My best friend used to live in an old house where something was always breaking or leaking. Evie always said nothing ever went wrong until evenings, holidays or weekends."

Rosanna continued putting groceries away, but

something in the tone of Cole's voice prompted her to say, "Evie?"

Surely whatever he'd gotten on his knees was gone by now. And yet he didn't look at her when he answered. "She was my partner Gary's wife. And she was right about things going wrong after hours."

Rosanna held perfectly still, waiting.

He was staring at a pipe wrench now, fiddling with the handle; his mind seemed to be miles, ages, away. "They had two little girls. Twins. God, they never stopped talking. And they rarely sat still. Two years ago, while Gary was bleeding to death—from a bullet that was meant for me—in a back alley and I was begging him to hold on, his girls were performing in their first dance recital."

The kitchen had grown so quiet, Rosanna could hear the deep breath Cole took. His eyes were still downcast, so she couldn't see the emotion in their depths. There was plenty of emotion in his voice.

"Evie saved him a seat. She didn't think anything of it. Hell, he was always late. She and I used to joke that he'd be late for his own funeral. Turned out he was early. Decades early. She brought the girls with her to the hospital when the call came. They showed me their dance routine while she went into Gary's hospital room. They were still in their muumuus or tutus or whatever the hell they're called."

Cole closed his eyes, the image as clear in his mind as the day it had happened. He didn't know why he was doing this. Dredging up the past sure as hell wasn't much fun. Now that he'd gone this far, he couldn't seem to stop.

"Evie fell apart. But me…I was a rock."

"Where are they now? Evie and the girls?"

"Moved to Cleveland. Evie got married again a couple of months ago. To a big brute of an ex-football player with shoulders a mile wide and a mustache that rivals Wally the Walrus's. I got quietly and thoroughly drunk at the wedding. By then I was getting drunk a lot."

"A delayed reaction," she said.

It was as if she understood. He didn't know what to say. He wished he hadn't said anything. "You should have been a shrink."

Rosanna waited to smile until he looked at her. It was either smile or cry. "That's what you think. I would have made a lousy psychiatrist. I'm patient with the kids, but not always with my peers. I've always wanted to fix people's problems, and I get exasperated when I can't. A psychiatrist? Me? Uh-uh. By the time I finished getting too emotionally involved, I would need a shrink, too."

He seemed to take her declaration in stride. He tried the faucet, peered underneath the sink to make sure nothing was leaking. She was glad he'd opened up to her, even if he had left a lot out. She'd known there'd been sadness in his past. But while he'd been talking, she'd heard regret, as if he was sorry it hadn't been him who took the bullet and died in that dark alley. She could have argued that having a wife and children didn't make one person's life more valuable than another's. God knew her mother always said Rosanna could have argued with the Pope. But she wanted to win back Cole's smile.

"Is this big ex-football player with the mustache a good man?"

He nodded. "I think Gary would have liked him."

Rosanna blinked back a tear. "Speaking of mustaches," she said, hitting the bull's-eye in her aim for a complete change of subject. "A man stopped in yesterday who was sporting a fake one. At least, I think it was fake. It was the funniest thing. His nose kept twitching, as if it tickled. He sure was adamant about renting the attic apartment."

Cole's nerves were shot. Dredging up the past always had that effect on him. "Somebody's interested in the attic apartment?"

She began folding brown paper bags. "He offered me twice, three times, four times what you're paying."

The hair on the back of Cole's neck bristled the way it always did when his temper was about to go through the roof.

"And money talks. Is that it?"

Her mouth dropped open. "I suppose, but…"

"You suppose? What were you going to do? Wait until Friday night to say, 'Oh, by the way, I've rented the room to somebody else so kindly pack up and get the hell out'?"

The wrenches clanked and clattered to the counter. And then he stormed up the stairs.

It didn't take long before Rosanna stormed up the stairs after him.

She didn't try to dodge any noisy floorboards today. The noisier her advance, the better.

"Listen, you…you hermit." She spoke the words loud, and pushed into the room without knocking. "When somebody picks a fight with me, I expect them to have the decency to stick around long enough for me to dish a little back, not to mention the chance to explain."

He tried to speak.

This time it was she who cut him off. "I didn't tell you about the man because I didn't rent him the room. I said I wouldn't, and I didn't. I'm as good as my word, and if you have a problem with that, tough. Maybe I should have told that man, Derek Drexler, that he could have it. I guess I've never had good taste when it comes to men."

She didn't rent the room? was Cole's first thought. His second was, Derek Drexler? The name sounded as fake as the mustache.

The first thought was sweeter, and returned, overriding everything else. *She didn't rent the room.*

He'd jumped to conclusions. Worse, he'd misjudged her.

"I'm sorry, Rosanna."

She was too revved up to listen, too busy reading him the riot act to cut him any slack. She'd mentioned a temper. He was witnessing it in action. She paced back and forth, her boots thudding over scatter rugs and old floorboards. She called him a lot of things, none of them particularly flattering. It didn't take him long to get fed up.

"Hold it right there," he yelled. "You're a damned attractive woman, Rosanna. With your legs and energy, you should have been a dancer, but you must be hard-of-hearing, because I said I'm sorry. Maybe you'd feel better if I got down on my hands and knees and kissed your feet."

For the span of two heartbeats, Rosanna was speechless. His mention of dancing started to soften her resolve. A long time ago she'd dreamed of becoming just that. But that was when she'd been young and naive. She was older now, and wiser.

"Don't tell me what I should have been." It thoroughly ticked her off that he'd reminded her of broken dreams and compromises. Max and Shiloh were everything to her, and they were worth everything she'd done, and more. "I'll have you know I don't want you kissing my feet or any other part of my anatomy. I don't so much as want you to touch me."

"Surprise, surprise."

"What's that supposed to mean?"

"I heard you the other night."

They stared at each other, chests heaving, eyes glittering with anger, the air so thick with tension it wasn't easy to breathe. "What are you talking about?" she asked.

"I know what I am, Rosanna. A woman like you

could do a lot better than a man like me. You don't have to remind me.''

Rosanna fought to control her swirling emotions. She detested losing her temper, because she knew better than anyone that words uttered in anger couldn't be called back.

"Look, Cole, I didn't mean…"

"Yes, you did."

He ran a hand through his hair, across his eyes, down his face. "Look," he said. "You don't owe me an explanation. You don't owe me anything. Kissing your feet was a figure of speech.''

"Of course it was…"

"Don't worry. I don't have a foot fetish. So kissing your feet, hell, touching you anywhere is the furthest thing from my mind." Cole was a liar. He wanted to touch her everywhere. Since he didn't have much except his pride, he said, "Let's just forget it, okay?''

"Sure. I mean, forget what?''

She didn't seem to expect him to smile. And he didn't.

"I'm sorry," she said. "For losing my temper."

"Yeah. Me, too.''

"I don't usually have a problem keeping it under control.''

"Me, either." Actually it had been a problem when he was younger. When he'd first hit the streets, he'd been known to lose his temper with drug dealers and pimps and strung-out hookers and thieves looking for an easy way to make a buck. But that was different. Rosanna hadn't done anything wrong. She was a mother, for cripes' sake. In another life, she might have been his friend. On another planet, she might have been his lover.

But not in this lifetime, and not in his world.

"You can stay until the end of the month if you want to. I was planning to tell you. I guess I should have mentioned it sooner. Do you still want to stay?"

He lowered his hands to his sides. Chin level, eyes steady, he said, "I guess I do."

"All right then." She glanced away, uncomfortable. "No hard feelings?"

"No," he said quietly. "No hard feelings."

She wavered him something that barely passed for a smile. Turning on those dancer's legs he'd mentioned, she left the room.

"Maxie. It's beautiful." Shiloh held the embellished flowerpot in her hands as if it were a sacred offering. Slowly turning it around, she whispered, "Mama's gonna love it."

"Don't drop it," Max said while she lowered it carefully into the box he'd found in the attic closet. "Or we'll have to start over."

They'd spent an hour gluing the ocean glass Shiloh had found to the outside of the pot. She was right. It sure was pretty. Their mother always said she liked practical things, but her eyes were going to sparkle as much as the flowerpot, he just knew it.

It was fun giving gifts, especially when you knew

a person was going to love them. He wondered what Mom and Shiloh were going to get him. Uncle Henry had talked about bikes a lot, so Max had a feeling he was going to get one of those. It didn't look like he was going to get a father, though.

Max didn't know what had happened, but something had gone wrong between his mom and Cole. Oh, they were polite. That was the problem. They said please and thank you and excuse me, but hardly anything else.

"Are you gonna make Cole a present?" Shiloh asked, holding her finger where Max indicated on the wrapping paper he'd just cut.

"I don't know what," he answered forlornly, tearing off a piece of clear tape.

"Me, either," Shiloh said gravely. And then, brightening considerably, she whispered, "Wanna see what I'm making Nadine?"

Uh-oh, Max thought. She was whispering again. That was never a good sign. "I guess."

"Okay," she said, going down on all fours and peering under her bed. "But you've gotta promise not to tell anybody."

Max was pretty sure he wasn't going to like keeping such a promise, but Shiloh refused to show him until he'd said, "I promise."

Grinning for all she was worth, she pulled a pair of high-heeled shoes from underneath her bed.

"What are you doing with Nadine's killer heels?" Max asked.

"Shh. Somebody might hear."

"Hey, kids." Cole rapped softly on the doorjamb. Shiloh let out a little yelp. Even Max jumped guiltily.

Cole had walked into the middle of enough covert actions to recognize one in progress. Max had almost dropped the gift he was holding, and Shiloh had spun around, her eyes huge in her narrow face.

"Shiloh," he said. "Aren't those heels a little high for a girl your age?"

She twirled around, as spry as a ballerina. "They're not mine, silly."

He strode farther into the room. "Whose are they?"

"They're Nadine's. Shiloh took 'em."

"Max, you promised not to tell. Besides, I'm gonna give 'em back. For Christmas. First, I'm gonna put glitter on 'em."

"You can't put glitter on Nadine's shoes," Max exclaimed. "Tell her, Cole."

"I can so," Shiloh declared, her chin raised stubbornly. "Nadine told me these were her favorite shoes. Sure-thing shoes, she called them. She says she's gonna hafta get a new pair on accounta these are getting scuffed up and aren't effective. What's effective mean, Cole?"

"Er, um, let's see. That's a tough one."

"Anyways, I'm gonna make them shiny as new with glitter, like Dorothy's ruby slippers."

Cole eyed the shoes dangling from Shiloh's fingertips. He knew why Nadine called them sure-thing shoes. They were sexy numbers, all right, with those pointy toes and four-inch heels.

"Shiloh," Max said. "You can't steal other people's stuff. Mom said."

"It's only stealing if ya don't give it back. Otherwise it's borrowing. Right, Cole?"

Max looked to Cole for help. Other than bringing up the little issue of getting permission, Cole was at a loss. Shiloh glanced from one male to the other. Sensing victory, she grinned guilelessly then returned the shoes to their hiding place underneath her bed.

Max and Cole shared a look men all over the world exchanged when dealing with a woman they didn't understand, let alone have a chance of coming out ahead in an argument.

Max rolled his eyes dramatically. It brought out a smile that felt foreign on Cole's face. "Your mom said it's time to eat."

"Are you gonna eat with us?" Shiloh asked.

Cole shook his head. "I think I'll get a burger someplace."

Max sighed. Cole hadn't eaten with them in a week. He kept the sidewalks and driveway shoveled, and every day something else got fixed in the inn, but most of the time, Cole stayed in his room.

"What do you want for Christmas, Cole?" Shiloh asked, out of the blue.

Cole shrugged, and Shiloh fired off another question. "Whatcha gonna get for Mama? Don't forget, whatever it is, it's gotta be homemade."

"What I'm going to get," Cole said, gesturing toward the door, "is in trouble if you two don't hightail it down to supper."

As if on cue, Rosanna's voice carried up the stairs. "Is anybody up there hungry?"

Racing to be first, the kids took the main stairs down to the first floor. At a much slower pace, Cole climbed the back stairs to the third floor. Shiloh's question was still echoing through his mind as he let himself into his apartment.

What was he going to get Rosanna for Christmas?

His gift to her was pretty straightforward. She didn't want him touching her. So he was keeping his distance.

Not that it had been easy.

Rosanna peered up at the top shelf where several boxes of Christmas decorations were stacked one on top of the other. The Midnight Inn was spacious even by Victorian standards. The previous owners had been eccentric spinster sisters who had spent their final years, as well as most of their money, painstakingly restoring the huge old house to its original glory. They'd sold it to Rosanna's mother for a fraction of what it was worth. They hadn't needed the money, they'd said. What they'd needed was a family to love their old house. A few months later, they died from the same flu virus, days apart. It was the kind of thing small-town people brought up from time to time after they'd exhausted the topic of how Marshal Hogan's car had been seen parked in front of MaryEllen Jacob's house the nights her husband Roy was out of town. It was the sort of thing that found a place in the town's history right alongside the heroic rescue of an entire fishing crew back in '83, and the mysterious disappearance of Verita Hicks's diamonds in '91. These were the things people talked about at graduations and birthday parties and while standing in line at the grocery store. They were the kind of things that gave small towns in general and the town of Midnight in particular, a personality, a heart and a soul.

Rosanna included the old ladies in her prayers of thanksgiving every night. Once or twice a year, she raised her eyes toward heaven and asked them what they'd been thinking when they failed to incorporate a little closet space on every floor.

Other than a tiny alcove in two of the six bedrooms, this cubbyhole in the attic was the only storage space in the entire house, which meant that everything had to be stored here. Retrieving stored items was always a dilemma.

She stared up at the high shelf. Hands on her hips, she decided that there were two ways she could do this: She could trudge down two flights of stairs, traipse out into the cold, feel around in the dark shed until she found the stepladder, then haul it into the house and drag it up two flights of stairs. Or, she could climb up the front of the shelves on the opposite wall, keeping her balance while she reached around and took down one box at a time.

Actually there was a third way. She could knock on Cole's door and ask him to help.

She couldn't count how many times the argument they'd had had crossed her mind. It stung her conscience every time. That was nothing compared to the way the memory of Cole's declaration that he didn't want to touch her stung her pride. Or was it her ego that was smarting?

They'd both apologized, but things had changed between them. He'd retreated inside himself. She didn't blame him. If anything, she blamed herself. Words spoken in anger could never be unspoken. No amount of apologizing could erase what they'd both said.

Asking for Cole's help wasn't really an option.

Which meant she was back to her first two options. Grasping the edge of a high shelf, she hiked her foot onto the lowest shelf, just as she did every year.

Did something just thud?

Cole turned his head, listening. He wasn't afraid of things that went bump in the night. But he was curious.

He opened his door. The hall was empty. And quiet.

It had been this way all day. Things normally got pretty loud when Max and Shiloh first got home from school. They must have gone someplace today because he hadn't heard a peep out of anybody all afternoon.

He'd closed the door all but the final two inches when he heard noises again. The sounds were coming from the end of the hall: the scrape of cardboard, the shuffle of boxes, the clink of glass and metal, an occasional "oomph."

He followed the sound around the corner, and peered inside an open door. Rosanna was perched on the middle of a series of shelves that reached from the floor to the ceiling. The fool woman had to lean back, contorting her body into an uncomfortable-looking position, and then go up on tiptoe to reach the top shelf. How the hell she kept her balance was beyond him.

"I had you pegged as a woman who had a little common sense!"

Rosanna jerked in surprise. In the millisecond it took her to glance behind her at the man who had startled the breath out of her, her fingers slipped off the shelf and her smooth-soled shoes slid from their toehold. She clawed at the air, but the pull of gravity won.

While she fell as if in slow motion, Cole moved like lightning. He shot forward, catching a pinecone wreath in one arm, and Rosanna in the other.

She was slight, but the impact propelled him backward. His arm tightened around her waist, and he pulled her to him so hard he felt her breath catch in her lungs.

He loosened his hold only slightly, and lowered her feet to the floor. "That was a fool thing to try."

Rosanna could have argued that it wasn't as if

she'd climbed out onto the roof. If she had fallen in the closet, she wouldn't have been seriously injured. The space was crowded, awkward, the shelves difficult to reach. But they weren't high enough to be truly dangerous. She could have broken a decoration or two, and she might have ended up with a bruise, but she wouldn't have been hurt. But she was too busy reacting to Cole's touch to utter a single word in her defense.

Awareness shimmered like light in the dim, shadowy room. The arm around her back was strong, the body molded to her own solid and warm.

"Cole?" she whispered.

"Hmm?" His jaw was set, his lips slightly parted, his eyes such a dark shade of brown they looked nearly black.

"You're touching me."

He lowered his face, easing closer one slow degree at a time. "Yeah, I know."

She knew he was giving her plenty of time to resist. By the same token, he was giving her time to acknowledge, to savor, to anticipate.

Almost of its own volition, her hand went to his cheek in a feather-soft caress. His skin was warm, tight and slightly rough with the beginning of a five-o'clock shadow.

His eyes closed partway, as if it had been a long time since he'd known tenderness. He made a sound deep in his throat, part frustration, part need, all male. And then, with a gentleness she'd sensed was as much a part of him as his broodiness and those features that made him rugged and strong, he touched her lips with his.

Chapter 4

Rosanna's eyelashes fluttered down, and her lips parted beneath Cole's. The man was not what he'd seemed, nor was his kiss what she'd expected. It was like a ripple on a glass-smooth lake, spreading outward in a pattern that was so beautiful and natural that when it was over, you wanted to toss in another stone just to witness it again. Poignant and sweet, it was the kind of kiss that poets wrote about and musicians sang about and scholars tried to make sense of.

His lips were firm, and yet his kiss was soft, thought-provoking, heartrending, gentle. It was the first time Rosanna had been kissed in a long, long time, the first time she'd ever been kissed exactly like this, as if she were precious, special, and in some way uniquely appreciated.

It was a healing kiss that hinted of passion, but didn't quite cross that line. It was a gift, one to be savored, but it wasn't the kiss of a man whose life was over, whose future was meant to be spent all alone. Oh, she knew he wasn't going to be staying, not here, not with her. He would be one of those people she thought about from time to time. One of those people she would miss, and yet would be glad she hadn't missed knowing.

Whether he remembered her or not didn't matter. This moment in time was all that mattered. And for this moment in time, Rosanna returned his kiss, matching it for tenderness, filling it with feeling.

She was as comfortable in his arms as she was in her home, the sound of his breathing as natural in her ears as the sound of the wind in the eaves, the rattle and creak of hundred-year-old beams, or the sound of Max and Shiloh clomping up the stairs. Her children's presence in the house reminded Rosanna of her responsibilities, and the promises she'd made to them, and to herself. She ended the kiss about the same time the squeaky boards in the steps let Rosanna know that Max and Shiloh had reached the second flight. She opened her eyes, and moved backward an inch at a time.

Cole felt her drawing out of his arms. It required a conscious effort to let her go. He glanced at the wreath he'd caught an instant before he'd caught her. It was a little worse for wear. The same couldn't be said for Rosanna. Her eyes were a brilliant shade of green, her lips wet and enticing and full.

"That was nice," she said.

Cole thought it was a damn sight better than nice. "Yes, it was."

While the kids were trudging up the last few steps, she took the wreath from him and said, "As far as icebreakers go, that was much more effective than 'I'm sorry.'"

Cole shook his head, shrugged and damned if his lips didn't curve of their own volition. Leave it to Rosanna to bring out a smile on a face that wasn't prone to any such thing.

"Hey, Cole!" Shiloh called. "Whatcha doin'?"

"Shh!" Max reprimanded. "He and Mom are talking. Don't bother them."

"They're not either talking. They're just standing there looking at each other."

Cole wondered how Rosanna was going to explain that. With an air of calm and self-confidence that he liked, she simply turned back to her task, saying, "Here. You guys can start carting boxes downstairs."

She handed Shiloh the wreath, and Max a larger box, giving them both strict instructions to be careful on the stairs. When the kids were well on their way, she turned to Cole. "Do you feel like doing me a favor?"

His imagination took a gigantic leap. "That depends."

Seemingly oblivious to the huskiness in his voice,

she said, "Max and Shiloh and I went to the Christmas tree lot and chose the perfect tree. The man at the lot helped us tie it to the roof of the van. But it would be an enormous help if you would bring it inside."

She handed him the keys to her van, then bent to retrieve a stack of boxes on the floor. Cole figured he could back the van around and bring the tree inside. It would probably be much safer to haul the tree in than to haul her off to bed. Although it couldn't possibly be as much fun.

Three hours later, red, green, yellow and blue lights twinkled up and down the nine-foot tree. The only room that could accommodate such height was the parlor. Even then, Cole and Max had had to chop a good foot off the trunk. It was the tallest tree Cole had ever helped decorate. It was the most fun he'd had in a while, too. Not as much fun as sex, maybe, but almost as tiring.

The kids had gone to bed at nine. Cole had come upstairs shortly thereafter. Now, it was slightly after eleven, and hours earlier than he ever went to bed in Miami. Night came earlier up here. There were no sirens, no traffic, no garish neon signs flashing fake daylight. Beyond the streetlights on the corners, there were only stars. The snow on the ground was thick, the night sky even more so. It was as if this tiny corner of the world was blanketed in peacefulness. Even the wind carried a quiet hush.

Cole yawned.

He ran a hand through his hair, took a hot wash-cloth to his face, made a couple of passes in his mouth with his toothbrush. And then he was tugging his white T-shirt from his jeans, and reaching a hand into either pocket, removing his loose change and a set of van keys.

He paused, staring at those keys. Rosanna would need them to take the kids to school in the morning.

Leaving his shirt untucked, he headed for the back stairs in his socks. He could see a light on in the kitchen, but the door was locked. He jiggled the handle, then rapped lightly on the wood.

Hmm. He wondered where Rosanna was. He could have jimmied the lock. God knew he'd done it often in the past. He remembered the keys. Why jimmy a lock when he could open it with a key?

Fitting the third key he tried into the lock, he opened the door and quietly called Rosanna's name. Again, he was met with only silence.

He padded around the kitchen table, stopping in the doorway between the kitchen and the living room. The double parlor doors were open on the far side of the living room. The Christmas tree lights were still on. The only other illumination was coming from the television where a black-and-white *I Love Lucy* rerun was playing.

"Rosanna?"

The only sound was the canned laughter coming from the television. He turned in a circle, searching for a clue as to her whereabouts. Strolling farther into the room, he discovered why she hadn't answered. Rosanna was fast asleep.

She was lying on her couch, a homemade pillow beneath her head, an afghan she'd said her mother had made pulled up to her neck. Her eyes were closed, her dark lashes casting a shadow on cheeks that looked pale beneath the faint glow of Christmas lights.

Cole squeezed the keys, then quietly placed them on the coffee table. He couldn't seem to take his eyes off her. She looked vulnerable in sleep. She gave so much, and it seemed a shame that a woman like her, so warm and responsive, had to fall asleep watching reruns of old situation comedies, and not in a man's arms.

He wondered what she would do if he skimmed his fingertips along her cheek, his lips along her forehead. Better yet, he wondered what she would do if he woke her with a kiss placed gently on her mouth. Would she wake slowly, returning his kiss from the drowsy place halfway between sleep and wakefulness? Or would she scream bloody murder?

He had no business being here, no business watching her sleep. He sure as hell had no business waking her with a kiss.

He'd barely straightened to his full height when her eyes opened. They homed in on his, drowsy, and so deep and warm and inviting he felt himself slipping in.

"Cole?"

He startled guiltily. "I brought back your keys."

"Oh."

The canned laughter covered the quiet, but it didn't quiet his thoughts. He was aware of the darkness, of the silence, the seclusion. It was as if those elements had wrapped the two of them in intimacy. And Cole wanted...

He wanted. And that wanting was a powerful, dangerous thing. "You like old comedies?" he asked, hoping his voice was steadier than he felt.

"Watching old *I Love Lucy* shows happens to be one of my two greatest passions."

He had to clear his throat in order to speak. "Gary loved *The Three Stooges*."

She sat up, pushed the hair out of her face. "That's one of the differences between the sexes."

Perhaps, Cole thought. But it wasn't the greatest difference. Or the most intriguing.

"Chocolate marshmallow ice cream."

His heart skipped a beat. "I beg your pardon?"

"That's my other passion."

His throat felt thick, and he was pretty sure something was wrong with his heart, and his lungs, and his brain. Her eyes were sinfully soft, her pupils so large and black only a thin circle of green surrounded them.

He eased closer, drawn to her like a freezing man to a glowing fire.

She held up a hand in a halting gesture. Shaking her head, she whispered, "I can't, Cole."

He stopped. She'd said she couldn't. Not *I don't want to,* or *I shouldn't,* or *I won't.*

I can't.

The low drone of voices and laughter coming from the television was at odds with the seriousness in Rosanna's eyes. "I know what kind of man you are. And it isn't what you think. There's a depth to you that few men possess. But your stay here is temporary. I know I'm a woman alone. Sometimes that means I'm lonely. But no one is going to take care of me but me. I fell in love with the wrong man once, a man who wanted to wander the earth and write his songs. If I ever fall in love again, it'll be with a man who wants what I want."

Suddenly Cole understood why she hadn't asked him what that kiss in the attic had meant to him. She was looking for forever. And a man who had no job, no plans, no responsibilities, a man whose greatest tie was to an attic apartment he was renting by the week wasn't a forever kind of man. Oh, there was attraction between them. But she wasn't going to act on it.

And neither was he.

His reasons had to do with his past. Hers had to do with her future.

"I understand," he said. Understanding made him want her more.

"I thought you would."

She made no apologies, no excuses. She wasted no time on wishing that things could be different. What was, was. And any more than a passing friendship between them wasn't meant to be.

Cole said good-night, and as he returned to his

attic apartment, he thought the men in Midnight, Maine, were either blind, or stupid, or both.

He stood at the window for a long time, thinking. Rosanna wasn't like other women. She didn't say things she didn't mean. She didn't make a lot of small talk. She was lonely, but she wasn't desperate. Once Max had said she sometimes watched TV in bed. He imagined her taking the tape out of the VCR and carrying it to her room.

He stared out into the night, his room dark behind him. Now that he'd been to the harbor, he could place some of the lights in the distance. Someone had strung Christmas lights on a ship in dry dock, and had placed a perfect star high atop its mast.

Christmas was just over a week away. That seemed amazing. Where had the month of December gone? He'd helped Rosanna and the kids decorate their tree, but he'd done nothing to prepare on his own. He had to find gifts for Evie and the girls. And his dad, and his uncle Lou. Hell, he wondered what chance any gifts he bought had of arriving at their destination before the big day.

While he was at it, he would try to find something for Max and Shiloh. And for Rosanna, too. It would have to be something special. Something to remember him by long after he was gone.

He drew away from the window slightly. A movement in the shadows far below brought him to full attention. The skin on the back of his neck prickled. His heart pounded. His breathing quickened. His vision blurred and pressure built in his chest.

He closed his eyes, immediately starting the relaxation technique he'd learned in Florida. His hands fisted at his sides. Consciously he flexed his fingers, relaxing them one at a time. He concentrated on his breathing—in through his nose, out through his mouth, in through his nose, out through his mouth—and on keeping his muscles from bunching—roll those shoulders, relax. Relax.

It used to take him an hour to master. Now it took him a matter of seconds. The precinct's psychologist said his condition was similar to one war veterans experienced. Doc Henderson had claimed it was due to trauma, and in his case, a combination of his childhood and feeling responsible for his best friend's death. Which just went to show what that framed piece of paper on the wall in the noted psychiatrist's office was good for.

Cole's father had been a career army man. After Cole's mother died, the colonel had coped by taking a position overseas. He'd left Cole in the care of his best friend's family. Cole hadn't minded. He'd loved Jim and Martha Davis. And Gary was the closest thing to a brother he'd ever had. He'd missed his mother, and his father, too, but it was the first time he'd had real roots. And no matter what the textbooks claimed, Cole didn't feel responsible for Gary's death. He'd relived the scene in his mind a million times, and he knew there was nothing he could have done.

The fear was real. And so was the remorse. But this feeling of helplessness stemmed from having his beliefs shattered. What the hell difference did it make if he was a good cop? The bad guys were winning. And the good guys were dying.

And there wasn't anything one lonely man could do about it.

He stared long and hard into those shadows, wondering what it was he'd seen. Nothing moved. Perhaps it had been the wind in the bushes. Or some animal foraging for food and shelter. Feeling drained, he decided to have a look in the morning. Exhausted, he crawled into bed.

Rosanna was baking Christmas cookies the next morning when Cole poked his head inside the cozy kitchen. The air smelled of cinnamon and ginger and warm applesauce.

"Hey, Cole!" Max said. It was Saturday, and the kids weren't in school. "This here's Lumpy."

Cole eased a little farther into the room and smiled at a pudgy kid sporting a baseball cap and a baggy sweatshirt. "How's it going?"

"Pretty good."

"Hey, sugar. Remember me?" Nadine called from the table where she was nursing a cup of coffee and leafing through a glossy magazine.

Cole wondered if she'd missed her killer heels yet. Which reminded him that he'd forgotten to mention Shiloh's latest nimble-fingered enterprise to Rosanna.

Max and Lumpy were sitting at the bar; Shiloh was standing on a stepstool on the other side of the counter, in her mother's way. Helping. Her hair was in a ponytail this morning. There was a smudge of flour on one cheek and a huge dusting of it on the front of her pink shirt.

"His real name's Daniel," she piped. "But everyone calls him Lumpy, on account'a he used to fall on his head all the time when he was little."

Thinking it was amazing that anybody survived their childhood, Cole winked at the boy who was studying him with serious blue eyes.

"Max says you used to be a cop."

"That's right."

"You ever kill anybody?"

The room, all at once, got very quiet.

Although he didn't look at them, he could practically feel the look Rosanna and Nadine shared. Nadine tried to divert the boys' attention by saying, "You boys watch too much television."

Rosanna, too, tried to smooth things over. She told Shiloh to go easy on the sprinkles, and asked Max and Lumpy if they were going to watch or help. The boys glanced at Rosanna, then looked Cole straight in the eye.

Cole considered his options. He could lie. At least then he wouldn't have to dredge up details and answer a dozen questions.

Although he didn't speak, he nodded his head one time.

Lumpy looked away, but Max held Cole's gaze. "That's what I thought."

Lumpy took a bite out of a gingerbread man. Max

pointed to a bowl of frosting and said, "Hey, Shiloh, hand me that knife."

That was it. No inquisition. No quest for morbid details. Just a calm acceptance of a simple answer taken at face value. The boy had a lot of his mother in him.

Nadine snagged Cole's attention, asking him a few questions regarding the weather. Cole kept his answers brief, and left soon after.

The wind was brutal this morning, flinging snowflakes that were so tiny they felt like shards of glass hitting his face. He zipped up his thick coat, turned up the collar, pulled on his gloves. Glancing up, he figured angles and gauged the portion of the yard he could see from the third-floor window.

The sidewalk ended several feet from the place he determined he'd glimpsed movement last night. He followed a set of men's footsteps around to the side of the house. He measured them against his own.

The prints could have belonged to the trash man or the meter reader. Except this wasn't where Rosanna kept her trash can, and there wasn't an electric meter in sight.

Cole wondered if there was a window peeper in the neighborhood. He glanced around with a practiced eye. Kids were playing in a snowbank across the street. And the woman who lived behind Rosanna was letting her poodle out the sliding glass door. Whoever had left those footprints was long gone. Deciding to keep an eye out tonight, he turned on his heel, and headed for his car and a shopping excursion in the larger and nearby town of Rockland.

Cole studied the darkness beyond his attic window. It was Wednesday. The gifts he'd purchased for Gracie and Glory were on their way to Ohio. He hadn't found anything for his dad or Uncle Lou, but the presents he'd bought for Rosanna and her kids were sitting on the table next to a huge conch shell. He'd kept his eyes and ears open since Saturday, but hadn't seen or heard anything unusual outside or in. He'd convinced himself the footprints had been a fluke, until he'd discovered more in the newfallen snow this morning.

Somebody wearing man's size ten cowboy boots had circled the entire house sometime after midnight last night. Cole knew, because that was when he'd turned in.

Tonight, he planned to extend his vigil. It was only six-thirty. And right now he was antsy, fidgety. Pacing had proven ineffective in relieving his pent-up nerves. What he needed was some exercise and a dose of fresh air. He'd dug a pair of running shoes out of his duffel bag, donned his last clean pair of jeans and headed downstairs.

He was on his way out the back door to take a long, hard run when he heard a voice. Female.

He stopped in his tracks. And tried to place the voice. It was slightly squeaky, terribly shaky, strangely muffled. It wasn't coming from outside the house, but from within.

Sweat broke out on his brow.

Rosanna?

He closed the outside door, and tried the inside door on the other side of the narrow entryway. It was locked tight.

What the hell was going on?

A voice in his head screamed for him to go faster. Over and over and over, it chanted, hissed, prodded. Go. Hurry. Before it's too late. Too late.

He jimmied the lock, pushed through the door, his stride long, his feet moving across the kitchen, down a narrow hall, closer to that shaking, muffled voice.

It was definitely Rosanna's voice. He knew it as surely as he knew his own name. Horrible images in living color shimmered through his mind. Like a psychedelic light, red flashed to white, back and forth and back and forth.

Red. White.

The red was blood, hot and sticky; it trickled to the gutter in a dark back alley. The white was snow. And in it were footprints made by pointy-toed cowboy boots, leaving a crisp, pristine trail leading nowhere. The two images flickered, dark to light, light to dark, over and over.

The hair on the back of his neck prickled. Heart racing, Cole had no time for a panic attack, no time for relaxation breathing techniques. He reached the bathroom door. Jiggled the handle. Good God, Rosanna was in there. And she was in pain.

"Rosanna. Answer me."

As if someone had flipped a switch, the bathroom went completely silent.

Instinct took over. He burst through the door with so much force wood splintered and the floor shook. Rosanna swung around, took one look at Cole and let loose a blood-curdling scream.

Chapter 5

The bathroom door banged against the wall about the same time Cole's heart banged against his ribs. One second Rosanna's scream had pierced the air. The next second there was only deafening silence.

Rosanna stood in the shower, Cole a few feet away, his hand still gripping the edge of the shower curtain he'd jerked open. They stared at each other, stunned.

She wasn't in danger.

But Cole was.

His gaze flicked down her body where goose bumps rose on flawless, olive-toned skin. Good Lord, she was fine-boned, delicate looking, her breasts pale and plump.

Hell and damnation. He was in danger, all right.

In danger of saying to hell with it and joining her in that shower.

"Cole?"

She sounded breathless. He was having a tough time breathing, himself. He finally managed to take his eyes off her breasts, only to get into even more trouble a foot or two lower.

The shiver that shook her entire body brought Rosanna to her senses. With a flick of her wrist, she turned off the shower. Quickly she reached for her towel, covering the front of her body.

Cole's features were chiseled, his expression serious and still. His eyes were dark and hooded, his lips set in a firm, taut line. His shoulders were taut, too, his fingers curled into fists at his sides.

"Cole," she said again. "What do you think you're doing?"

His stance was wide, his feet planted, as if he was ready for battle. "I thought you were in trouble."

"In trouble, how?"

"I heard you. And I thought…I thought you were in pain."

Somebody nudged him on either side. He jumped, reached for a gun he no longer carried, and swore all over again.

"Whatcha doing, Cole?" Shiloh asked.

"Why doesn't everybody come on in?" Rosanna called.

Her sarcasm was completely wasted on Shiloh, who sashayed closer and innocently asked, "Cole? Why are ya watchin' Mama in the shower?"

He came to his senses, only to take a backward step, bumping into Max. Rosanna had been taking a shower. Alone. She wasn't hurt. Or bleeding. The only danger she was in was coming from him, and what he wanted to do, where he wanted to touch her, and how badly he wanted to make love to her.

He considered his options. He could turn tail and run. He would have preferred to close the door on the kids and whisk that towel out of Rosanna's hands.

"Yeah, Cole," Max said. "Why are you watching Mom in the shower?"

He finally managed to pry his eyes off her thighs and try to explain. "I heard something...and I thought...I mean, it...sounded...like she was...in trouble."

"Mama wasn't in trouble," Shiloh said. "She was singing. Tell him, Maxie."

"Shiloh's right. Mom was just singing in the shower. She does it all the time."

"Singing?" Realization dawned. "That was singing?"

"Get out." Rosanna's eyes were suddenly a stormy gray.

Cole and the kids took a backward step.

"I didn't know," Cole said. "How could I have known? I thought somebody was hurting you...but that's what you were doing. Singing."

"Grandma used to say you had a voice like a frog's, didn't she, Mama?"

"Everybody. Out!"

Cole and Max jumped to attention, but her darling daughter remained, nonplussed. "We're going," she said. "In a minute. When the windows are open in the summer, cats howl when Mama sings in the shower. Right, Mama?"

"*Out!*"

Like puppets tied to the same string, Cole, Max and Shiloh backed the rest of the way out of the room, only to stand in the doorway, staring. Rosanna slammed the door.

With the sound of that slam still echoing in his ears, Cole's lips quirked. "Cats have really been known to yowl when they hear your mother sing?"

"Yup. Mrs. Zuker's cats yowl every time. Don't they, Max?"

Max nodded sagely. "They aren't the only ones, either. She got kicked out of the church choir when she was little. Lumpy's mom said the choir director said she couldn't carry a tune in a basket."

Cole was in grave danger of laughing out loud. "That's too bad."

"Mama doesn't mind," Shiloh said. "She says God created the croak of the frog just as surely as He created the twitter of songbirds."

"Don't tell Mom," Max said, "but I think songbirds are a lot easier on the ears."

"I heard that!" On the other side of the door, Rosanna shook her head and rolled her eyes toward heaven. Rubbing the threadbare towel over every inch of her body, she sputtered to herself. Was nothing sacred? Did she have no secrets? No privacy?

Laughter carried to her ears through the closed door. She would never tire of hearing Shiloh's giggle and Max's boyish chuckle, but tonight it was the sound of Cole's laughter that drained her embarrassment and ire away.

Perhaps being the butt of a joke wasn't all bad. If it meant hearing Cole laugh, she would do it all over again.

Rosanna swiped a towel over the steamy mirror and stared at her reflection. She'd seen the heat in Cole's eyes when he'd first burst into the room. She could still feel the answering ache deep in her body.

He would be easy to love.

She closed her eyes against the rush of emotion that flooded into her. She had her pride. And she had her priorities firmly in order. She wasn't falling in love. She was falling in like. She liked a lot of people. Liking Cole was no big deal. He was a likable man.

Who was going to leave.

While she took the clip from her hair and donned her robe, she told herself there was no reason to feel weepy, no reason to panic. She was strong and resilient. She would find the strength to resist him, and the resilience to go on with her life after he was gone.

She'd already put the color of his eyes, the stubborn angle of his chin and his slow, rare smiles to memory. Listening intently, she memorized the mellow sound of the deep voice blending so effortlessly with Max's and Shiloh's laughter. Everything was going to be all right. She just had to be strong a little while longer.

Cole and the kids meandered en masse into the living room. The musky scent of evergreen hung heavy on the air. Somebody had plugged in the lights on the Christmas tree in the parlor, and it looked like Rosanna had finished decorating the rest of the house.

It was nearing evening. Here in Maine, it was the quiet time of the day. Cole still hadn't taken his run. He started to make noises about doing just that when Shiloh said, "Mama sure can scream."

Cole barely kept his grimace to himself. Uncomfortable with the turn his hormones had taken, he would have preferred to let the subject drop. Shiloh seemed intent upon rehashing the entire episode. For the first time he noticed that the kids were dressed up. Max's hair was neatly combed, his shoes polished, his navy chinos creased. He wore a forest-green sweater a shade or two darker than Shiloh's velvety dress. Her shoes were black patent leather and buckled on the side. A big white bow tied up her curling hair. A matching white ribbon circled her waist. Evie used to deck Glory and Gracie out like that. She probably still did. He missed the girls, wondered how they were.

"What would you have done, Cole?" Shiloh asked, climbing onto the sofa in the living room. "If Mama hadn't been singing at all. If she'd been screaming like you thought."

A heaviness centered in Cole's chest. He swallowed, trying to form an answer.

Rolling his eyes, Max answered for him.

"He woulda rescued her," he said in that know-it-all voice even brothers who liked their little sisters used.

Cole's heart pounded like a fist on a drum. It wasn't the same as a post-trauma episode, but it was nearly as unsettling. Suddenly he felt as if he'd been treading water in a shark-infested ocean for months. Just when he was certain he was going under, someone had thrown him a lifeboat. Rosanna and her children were holding the rope.

Day by day, they were getting to him. He was starting to care about them. How in the hell had that happened?

"Are you gonna come watch us in our Christmas program at school, Cole?" Shiloh asked.

He glanced at both kids. There was so much open longing on their faces that he had to look away. They thought he was a hero. Couldn't they see that he was just a man? He couldn't protect them. Not from the evils of the world. But he could protect them from himself. With a shake of his head, he said, "Christmas programs are for families."

"What will you do all by yourself?" Shiloh asked.

Cole shrugged. "Maybe I'll take a nap."

Shiloh pulled a face. Cole was pretty sure he'd dropped a notch or two in Max's estimation, too.

So be it.

He wasn't father material, and no matter what Max thought, Cole wasn't a knight sent here to rescue him or anyone else. He'd left Miami to get away. From crime. From responsibility. From the gut-wrenching knowledge that he just plain couldn't do it anymore.

He excused himself. Instead of going immediately for a long, hard run, he went up to the attic to think. Darkness fell while he was peering out the window. Lights came on in the houses up and down the street in the same order they always did. Somebody ought to tell these people to vary the sequence a little. Hell, a crook would have a field day on this block.

Cole didn't like the dull ache of foreboding that crept into his chest. There it sat, as cold and heavy as a slab of concrete. He was no longer in the business of matching wits with crooks. And he was getting much too emotionally involved with this family.

He thought of the way Rosanna had halted his forward motion when he'd been intent to kiss her a few nights ago. She didn't want to get involved with him because she knew he wasn't going to stay. The last thing she needed was a romantic interlude that could only end quickly and badly. He'd understood that. And he'd been perfectly willing to keep his distance. Then he'd seen her in the shower. During that brief moment when their eyes had locked, their bodies had communicated with each other, acknowledging the attraction, the desire. The longer he stayed, the more difficult that attraction was going to be to fight,

It was time for Cole to leave.

The thought came out of nowhere, and yet it seemed as if it had been there all along. He knew what he had to do.

It took him five minutes to throw his belongings into his bags. Giving the room a cursory glance, he spied the gifts he'd selected for Rosanna and the kids. He considered taking the time to wrap them. In the end, he left them on the table next to the conch shells for them to find.

He listened intently at the bottom of the stairs. The house was quiet, and other than the light over the stove, it was dark. He'd planned to say a hasty goodbye and then be on his way. Since his goodbyes were going to have to wait until the Fitzpatricks returned, he stashed his bags in the hall, ran the zipper up on his jacket and headed for the back door for a long, much-needed run.

The cookies.

Rosanna forgot the cookies.

First, she'd almost forgotten her purse. Then she'd had trouble finding the keys. And now the cookies. Good heavens. She'd been restless and giddy and nervous and forgetful. All because Cole had seen her naked.

She should have been upset with herself. Every time she mustered up a degree of self-reproach, soft-touched thoughts shaped her smile. It was happening right now.

She circled the block, and pulled back into her

own driveway. Throwing the shifting lever into Park, she turned the key, opened her door and told the kids she would be right back.

Her shoes clicked over the cement driveway. A cold wind billowed her long wool coat behind her, and yet she didn't feel cold. Far from it; she felt sensual, desirable, warmed from within. All because Colter Remington Monroe had seen her naked.

It was crazy. She knew how she looked. Her tummy would never be as flat as it once was. And she'd always thought her bustline could have used a little enhancing. But there had been no revulsion in Cole's eyes when he'd looked at her. His gaze had been sensual, possessive and infused with so much heat she'd felt branded, and infinitely sensual in return.

She told herself it didn't change anything. He was still going to leave. And she was still going to stay. In the meantime, it looked as if she was going to be forgetful, and excitable, and oh, what the heck. It was almost Christmas. Wonder was in the air, and magic and fun. As long as she didn't act upon her feelings, what harm could there be in enjoying the interim?

Now, she had to retrieve that plate of cookies she'd been asked to furnish for the social hour following tonight's program. As long as she didn't tarry, she and the kids would still be on time.

She came face-to-face with Cole while she was going in and he was coming out. Their gazes met, held. Feeling strangely tongue-tied, she smiled. "I forgot the cookies. Max is certain I'm getting senile."

He grunted an answer.

She gave him a quick once-over. His face was closed, as if he was guarding a secret. That wasn't unusual. Communicative, he wasn't.

He was dressed for a run in faded jeans, a heavy coat and athletic shoes that had seen better days. So she wouldn't have had to say, "Going someplace?" But she said it anyway, only to clamp her mouth shut the moment it slipped out. Honestly, she hadn't been this giddy at fourteen.

He started guiltily. "What? Oh. Yeah. I guess I am."

A dull sense of foreboding crawled down her spine. "Is something wrong, Cole?"

"What? No. I'm going to get some exercise. Thought I'd head on down to the harbor."

"That sounds nice." Letting him pass, she said, "Whatever you do, don't tell Max. Or he'll want to go with you, and I'll never be able to get him to participate in the Christmas program at school."

"Don't worry, my lips are sealed."

She watched him go, thinking something had changed. She couldn't put her finger on what it was, but for some reason, she could no longer muster up a smile. She watched as he waved at the kids, then headed in the opposite direction.

Giving herself a mental shake, she turned toward the kitchen. The sight of the bags on the floor in the back room stopped her in her tracks.

They were old, faded and stuffed to capacity. Cole was leaving. Not this minute, but probably tonight.

She hadn't even realized hope had sparked in her chest until it flickered out. Her mind cleared, her giddiness little more than a distant memory.

She let herself into the kitchen, telling herself that Cole's leaving was inevitable. She'd known it from the start. She'd thought something had happened when he'd walked in on her in the shower. At the time, it had felt as if his gaze had branded her. It had certainly brought her alive in a way she hadn't felt in a long, long time. She'd known he was going to leave. And she'd assured herself she could handle it. In the meantime, she'd planned to enjoy the interim. It looked as if this was going to be the shortest-lived interim in history.

She felt bereft. And he hadn't even gone yet.

No, she didn't. She was fine. Everything was fine.

Taking the bag of cookies the kids had helped decorate, she retraced her steps, locking the door behind her. The wind blew through her hair, billowing her coat behind her. Rosanna shivered, suddenly chilled to the bone.

Cole dug deep into his coat pocket, bringing up several bills, along with Gary's badge. He tossed the bills on the Formica-topped table in the tiny fish restaurant, and squeezed the badge in his hand.

A dozen thoughts clambered over one another. He remembered the day Evie had pressed Gary's badge into his hand. He'd tried to refuse it, telling her she should save it for the girls. She'd said he needed it more. She'd been right, but then, she usually was.

Months later, another woman had done the same thing, returning the badge her daughter had "found." He'd been surly, temperamental, a basic jerk. Rosanna had seemed unfazed. She'd been friendly and honest, turning an awkward situation into a tolerable one.

She'd been wearing green that night. It had matched her eyes. It was strange. He didn't usually remember those kinds of details. And yet he remembered everything about that first meeting with Rosanna with a clarity that surprised him.

Saying goodbye wasn't going to be easy. Forgetting her was going to be impossible.

He took a deep breath, inhaling the scent of hot oil and herbed fish and battered shrimp. Deciding a long walk better suited his needs tonight, he'd wandered down streets named after either fish or trees, and had ended up at this small table in a family-owned restaurant near the harbor.

It had been a good choice, the ocean perch the best he'd ever tasted. Bells over the doorway jingled every time somebody came or went. Sometimes Cole looked up, sometimes he didn't. Several of the diners made a fuss over the two-foot-tall Santa Claus that danced a hula at the touch of a button. And everyone except Cole looked out the window when sirens sounded in the distance.

Cole sipped his coffee in silence, thinking. Sirens

were such an everyday occurrence down in Miami that most people didn't even look up anymore.

He wondered where he should go next. Up the coast? Or down? Finishing his meal, he eyed his watch. Rosanna and the kids had probably been home for a while now. It was time for him to say his goodbyes.

He paid for his meal, zipped up his coat, turned up his collar and stepped out into the night. The air was so cold it stung his face, and made him hurry.

He crossed Mackerel Street, took a left at Harbor Avenue, and cut over to Oak. The flashing lights up ahead brought him to attention. It almost looked as if that police car was parked in Rosanna's driveway.

Sweat broke out on his forehead.

It *was* parked in Rosanna's driveway.

He cut through a lawn, jumped a low hedge and burst into the inn. Rosanna, Max, Shiloh and two police officers looked over at all the commotion.

Cole did a quick appraisal. Rosanna and the kids appeared to be unharmed. Striding to the center of the room, he asked, "What the hell is going on?"

Chapter 6

Shiloh, Rosanna and Max all jumped to their feet the instant they saw Cole.

"Somebody broked in!"

"We're all fine, but we've had a burglary."

"Busted the lock right out of the door."

It would have been easier to make sense of their explanations if they hadn't all spoken at the same time. Still, Cole got the gist of what had happened.

"A burglar?" he asked, his gaze sweeping the entire room, encompassing two police officers who were watching him openly. "Did anybody see anything? What's missing?"

Rosanna started to answer, but the younger policeman cut her off. "You're not from around here, are you?"

The guy eyed Cole shrewdly. Great. Cole was a suspect. That figured. His fingers flexed at his sides. Rather than waste precious time being uncooperative, he said, "My name's Colter Monroe. I've been renting the attic apartment the past few weeks."

The other man clicked his pen and patted his handcuffs. Cole had seen guys like him before. He was five foot five and on an obvious power trip. Doc Henderson would have said his was a prime example of a textbook case of Napoleon complex. Cole pegged him as a prime example of a jerk.

"Those bags I saw in the back room belong to you?"

Cole felt like pacing. Better yet, he felt like throwing the little weasel up against the wall. Swallowing a stack of nerves that had lodged sideways in his throat, he nodded. "They're mine."

"Quite a coincidence, don't you think?"

"I don't believe in coincidences."

That got a rise out of the younger man, but before he could act on it, the older officer asked, "What size shoe do you wear, son?"

The gray-haired policeman's gaze was steady, his question direct, his attitude steadfast and nonjudgmental. Cole liked him immediately.

"Eleven and a half."

Cole's answer obviously took the wind out of the young policeman's sails. He actually looked disappointed. If all the men in Midnight were like this one, it was no wonder Max hadn't found a suitable father yet.

"The man who broke in was wearing cowboy boots," the lieutenant said. "Size ten. He left his footprints all over the place, and he broke the lock in the back door."

"Yeah," Max interrupted. "He must be stupid, because he coulda just looked under the mat and found the spare key. Everybody in Midnight keeps one there. Too bad you weren't here, Cole. You coulda stopped him."

Pressure built in Cole's chest all over again. Dammit, he'd lost all patience with these stupid episodes. Shaking his head to clear it, he could have told the kid that he was wrong. Colter Monroe was no longer in the business of stopping bad guys or protecting the innocent.

He eyed both kids, then Rosanna, and finally the senior officer. "Any idea who did it?"

"Other than his footprints, he didn't leave any clues. Whoever he is, he's inept, but not vicious or particularly threatening. A lot of things were overturned, but nothing was destroyed. And nothing seems to be missing."

"What do you mean nothing's missing?" Cole asked.

The other policeman piped up. "This wasn't a typical B and E. Drawers were dumped, floorboards in the attic pried loose, closets searched. Seems he was looking for something specific."

Rosanna added, "He didn't touch the antiques or the money he found in my top drawer."

"An honest thief?" Cole asked.

Making noises about reports that had to be filed, the policemen headed for the door. The younger one told Rosanna to get her locks changed. The older one looked Cole in the eye and asked, "Those bags packed for a reason?"

Looking from one man to the other, Max caught on. "You aren't leaving, are you, Cole? You're not. Are you?"

Rosanna held her breath. The knowledge that someone had broken into her home and had gone through her personal things was disconcerting and emotionally draining. But that wasn't the reason behind the nerves dancing across her shoulders. She'd seen how pale Cole had been when he'd first burst into the house. His breathing had been labored, a muscle working in his jaw, a vein pulsing in his neck. She hated the idea of a stranger wandering uninvited through her home, but this sense of dread had been with her ever since she'd noticed the bags, ready and waiting near the back door.

She'd told herself she was prepared for Cole's imminent farewell. She'd clapped along with the other parents in the audience tonight. She'd smiled and made small talk afterward. Inside, she'd been trying to prepare herself to let go. Looking into Cole's eyes now, she waited to see what would be.

Shiloh tugged on his coat. Looking up at him as if he were a giant, she said, "The crook broke my night-light. The jerk."

Cole's eyebrows rose fractionally, and a glimmer,

like moonlight, flickered in his dark eyes. "I guess we're just going to have to buy you another one."

Rosanna heard the words, and felt the implications. Cole had said "we." He wasn't leaving. At least not yet. She was far more relieved than she should have been, but she couldn't muster up anything other than extreme relief and a warm glow that felt suspiciously like a second chance.

Looking the older officer in the eye, Cole said, "It looks like I'll be staying on for a while."

With a tug at their hats and a quickly mumbled, "We'll be in touch," the police officers left.

Max waited until Rosanna had closed the door to say, "What a pipsqueak."

"Max," Rosanna reprimanded.

Cole held the boy's gaze as he said, "My partner was five-six, and he was the biggest man I've ever known."

Max sighed, duly chastised.

In an effort to fill the ensuing silence, Rosanna smiled at Cole and said, "You missed quite a performance tonight."

With a lift of her little chin, Shiloh exclaimed, "I sang 'Up On The House Top' all by myself."

Max ran into the parlor to plug in the Christmas lights, and Cole said, "Did you make any cats yowl?"

Rosanna cast him a stern look. "That's not funny."

Max chuckled. Shiloh giggled. And Cole smiled. The combination turned Rosanna's heart over.

There, on the very bottom, where a woman's heart was the most tender, a gentle emotion nudged her. Just as the Christmas tree lights burst on, she gave in to the emotion. Rosanna was in love.

"Hey, sleepyhead." Rosanna bent close to Max, who'd fallen asleep in the recliner. "What do you say we move you up to your bed so the sandman will know where to find you?"

He opened his eyes, and roused enough to allow her to lead him from the living room. Cole scooped Shiloh from the sofa, following close behind.

School was out until after the holidays. And Rosanna had let Max and Shiloh stay up as late as they wanted. At first the kids had followed her and Cole like shadows, asking dozens of questions while the adults restored order to drawers and closets. An hour or so ago, they'd retreated to the living room to watch their favorite Christmas videos. Shiloh hadn't lasted through Frosty's meltdown. Max had dropped off while Rudolph had been visiting the island of misfit toys.

Rosanna had expected them to show more fear concerning the break-in. They'd been curious, and indignant that somebody had dared to trespass on their territory. But they'd been amazingly unafraid. It was probably partly due to the fact that the interloper hadn't been destructive or vicious. Rosanna thought it was largely due to the fact that Cole was here.

They felt secure having a man in the house. It

didn't matter to them that Cole believed he'd lost his edge. He was here. And they were glad.

Rosanna was glad, too. But for different reasons.

It was the eighth day before Christmas in her twenty-ninth year. And she was in love. She'd been in love before. Then, she'd naively believed it would last forever. It hadn't. Her feelings for Cole might last through eternity, but the relationship wouldn't. Because he was leaving. Not tonight, but soon. That didn't change the fact that she loved him, but it did change the beating rhythm of her heart. It brought about a quiet urgency not unlike the heaviness in the air before a storm. Along with the urgency was desire, so thick she could smell it, taste it, revel in it.

She led Max to his bed, helped him take off his shoes, tugged his sweater over his head and handed him his flannel pajamas. After a hundred washings, the fabric had become so faded that the lobsters were barely discernible from the fish. Someday he probably wouldn't want to wear flannel pajamas with fish on them. He'd been a pudgy, dimpled, adorable baby. He was only nine years old, but he was sturdy and strong. Time was passing.

Closing her eyes, she kissed his cheek, tucked the blankets underneath his chin, then turned toward the door where Cole was waiting with Shiloh. Their gazes met, held. Neither of them looked away.

They'd worked together to put the inn back in order. Sometimes they talked. Sometimes they were silent. Certainly neither of them had mentioned the attraction that glowed so strong between them that it took on a presence all its own.

He carried Shiloh into the next bedroom. With infinite tenderness, he lowered her to the bed. Rosanna went to work removing her daughter's buckle shoes, her tights and her Christmas dress. Unlike Max, Shiloh didn't so much as open her eyes. She was as loose-jointed as a rag doll. Getting her into her pajamas wouldn't have been easy if Cole hadn't been there to lift her while Rosanna tugged her clothes off and her nightgown on.

Cole peeled the blankets back from one side of the narrow bed. Rosanna tucked them around Shiloh from the other side. They straightened, as if in one motion. Their gazes met all over again.

She'd sensed that he'd been fighting the attraction that had been shimmering between them all evening. But he hadn't retreated to his room upstairs, at least not for good. Rosanna didn't know what she would have done if he had. Perhaps she would have followed him there. For time was passing. And she didn't want this one night to pass her by.

Walking around to the foot of Shiloh's bed, she whispered, "They're both out for the night."

Cole swallowed. He was pretty sure a fist had a hold of his heart. That didn't stop it from beating a slow rhythm, steady and strong. He'd told himself countless times to get the hell out of there and head back to his room in the attic. A power greater than his conscience held him here.

There wasn't a man alive who wouldn't have

known what Rosanna had on her mind. Cole doubted there was a man alive who could have resisted her small smile.

For her sake, he had to try.

He searched his mind for something to talk about, and ended up with a topic that came out of the blue. "I meant to tell you," he whispered huskily. "It's possible that Shiloh might have taken something out of Nadine's house without asking."

"Oh, no. What did she take?"

"A pair of shoes. I'm pretty sure they're all wrapped and under the tree. Last I knew, Shiloh had plans to turn them into ruby slippers."

"Do you think hardened criminals start like this?"

He beat her to the doorway, then stood to one side to let her pass. The hem of her dress brushed his pant leg. The faint scent of her perfume found its way to his nose; her hand found its way into his.

Cole had to remind himself to breathe.

"I don't see her doing hard time for putting glitter on a pair of old shoes, if that's what you mean."

Her deep sigh had to be heartfelt. "You have no idea what a relief that is to hear."

He'd bet his car she knew exactly what her husky whisper was doing to him. Her hair was a deep, dark brown. Normally she wore it long and loose around her shoulders. Tonight, she'd twisted it and fastened it high on the back of her head with a shiny black clip. She'd taken her heels off hours ago. At five foot six, she wasn't a short woman, and yet she made him feel big and tall. And that wasn't all. She made him feel strong, good and in some strange way, accepted.

There was something different about her tonight, something besides the hairstyle, the blush on her cheeks and the faint dusting of shadow on her eyelids. Her dress was red, loose fitting, soft looking. The collar and cuffs were trimmed in black. She looked good in red, and black, and nothing.

He clamped his mouth shut, even as he followed her toward the main stairs. "Well," he said, grappling to find something safe to say. "The kids handled tonight pretty well."

She nodded, but made no reply.

His gaze strayed to her lips. His heart skipped a beat. "I guess I'll turn in."

Her hand fluttered to his arm, her touch so gentle it couldn't have held back a flea. And yet it held him perfectly still. "Rosanna, I..."

She touched a finger to his lips.

Rosanna heard Cole's sharply drawn breath. She felt the tension in him, and the desire he was trying so desperately to control.

"I know what you're going to say, Cole. I've said it to myself a hundred times. I thought I could deny this attraction. I thought I should. But I can't. I don't want to. Do you?"

"This is dangerous, Rosanna."

He'd helped her restore order to every room in the house, except one. He'd slipped up to his apartment to take a shower while she'd put the drawers in her bedroom in order. It was as if he hadn't trusted himself to be alone with her there.

She shook her head. It hadn't mattered. Oh, it might have prolonged the evening, but it hadn't altered the final outcome or changed the way she felt.

"I saw your bags earlier," she whispered. "And I thought you were leaving. And I was sorry. For waiting too long. For missing the chance to be with you."

He closed his eyes, as if it hurt him to listen. She didn't want to hurt him. "I don't want to miss the chance again."

"I'll stay a few more days. But that's all, Rosanna. I'm not making any promises."

She knew what the words cost him. The man was nothing if not honest.

"I know, Cole."

They were only a few feet away from her bedroom when he said, "I can't protect you and the kids from harm, Rosanna."

"I can take care of myself and my children, Cole. Just so you know, this has nothing to do with protection."

"That makes it even more dangerous," he said, even as his arms went around her, locking her in an iron embrace.

She felt the effect desire was having on his body. Physically he posed no threat to her. After all, she wanted this as much as he did.

Emotionally was a different story. In that aspect, he was dangerous. She'd known it the first moment they'd met. No matter what he thought, it wasn't the threat of murder or mayhem. It was more like the lure of darkness, the thrill of the unknown.

He was dangerous. She knew it as she lowered the zipper down the back of her dress. And yet, as he pulled her hard against him, and pressed his lips to hers, she knew she'd never felt anything quite like this.

He was dangerous. Not because of anything he'd done or couldn't do, but because of how he made her feel. With him, she felt beautiful. With him, she felt smart. With him, she felt witty, and young, and free. It wasn't in any way superficial, for her feelings went soul deep. With him, she was in danger of falling completely and irrevocably in love. With him.

Hands clasped, they strolled the remaining distance into the bedroom where she'd slept, alone, for the past six years. She shivered. Not because she was cold, but because it had been a long, long time since she'd known passion, or desire, or love.

Cole kissed her softly. Tugging his shirt out of his jeans, he glanced around. She'd turned the lamp on earlier, and folded the covers back, as if she'd been anticipating this moment.

He looked at her, and damned if the little tart didn't smile. "Once you saw me naked, this was inevitable."

Could she read minds, too? Deftly unfastening the final button on his shirt, he said, "I can't help it that you can't sing."

Her dress swished to the floor about the same time she said, "I've never been so glad about that in my life."

God, she was provocative, playful. "You're incorrigible."

He spoke the words on a rasp close to her ear, his hands cupping her bottom, drawing her closer, exactly where he wanted her.

"Is that a good thing or a bad thing?" she asked, pushing his shirt off his shoulders, anxious to feel flesh against flesh.

"Do you hear me complaining?"

What she heard was his rasp, and his labored breathing. Before she could answer, his hands went to her shoulders, gliding her bra straps down, whisking it away. For a long time, neither of them spoke. Certainly neither of them complained. They were too busy tasting, touching, enjoying, reveling in secrets they learned one at a time.

They closed her door, turned the lock and stretched out on her bed, a tangle of arms and legs and kisses and sighs. One minute he was straddling her, pinning her to the mattress, and the next she was on top of him, torturing him with her hands and lips and body. He kissed her senseless, and she, him. They touched each other in fevered frenzy, their breathing ragged, their bodies straining for more, so much more.

Cole told himself that the only reason this felt so utterly poignant, so incredible and perfect was that his mind wasn't blurred with booze. Completely sober, he was better able to enjoy, to savor, to take and to give.

And maybe she was just a little bit unforgettable. After all, Rosanna was a study in contrasts, gentle one minute, aggressive the next, her kiss soft, her touch bold. She laughed brazenly, smiled sweetly. She wasn't a quiet lover; her cries were lusty, honest. She knew exactly what she was doing. What she was doing was driving him insane.

"Now, Cole," she whimpered, her hands reaching out to him.

"Easy," he whispered, trying with all his might to keep this from ending too soon. He outweighed her by fifty or sixty pounds, and yet she accepted his weight as if she'd been made for him. Finally he joined them in that age-old way God created. He held still for a moment or two, letting her body adjust to his.

Rosanna's eyes drifted closed dreamily. It would have been so easy to give in to the fog swirling in her brain. She fought it, forcing her eyes open. She wanted to see how beautifully intense Cole's features were in passion. She wanted to watch the way need etched itself in the line of his lips, the sweat that broke out on his brow. She wanted to memorize the way his eyes closed as if in rapture.

He started to move, and she forgot all about watching, seeing, memorizing. She squeezed around him, and called his name. She must have called it again and again, for she heard it in her ears. And then she couldn't hear anything but the roaring of her own heart, the gasp of her own breathing, the cry of her own release.

His movements finally stilled, and more gradually, hers did, too. She surfaced slowly, stretching her legs languidly. He slid to his side, draping one arm and one leg over her body.

She was glad he didn't leave her completely, for she wasn't ready to be completely alone. No matter what Cole had said about being unable to protect her, he'd protected her tonight. In the most elemental of ways. She loved him for it, even while she acknowledged her remorse because she knew they would never have a child together. Not that she needed more children. Max and Shiloh fulfilled all but the faintest traces of her maternal instincts. There was just something about the idea of bringing a child into the world, a child born of two people in love.

The thought brought her mind to a screeching halt. She was in love with Cole. He'd said nothing of loving her in return.

"You okay?"

She stored reality away, and nudged him with her shoulder. "How mind-boggling would sex have to be in order for you to not have to ask?"

She felt his smile where his lips rested along the top of her head. "You know what I meant."

"I'm fine, Cole." She raised her head off his chest in order to look at him. "How are you?"

"Whipped, spent. My mind's been erased, my heart has exploded and I can't quite see."

"You're welcome."

He chuckled, and so did she.

"I like laughing with you, Cole."

His hand paused where it had been making circle patterns in the small of her back. After everything they'd just done together, she liked *laughing* with him. "Be careful of my ego," he said.

"This doesn't have anything to do with ego. It has to do with being comfortable together. My mama used to say pleasure can be bought, but comfort has to be given."

"Uh, Rosanna?"

She made a sound that meant what?

"The kind of pleasure we just experienced together can't be bought."

She smiled, and snuggled into the blankets he pulled up around her shoulders. He climbed out of bed and walked away, completely comfortable with his nakedness.

Fluffing the pillow beneath her head, she knew what he was doing, what he had to dispose of. She wondered how many he'd brought with him. And she was trying to decide if she had enough nerve to ask.

The phone rang on the bedside table. With her mind somewhere near the moon's orbit, she reached for the phone and placed it near her ear.

"What have you done with my diamonds?"

The question was so far-removed from her reality that she didn't even panic. "What?" she asked.

"You heard me."

She was listening intently now.

"Those diamonds are mine. I know where I left them. I came back for them tonight. And they were gone. Where are they?"

"I don't have any diamonds!"

"They've got to be there, somewhere."

The line went dead moments after Cole came back into the room. He must have read the expression on her face, because he said, "Bad news?"

"I'm not sure."

"A prank phone call?"

She shook her head.

"Give me a hint here, Rosanna. I take it that wasn't a friend of yours."

She closed her gaping mouth and hung up the phone. Trying to make sense of the conversation, she said, "I'm pretty sure that was the burglar."

"The burglar? What did he say?" His voice had a cutting edge to it now, his eyes were suddenly razor sharp.

Even the sight of a completely naked, virile man didn't cause her to lose her train of thought. At least not much. "He said he wanted his diamonds."

"His diamonds?"

She nodded. "I think I heard a cat meowing in the background. What kind of a bad guy keeps a cat? I swear I've heard that voice before."

Cole lowered to the edge of her bed. "Where?"

"I don't know. But I recognized that voice."

"From a long time ago? Or recently?"

She turned her head, slowly meeting his gaze. "Recently I think."

He was thoughtful for a moment, as if trying to put the pieces together. "It looks like we know what your bungling burglar was looking for."

"But why would he think I had diamonds?"

"He pried up the floorboards in the attic. He must have thought he knew something you didn't know."

"He thought there were diamonds hidden in the attic? Why? How?"

"I was wondering that, myself. I'll do a little checking tomorrow."

Rosanna thought about that voice. She wasn't happy that the crook knew her phone number, and she was anxious to get this mystery solved. But she didn't see what she could do until tomorrow. She gave Cole a quick once-over. "Did you have any plans for tonight?"

His brown eyes darkened, his lashes lowered and his lips parted slightly. "It's funny you should ask."

The light in his eyes turned her thoughts hazy, the brush of his lips on hers weakened her limbs. He joined her underneath the covers, and loved her all over again.

Rosanna responded just as thoroughly and completely the second time. All the while she was responding, reacting and returning his kisses, his touches, his sighs, she felt an ache deep in her heart. She was in love with a man who was going to leave in a matter of days.

Pressing her body to his, she moaned his name. He was here now. And she didn't want to waste a moment on wishing, or on what if. He was here now. And for now, he was hers.

Chapter 7

"Yoo-hoo—" Nadine blew into the inn's kitchen
on a blast of frigid air "—is anybody home?"

The last portion was spoken in a whisper, a direct
response to the finger Rosanna placed to her lips as
she said, "Shh. You'll wake them."

Hurriedly closing the door, Nadine tiptoed over
to the cardboard box Rosanna had dragged up from
the basement. Peering over Rosanna's shoulder at
the special delivery that had arrived an hour ago,
Nadine said, "A puppy *and* a kitten? Are you
crazy?"

"They're Christmas gifts for Max and Shiloh
from their father."

Five concise, single syllable words spewed out of
Nadine's mouth.

"Now, Nadine, you've never actually met Darrell's mother."

Nadine shook her head and sputtered, "I don't suppose he sent along a year's supply of cat and dog food, or had them vaccinated before he had them delivered."

Rosanna sighed. She'd been doing a lot of that this week. "It would have been nice if he would have at least delivered them himself. Shiloh barely remembers what he looks like. But the kids are going to love them."

Nadine relented, and very nearly crooned. "They're positively adorable." Glancing all around, she said, "Max and Shiloh aren't here?"

Rosanna shook her head. Cole took the kids with him to Rockland. He'd already spoken to Verita Hicks regarding the theft of her uncut diamonds six years ago. He'd been in close contact with the police department, too. Today, he hoped to garner information via old newspaper articles that had been kept on microfilm in the library in Rockland. He was convinced the break-in, those diamonds and the man on the telephone were connected in some way. Rosanna was all for solving the mystery. Except for one tiny thing.

As soon as the burglar was captured, Cole was going to leave.

Sighing again, she said, "How was your trip?"

Nadine worked for a leading makeup manufacturer, and had just returned from an intense round of meetings at corporate headquarters in Boston.

"The trip was uneventful. I can't say the same for my life since I returned yesterday."

Rosanna recognized the light in her friend's eyes. Nadine was in the mood to talk. Since listening was better than trying to tell herself that she wasn't going to be devastated when Cole left, she rose to her feet and started a pot of coffee.

When the coffee was done, Rosanna poured it into two mugs. She tried to listen to Nadine. It wasn't easy, because her mind was prone to wander these days. Every night Cole came into her bedroom, locking the door and the world behind it. Beneath lavender-scented sheets and her homemade quilt, she and Cole created a world all their own. In the wee hours of the morning, he crawled out of her bed, donned his clothes and retired to his own room upstairs. Every night, she told herself it was enough.

Every night, she reminded herself that she needed to be objective. It wasn't easy. Objectivity tended to disappear when a woman found herself head over heels in love.

"As you know," Nadine said, "I got home the day before yesterday. Since I didn't have any food in the house, I decided to go to Rocky's Diner for an early supper. I was just minding my own business, having a lonely meal, bemoaning the fact that I'd reached my sexual peak and I had nobody to appreciate it, and in walked this interesting guy. I've always just loved a man with a mustache."

Nadine just loved *men*. Rosanna didn't see any

reason to state the obvious, so she simply nodded encouragingly.

Nadine was completely willing to oblige. "I couldn't believe my luck. And I wasn't even wearing my sure-thing shoes. Not that I hadn't tried to find them. I searched my entire house. I can't imagine where they went."

Rosanna reacted with a jerk, which caused her coffee to slosh over the rim of her mug. Nadine didn't notice. "Turned out I didn't need those shoes to find a man. Actually, Rexy found me."

"Rexy?"

Nadine winked broadly, whispering, "Sexy Rexy."

"Sexy Rexy?" Rosanna repeated. Just then, Cole and the kids walked in.

Max and Shiloh pushed out of their coats, dropping them onto a chair. "Hey, Nadine," Max said.

Shiloh sashayed over. Blithely climbing onto Nadine's lap, she held up one bandaged finger. "My finger got pinched."

"In what?" Nadine asked.

Shiloh clammed up, and Max blurted, "In Mom's jewelry box."

"Aw, sweetie, that's rough. Want me to kiss it and make it better?"

Shiloh shook her head bravely. "Mama already did. She kissed Cole, too. And you know what else? Cole saw her naked."

Rosanna glanced at Shiloh, at Max, at Nadine and finally at Cole. He was as stunned as she was. It seemed everyone was exchanging furtive glances, but nobody said a word. Rosanna wanted to drop her face into her hands. Leave it to her darling daughter to bring that up, and completely fail to mention the break-in.

Two little yips, followed closely by a faint meow broke the uncomfortable silence.

Five heads turned at nearly the same time. "What was that?" Shiloh asked.

The yips came again, louder, in closer succession, practically drowning out the squeaky meows. "Mom," Max said. "What's in that box?"

Shiloh scampered off Nadine's lap, arriving at the edge of the cardboard box two steps behind her brother. "Shiloh. Look."

Max handed a scrawny white kitten to Shiloh, then scooped a pudgy, brown-and-white puppy into his own arms. Gliding down to her knees, Rosanna showed Shiloh how to hold the kitten, and pet her softly. The kitten looked up at Shiloh with unblinking blue eyes and purred. Shiloh was unequivocally lost, and completely in love.

When the puppy whimpered, Max tucked him close to his chin. The little guy took that as a sign and started licking Max's neck. Max giggled so much even the adults had to join in.

The pets were oohed and aahed over, and declared the smartest, cutest cat and dog in the universe. Names were discussed, and discarded. In the end, Max named the springer spaniel Rudy, after a flying rcindeer, and Shiloh called her kitten Frosty, after a magical snowman come to life.

When things had died down a little, Nadine said, "So, Cole. You thinking about sticking around? Maybe staying in Midnight?"

Everyone, even Max and Shiloh, turned to look at Cole. Rosanna doubted she would ever forget that moment. Cole looked as if somebody had shot him with a stun gun. He'd probably opened the refrigerator fully intending to put the six-pack of cola inside. Nadine's question held him immobile.

He'd changed slightly since Rosanna first saw him. When she'd mentioned it to him a few days ago, he'd said her cooking agreed with him. It was true that he'd lost his haggard look, but his face was still lean and hard and handsome. And his eyes were still hooded, with regret, with remorse, most likely with something from his past he hadn't worked out yet. She wasn't certain he ever would.

"No," he finally said when Rosanna nudged him aside and took the soda from him and put in the refrigerator. "I'm not planning to stay here indefinitely."

Max and Shiloh looked from Cole to each other. Together, they sighed. Suddenly Rosanna was glad Darrell had given them the puppy and kitten. She loved Cole. She'd never expected to feel this way, and it was unlikely she'd ever feel this way about any other man. Therefore, Max and Shiloh weren't going to get a new father. Maybe the puppy and kitten would ease the transition after Cole left. At least for them.

After Cole left, Rosanna planned to give up on men.

She wasn't antiman. Not at all. Oh, she didn't take a different man to bed every time she changed the sheets like Nadine did. In fact, she'd only had three lovers, and then only if she counted Billy Andrews who had technically been her first the summer after she graduated from high school. Billy had known little about sex and even less about girls. Of course, Billy had been a boy.

Cole was a man, all man. Oh, he thought the rest of his life was a crapshoot gone bad, but his manhood was A-Okay. He was good at being a man, at throwing on clothes he'd already worn, leaving his hair to grow too long, grunting a gloomy good-morning and then opening the refrigerator and just standing there while he woke up. Yes, he *was* good at all those things, but his goodness went deeper than gender and masculine trappings.

Colter Remington Monroe was good at being a good guy. Even when he didn't want to be. No matter what he claimed, he was watching out for her and her children. He'd installed new locks in the inn, and he'd talked to Rosanna's neighbors about finding a better place to hide their spare keys. He was "protecting" them. He claimed Max scared the daylights out of him, but Cole listened to that boy. And Shiloh, well... Her little girl had that man wrapped around all ten of her fingers.

He'd gotten to Nadine, too. Although that wasn't particularly noteworthy. Most men got to Nadine. But he'd gotten to Rosanna. And that was rare.

Every time he looked at her from beneath those heavy lids, every time he laughed with her children, every time he kissed her and touched her, she fell a little further in love.

Yes, the problem with Cole was that he was a man. A very special man. A man whose bags were packed.

Nadine finished her coffee, then headed home to get ready for a hot date. Rosanna and the kids were on the other side of the kitchen, talking amongst themselves. Cole's chest felt heavy. It wasn't like a post-trauma episode. It had been weeks since he'd had a full-blown one of those. This was different.

The kitten was sound asleep, curled in a ball on Shiloh's lap. Max and Rosanna were scurrying to spread some newspaper on the floor. They finished in the nick of time.

Maybe standing across a kitchen while a green-eyed woman patiently showed her kids how to care for their new pets was the reason his chest ached. Rosanna glanced over at him, and his heart rate quickened. Coming to his senses, he grabbed an apple and a cola and closed the refrigerator door. He never stood in the refrigerator back in Florida. Of course, there was never anything in his refrigerator back in Miami. He was developing some nasty habits up here. He felt antsy, itchy, like he might come out of his skin. Being a hermit wasn't all it was cracked up to be.

There was more to this than that. Cole knew it. Rosanna seemed to know it, too.

He ran a hand through his hair. Excusing himself, he took the apple and can of cola and went up to the attic apartment. He felt guilty. He felt at loose ends. He hoped the police caught the man who'd broken into the inn soon. Maybe then his chest would stop aching like a damp cave on a cold day. Maybe then, he could leave without looking back.

Rosanna crawled into bed and closed her eyes. It was midnight. The stockings were filled, Santa's milk and cookies eaten, the gifts spread out beneath the tree. Everything was ready for the brunch she prepared every year. Nadine would be over at ten. This year, she was bringing her new friend, Sexy Rexy.

Rosanna hadn't seen Cole since the kids had fallen asleep two hours ago. She'd heard him pacing overhead, heard floorboards creak as he made his way downstairs. Listening intently, she told herself he had every right to go directly back to his room and go right to sleep. When the footsteps came closer, pausing outside her door, she bit her lip, and waited.

The door opened on silent hinges. She and Cole looked at each other just as silently.

"Hi," she finally said.

"Hi," he answered.

A muscle worked in his jaw.

"Is something wrong, Cole?"

"What? Oh. No. That is, I put the gifts I got for you and the kids under the tree. I hope that's okay."

"That's fine. You didn't have to get me anything." He shrugged, and she added, "I didn't get anything for you."

It was her way of letting him know there were no strings attached to what they shared. He seemed to breathe a sigh of relief. And then, as if he couldn't help himself, he started toward her.

She rose up out of bed like a spirit rising out of a mist, meeting his kiss, her fingers going directly to the buttons on his shirt. There was a place deep in her chest, a dark, needy place she'd always managed to steer clear of. Tonight, that deep-seated need threatened to swallow her whole.

Cole's kisses filled that place. His touch, his sighs, his murmurs filled her senses. She tried not to think about what was going to happen to that place after he left.

The moment he was undressed, he joined her under the covers. He kissed her face, her neck, her shoulders, as if he couldn't get enough. "You're an incredible woman, Rosanna Fitzpatrick."

"You'd better believe I am." She ran her hand down his chest, slowly finding what she was after. He sucked in a ragged breath.

"Okay," he whispered, his voice a quiet rasp. "You have my undivided attention. Care to tell me what you want?"

"You know what I want."

A rush of sexual desire flooded into Cole. He closed his eyes. Swallowing a lump that had risen to his throat out of nowhere, he took her face in both his hands and kissed her in a manner that let her know just how precious he thought she was. And then he proceeded to give her what she wanted. What they both wanted.

The mattress shifted, legs and arms entwined, lips clung, fingers sought, breaths mingled, sighs meshed. Afterward, he tucked her close to him, covered them both with the blankets, and held her as she fell asleep.

Staring at the dark ceiling, Cole knew that, no matter what she said, she was giving him something for Christmas. By not clinging, or making demands, she was giving him the greatest gift he'd ever received.

He thought about the complete set of *I Love Lucy* tapes he'd put under the tree tonight. Compared to her gift to him, it seemed small and insignificant. He was afraid there was something else he was going to give her for Christmas. A saddened heart.

He'd thought about staying. But every time he did, pressure built in his chest.

He'd been in close contact with the police department regarding the break-in. The man he believed was responsible had called a second time. Rosanna had listened to the recording dozens of times. Although she was certain she'd heard the voice before, she hadn't been able to place where or when. She put on a brave face, pretending to be unafraid of the threat of another breaking and entering. She bravely assured Cole that he was free to leave whenever he needed to, as well.

He'd never come across anyone like her. He just didn't have anything to offer a woman like Rosanna. He'd lost his edge. And in the process, he'd lost himself. Until he got it back, he had nothing to give. If he got it back.

Climbing the steps to the attic apartment, Cole worried that he never would.

Chapter 8

It was Christmas morning.

Cole had never been in the midst of so much chaos. He'd thought Gary's girls were noisy and active. They couldn't hold a candle to Max and Shiloh. Okay, maybe they weren't solely to blame. Perhaps having a new puppy and a new kitten in the house had something to do with the pandemonium that bordered on mayhem.

He didn't know why Rosanna bothered tuning in the Christmas music in the background. Nobody could hear it, anyway. Wrapping paper and ribbons were everywhere. A bucket of water was sitting near the wall; a chair had been placed over the wet spot in the carpet, compliments of Rudy, the dog.

Rosanna had taken it in stride, but even she had

nearly come undone when Rudy chased Frosty the kitten up the Christmas tree. Christmas ornaments dropped like flies, the treetop teetering precariously while Max, perched on Cole's shoulders, had extricated the animal from Christmas lights and garland.

The kitten had played with a ribbon while Shiloh opened her gifts. Of course, Shiloh proclaimed to love everything she received. She must have truly liked the Wizard of Oz dress and ruby slippers Cole had given her, because she'd put it on right over the top of her pajamas, and she'd been wearing it ever since.

Max hadn't even tried to contain his excitement when he'd opened the box containing a book about whales and a gift certificate for a whale watching excursion. Rosanna hugged each of the kids when she'd opened a flowerpot they'd lovingly decorated with their own hands. She hadn't been nearly as effusive when she'd unwrapped the complete set of *I Love Lucy* videos, although she had smiled as she'd thanked him.

Cole thought her smile looked out of place on her pale face. Her green silk shirt brought out the green of her eyes, but it didn't hide the shadows beneath them.

Shiloh's gift to Cole was a crayon drawing of him holding Gary's badge, along with a whispered apology for borrowing it in the first place. Max gave Cole a pair of earplugs and a homemade book of coupons good for a personalized car wash, a shoe shine and an offer to accompany him to the harbor whenever Cole wanted.

After the kids finished opening their gifts from Santa, Cole helped Rosanna clean up the discarded wrapping paper and ribbons and bows. Shiloh introduced her new doll to her kitten, retreating into her land of make-believe.

"Max," Rosanna said. "You simply cannot ride the bicycle Uncle Henry and Aunt Maggie gave you in the house."

A timer went off in the kitchen just as the doorbell rang. Glancing over her shoulder at her son, who was promising to be careful, she said, "I know you like the bike. But rules are rules, kiddo." She opened the door, and there stood Nadine and her date.

The women hugged. "Merry Christmas."

"Merry Christmas to you, too." Rosanna included the man who was standing behind her best friend in the greeting.

"Won't you come in? Welcome to chaos."

Nadine handed Rosanna the quiche, and introduced Sexy Rexy Devoe. "Pleased to meet you," he said.

Even Max and Shiloh stopped playing with their toys at the sound of Rex Devoe's deep voice. "You'll have to excuse me." His rasp was reminiscent of Marlon Brando in *The Godfather.* "I seem to have caught a cold."

Nadine winked at Rosanna. "I'm afraid I'm to blame for keeping him up so much."

Rosanna did her best to smile at the joke. Cole did his best not to throw up.

Ears flapping, the puppy bounded over, sniffed Sexy Rexy's pant leg and promptly wet on his shoe. Cole had to hold in his chuckle. Since Rosanna looked ready to collapse, he offered to clean up the mess while Nadine whisked Rosanna into the kitchen to get her friend's impression of her new beau.

"Well? What do you think of him?"

Rosanna turned on the oven and put the quiche inside to warm. "For heaven's sakes, Nadine. I just met him, but he seems nice enough."

"Isn't he just the most handsome man?"

As far as Rosanna was concerned, Cole was better-looking. Not that there was anything wrong with Sexy Rexy. Separately, his features looked fine. He was of average height, average build. But his hair was a lot darker than his eyebrows. He was probably one of those men who dyed his hair to cover the gray. She couldn't see Cole doing that. But then, she wouldn't see Cole when he was gray.

"There's something about him that looks familiar," she said. It couldn't be his eyes. She'd never seen eyes quite that blue.

Carrying six plates to the table, Nadine said, "You wouldn't believe what I found in his overnight case."

"You snooped in his overnight case?"

"A girl can't be too careful." Nadine came back for the silverware. "He was in the shower."

"What would you have said if he'd caught you looking?" Rosanna put the peach marmalade in the center of the table.

"I don't know. Do you want to know what I found or don't you?"

The puppy bounded in, once again hot on the kitten's trail.

"What did you find?"

Frosty streaked right on past Rosanna, and made a beeline for Nadine's leg. "A mustache. Yeek. Ouch. There goes a perfectly good pair of nylons."

"I'm sorry, Nadine."

Nadine extricated the kittens sharp little claws from her leg, then carefully set the one-pound monster on the floor. "Don't worry about it. 'Tis the season. Besides, we can add them to Darrell's bill. You are keeping a running total of all the added expenses his Christmas gifts to the kids are incurring, aren't you?"

Rosanna shook her head, but she couldn't help smiling. Nadine really was a good friend.

In the parlor, the kids were showing their guest their gifts. Cole took advantage of the reprieve to stand back and catch his breath, so to speak. While he was at it, he tried to figure out why the skin on the back of his neck was prickling.

His instincts were shot. They had been for months. Add to that the fact that he wasn't getting much sleep...

Not getting enough sleep was the best part of his life.

"This is my new doll. I don't know her name yet. And this is a sweater from Mrs. Fergusson. Mama says her husband curses and endures with equal parts embolism."

"Enthusiasm," Max corrected. "With equal parts enthusiasm."

"Oh, yeah."

Cole almost felt like smiling.

"This is the picture I colored for Cole. And this is the flowerpot me and Maxie made for Mama. She says the best gifts are the ones that come from the heart."

Cole rested his hands on his hips. That little kid was a talker. With her "Mama says this" and "Mama says that," she was as precocious as they came. Shiloh held up the flowerpot just as the puppy noticed Cole's shoelaces. In no time at all, his left shoe was untied. Max caught Cole's attention, and the two of them shared a smile.

Sexy Rexy didn't seem to notice. All his attention was trained on the flowerpot in Shiloh's hands. Cole looked closer. At the flowerpot, and at the man.

He was on the verge of putting something together in his mind when Nadine appeared. Looping her arm through Rex's, she gently tugged him toward the kitchen. "Brunch is ready. Wait until you taste it. Rosanna has outdone herself, just like she does every year."

Cole turned his head, but kept Rex in sight from

the corner of his eye. Shiloh placed the flowerpot on the low table, then skipped into the kitchen in her ruby slippers. The last thing Cole noticed before following the kids was the furtive glance good old Rex gave that pot.

Nadine was right about the brunch Rosanna had prepared. It smelled wonderful, and tasted even better. Nadine and the kids kept up a steady stream of chatter. Which was a good thing, because Rosanna was unusually quiet. Cole never had been much of a talker. And Rex seemed distracted.

Cole buttered his roll with precision and care. Although he couldn't say why, he wasn't surprised when Rex asked for directions to the bathroom then hoarsely excused himself.

"Isn't he the best?" Nadine asked from the other side of the table.

Cole shrugged. Without explanation, he rose to his feet, and quietly followed the path Rex had taken. Being careful to step over the squeakiest floorboards, he crept into the living room.

At first he thought he'd been wrong. The living room and parlor seemed to be empty. But then he heard a low growl, and a man who definitely wasn't hoarse sputtered, "Damn dog. Get away from my shoes."

Cole crept to the doorway leading to the parlor. Rex, if that was his name, gave the puppy a kick, and headed for the door, Rosanna's new flowerpot tucked beneath one arm.

"Hold it right there!"

The man with the bad dye job spun around, his feet moving faster. Cole hit the parlor on a run. He jumped over Max's shiny blue bicycle, and tackled Sexy Rexy from behind. The flowerpot flew to the right, Cole and Rex to the left. They landed with a thud just as the pot shattered into a hundred pieces.

The puppy yipped; Rosanna, Nadine and the kids ran into the room to investigate the strange noises. "Cole, what are you doing to my boyfriend?"

"Those diamonds are mine!" the man sprawled beneath Cole sputtered.

"Diamonds?" Rosanna asked.

"I've waited six years to get out of prison to come back for them."

"Prison!" Nadine exclaimed.

"Hey," Max yelled. "What happened to Mom's flowerpot?"

"Cole," Shiloh quipped. "Mama says no wrestling in the house."

Grappling to sit up, Cole placed one knee in the center of Sexy Rexy's back. "Here's your burglar," he said to Rosanna.

"That voice," Rosanna said. "Of course. And the fake mustache, and unusual eye color. Colored contacts."

"Burglar!" Nadine squeaked.

Eyeing all the people staring at him with their mouths open, Cole said, "Do you think one of you could call 911?"

Forlornly Nadine took a sip of tea. "I really thought this was the one." She sat in the corner of the sofa, her feet underneath her, a hand-crocheted afghan tucked around her. "An ex-con. And a diamond thief."

Max and Shiloh eyed each other speculatively, then quietly rose to their feet. It wasn't that they meant Nadine any disrespect. It was just that she'd already said the same thing a dozen times.

The police had arrived in two separate cars an hour ago. The first batch had led Rex Devoe, alias Derek Drexler, alias Burt Axelrod away. The second set of officers had stayed behind to take everybody's statements. Max and Shiloh already gave their versions of what had happened. Cole and their mother had, too.

Max didn't know exactly what the funny looks his mom and Cole kept giving each other meant, but he had his fingers and toes crossed, just in case. Right now, Rudy was sleeping on Max's lap. Cole said the dog was a hero, and he was barely seven weeks old. Max was so proud he could hardly stand it. As soon as Rudy woke up, Max was going to call Lumpy and tell him all about it.

The doorbell rang. Not about to disturb such a sleepy hero, Max told Shiloh to answer it. She rose to her feet the way she always did, as blithe as a ballerina, even if she still had her pajamas on underneath her Dorothy dress-up clothes and ruby slippers.

Keeping her kitten tucked carefully in her arms, Shiloh opened the door. A lady wearing a long fur coat and a hat with a daisy in it said, "Hello, there. Is your mother home?"

Shiloh turned around to call her mother, but Mama was already there, laying a soft, reassuring hand on her shoulder. She liked it when Mama did that.

Rosanna smiled down at her daughter before peering at the gray-haired woman in the mink coat. "May I help you?"

The woman's eyes crinkled happily. "My dear, you already have."

She brushed past Rosanna, entering the house as if she owned the place the way rich people were inclined to do. Turning with a flourish, she beamed at Rosanna and Cole, who had joined them in the front room.

"I'm Verita Hicks. Those uncut diamonds you recovered belong to me. They were the last gift my dearly departed husband gave to me before he died. And I can't tell you how much it means to me to have them back."

Rosanna smiled at the other woman. Verita Hicks was on the tall side, large boned, not heavy, not thin. Everything about her said "money," but the warmth in her eyes was genuine. It seemed Sexy Rexy had been a gardener at the Hicks mansion six and a half years ago. He'd been Rosanna's mother's first boarder. He'd gone on working for Verita after he'd stashed the diamonds under a floorboard in the attic in the Midnight Inn. Earlier today he'd told police that he'd gotten nervous when the cops started poking around, asking questions. So, when winter came, he moseyed on down to Alabama, leaving the diamonds in his hiding place in Maine. He'd gotten caught red-handed trying to steal jewelry from another old woman in Mobile. He really was an inept thief. He'd done five years, and had gotten out of jail on good behavior two months ago.

There were already rumors floating through Midnight that Verita had taken a liking to the thief and was considering helping him. And Rosanna had thought Nadine was gullible when it came to men. Still, Verita had kind eyes, and Rosanna hadn't always used the best judgment when it came to men, herself. Smiling at the older woman, she simply said, "You're welcome."

She wanted to close the door. She was in a hurry to talk to Cole. Actually, she was in a hurry to listen, because Cole had started to say the most amazing things.

And then the doorbell had rung.

"Wait." Verita held up one kid-glove-ensconced hand. Reaching into her fine leather purse with the other, she drew out what appeared to be a check. "This reward money is yours."

"I don't want your money, Verita. I'm just happy you have your diamonds."

Shiloh tugged on Verita's expensive coat. "Mama says money spoils people. Like hamburger, only different."

Rosanna gasped. Hoping Verita hadn't taken offense, she said, "What my daughter means is…"

Verita winked, first at Rosanna and then at Cole, who was standing close to Rosanna's side. "I know what she means, dear."

Pressing the check into Rosanna's limp hands, she smiled again. Turning on her heel, she disappeared the way she'd come.

Shiloh closed the door. It was a good thing, because Rosanna couldn't seem to move. All she could do was stare at the amount on the check. It was obscene. She could put away enough to put both kids through college and have enough left over to pay off the mortgage on the inn, and still have money left. She couldn't accept it. After all, Cole was the one who captured the crook.

Cole.

Her heart swelled just thinking his name. She looked up at him, and very slowly handed him the check.

He shook his head. "Oh, no, you don't."

Christmas music was still playing in the background, a sweet sounding children's choir singing "Joy To The World." The song was fitting, for when she looked up into his dark eyes, she saw such tenderness and joy, she couldn't speak.

His eyes were so different than they'd been a month ago. Then, they'd been flecked with disappointments from his past. Today, she saw yearning for his future. "But, Cole. The reward money's yours. You deserve it."

He eased closer. His expression shimmered like light and felt like passion.

And closer.

His pupils were dilated in the dimly lit room, so that only a ring of brown encircled them. "If I accepted that check," he said, his voice husky and deep, "how would I ever know if you married me for love or for money?"

She knew her mouth was gaping. She clamped it shut, only to open it again to whisper, "Marry you?"

He smiled. And she melted.

"All this time I've thought I had nothing to give. And then I met a woman who asked nothing of me. The less you asked, the more I wanted to give. I'm not certain I deserve a woman like you, but if you'll have me, I'll give you whatever I have, no matter how great or how small. I love you, Rosanna."

"Oh, Cole."

Before Cole's eyes, Rosanna rose up on tiptoe and pressed her lips to his. She kissed him, not in the wild, frenzied way he'd expected, but tenderly, and so damn sweetly he couldn't keep the sigh from drifting up from his lungs.

She lifted her head dreamily, and he heard himself say, "Was that a yes?"

She raised her face and laughed. God, what had he done to deserve her?

"Yes. Yes, yes, yes."

He rested his forehead on hers, then just held her the way he wanted to for the next eighty or ninety years. "Merry Christmas," he whispered.

"Merry Christmas," she answered.

Max stood around the corner. From his position, he could see into the parlor where his mother and Cole were talking about wedding plans and whale watching and whether or not Max and Shiloh would like a baby brother or sister. Max didn't care if he had a brother or sister. All he cared about was that he was getting the father he'd asked for. He'd known Cole was the one the instant he saw him. Grinning for all he was worth, Max ran to the phone and dialed Lumpy's number.

In the living room, Nadine was at it again, flirting with a police officer who was smiling back at her sweetly.

On the other side of the Christmas tree, out of sight of everyone, Shiloh slipped a shiny pen into the big pocket on her Wizard of Oz dress.

Max started to put the phone down, getting that pained big-brother look on his face. She pressed a finger to her lips, and signaled for Max to keep her secret. He shook his head. Shiloh grinned.

And they both started to laugh.

It was the most unusual Christmas any of them had ever had. It was truly a Christmas to remember, a Christmas to treasure.

* * * * *

Be sure to look for Sandra Steffen's next book, LONE STAR WEDDING, part of THE FORTUNES OF TEXAS series available in April from Silhouette Books.

Dear Reader,

When it comes to Christmas, I want to be a kid again. Not a kid at heart. I want to be a genuine, bona fide kid. Because, let's face it, kids have it made at Christmas.

My brothers and sisters and I loved Christmas. We made lists. We counted the days. We wrote letters to Santa and listened for sleigh bells. And we tried to imagine a girl riding a donkey in a foreign land. Mostly, we could barely suppress our excitement. And then, miraculously, the day arrived. And everyone was happy.

I used to believe that I grew up in a simpler time. After all, Christmas wasn't a huge production in our house. In those early years, we didn't get dressed up. Honestly, there are pictures of me opening my gifts wearing juice cans in my hair. A few years ago I took a closer look at my mother in those pictures. She looked exactly the way I look on Christmas now. Frazzled. Exhausted. Of course Christmas was simple for me. I was the kid.

Now I'm the mom, and no matter how much I try to simplify, Christmas isn't simple. But I still love it. As a mom, I've experienced the wonder, the magic, the sheer joy and honesty of the season through my children's eyes. As a writer, I live it through the characters I create. Christmas is a wonderful time to connect with the people I care about. I'll give many gifts this year. "A Christmas to Treasure" is my gift to you, dear reader. If your Christmas can't be simple, may it be joyful.

Merry Christmas!

Sandra Steffen

**Start celebrating Silhouette's 20th anniversary
with these 4 special titles by
New York Times bestselling authors**

Fire and Rain
by Elizabeth Lowell

King of the Castle
by Heather Graham Pozzessere

State Secrets
by Linda Lael Miller

Paint Me Rainbows
by Fern Michaels

On sale in December 1999

Plus, a special free book offer inside each title!

Available at your favorite retail outlet

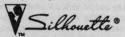

Visit us at www.romance.net

PSNYT

If you enjoyed what you just read,
then we've got an offer you can't resist!

Take 2 bestselling love stories FREE!

Plus get a FREE surprise gift!

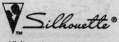

WHO'S AFRAID OF THE BIG BAD WOLFE?

Certainly not you—not when the Wolfe happens to be a sexy, dynamic lawman!
Pick up

And meet two of the Wolfe brothers, who know all the laws of seduction and romance.

Joan Hohl, one of Silhouette's bestselling authors, has thrilled readers with her Wolfe family saga. Don't miss this special two-book collection featuring the first two Big Bad Wolfe stories.

Look for *Big Bad Wolfe: Ready To Wed?* on sale in December 1999.

Available at your favorite retail outlet.

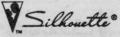

EXTRA! EXTRA!

The book all your favorite authors are raving about is finally here!

The 1999 Harlequin and Silhouette coupon book.

Each page is alive with savings that can't be beat!

Getting this incredible coupon book is as easy as 1, 2, 3.

1. During the months of November and December 1999 buy any 2 Harlequin or Silhouette books.

2. Send us your name, address and 2 proofs of purchase (cash receipt) to the address below.

3. Harlequin will send you a coupon book worth $10.00 off future purchases of Harlequin or Silhouette books in 2000.

Send us 3 cash register receipts as proofs of purchase and we will send you 2 coupon books worth a total saving of $20.00 (limit of 2 coupon books per customer).

Saving money has never been this easy.

Please allow 4-6 weeks for delivery. Offer expires December 31, 1999.

I accept your offer! Please send me (a) coupon booklet(s):

Name: _____

Address: _____ City: _____

State/Prov.: _____ Zip/Postal Code: _____

Send your name and address, along with your cash register receipts as proofs of purchase, to:

In the U.S.: Harlequin Books, P.O. Box 9057, Buffalo, N.Y. 14269
In Canada: Harlequin Books, P.O. Box 622, Fort Erie, Ontario L2A 5X3

Order your books and accept this coupon offer through our web site
http://www.romance.net
Valid in U.S. and Canada only.   PHQ4994R